Time of My Life

ALSO BY ALLISON WINN SCOTCH

The Department of Lost and Found

Time

ALLISON
WINN SCOTCH

of My Life

A NOVEL

Shaye Areheart Books
NEW YORK

Copyright © 2008 by Allison Winn Scotch

Published in the United States by Shaye Areheart Books, an imprint of the Crown Publishing Group, a division of Random House, Inc., New York.
www.crownpublishing.com

Shaye Areheart Books with colophon is a registered trademark of Random House, Inc.

Library of Congress Cataloging-in-Publication Data
Scotch, Allison Winn.
Time of my life : a novel / by Allison Winn Scotch.—1st ed.
p.   cm.
1. Self-realization in women—Fiction.   2. Life change events—Fiction.
3. Psychological fiction.   I. Title.
PS3619.C64T56 2008
813'.6—dc22   2008010628

ISBN 978-0-307-40857-0

Printed in the United States of America

Design by Lynne Amft

10 9 8 7 6 5 4 3 2 1

First Edition

For Adam, to whom I tell my stories.

*And for Campbell and Amelia, who hold
the answers to life's many questions.*

Now for the other life. The one without mistakes.

—Lou Lipsitz

Chapter One

Ding. *Ding. Ding. Ding. Ding. Ding. Ding. Ding. Ding.*

Somewhere in the tunnels of my left ear, I hear my car alerting me to the fact that my door is open. I take vague notice of my brain accepting the message, then I quickly ignore it. The dinging, to which I am now immune, as if someone were pinching me on my arm over and over again until that same spot becomes numb, continues.

I run my hands over the cool wood of the steering wheel, then onto the buttery leather seat below, flicking my hands underneath the sweat-basted backs of my thighs. The brochure to this car—the one that was filled with a couple who so closely resembled Barbie and Ken that my daughter actually pointed to them and said, "Barbie," which my husband and I applauded to the point of revelry (such that people in the dealership craned their necks to see if we'd been given a free car or something), because my daughter's vocabulary consisted of, to date, approximately seventeen words, so "Barbie" was another milestone—actually made you believe that if you bought the car, you could also buy the life. As if on the weekends, we'd be careening down sides of mountains or hurtling through white-water-filled rivers or picnicking in a dewy,

crisply green meadow at sunset with a field of sunflowers just behind us.

Ding. Ding. Ding. Ding. Ding. Ding.

Mama.

More.

Dog.

Dada.

No.

Yes.

Kiss.

Milk.

Ball.

Up.

Balloon.

Hi.

Bottle.

Cup.

Bye.

Down.

Sleep.

I run the list of Katie's words over in my mind. I have them
down cold, of course, because I was the mother who knew these
things. I was the mother who dutifully jotted down every milestone
("4 months, 3 weeks: Katie rolled over today! Far ahead of the
6-month target!"), who nursed her until her first birthday exactly, per
the American Academy of Pediatrics' recommendation ("I'm so sad to
give it up," I told friends as wrinkles washed across my forehead to
note my air of sincerity), and who, as I have mentioned, tallied up
Katie's vocabulary to ensure that she was on track to fulfill her potential. Seventeen words. A gasp ahead of other eighteen-month-olds.

And now, we also had "Barbie."

Ding. Ding. Ding. Ding. Ding. Ding. Splat.

My eyes whip over to the upper corner of the windshield, where mildew-colored bird shit slowly oozes down. *Great*, I think. *Just fucking great. There's never any bird shit in the goddamn brochure.* I inhale and try to release the stress, as my Pilates teacher had taught me to do every Monday, Wednesday, and Friday morning from 10:00 to 11:00, after my nanny had arrived, and just before I went to the grocery store to pick up ingredients for dinner. I feel the air fill my chest, and it expands like a helium balloon.

I count to five and try not to gag. It's hard, after all, to clear my mind when the scent of fetid milk is wafting from the backseat. On the way home from a playdate yesterday, Katie had dumped her sippy cup on her head, for apparently no reason whatsoever, and since I'd already exhausted myself pretending to dote on the kids at this seemingly never-ending excruciatingly boring playdate, during which all the moms discussed diaper changes and nanny problems and potential preschool applications, I opted not to clean her car seat. *Fuck it*, I told myself, as I pulled my darling daughter and her crisp near-black curls from her saturated seat and called her a "silly willy" for dousing herself despite knowing better. *Just fuck it.*

And so I did. Which is why my Range Rover, which should have still smelled like a fine blend of lemon cleaner and shoe polish, now reeked like petrified puke.

The bird shit is snaking its way into the crack between the windshield and the side of the car when I notice that Mrs. Kwon is waving at me from inside of the dry cleaner. She is frantically, frantically flashing her hand through the air, with an alarmed, toothy smile that she wears just about every time I see her. Sometimes the alarm fades into cunning, but the toothiness remains the same.

Ding. Ding. Ding. Ding. Ding. Ding. Ding.

I heave myself from my car and make the steep step down to the pavement. I turn and look at the backs of my legs: They glisten from the perspiration and are pocked with marks from the seat, such that they form the perfect illusion of sheeny cellulite. I slam the door shut.

Suddenly, there is quiet. I couldn't hear the dings. But now, I do hear the quiet.

☙

"You no look so good," Mrs. Kwon says to me. The rack of clothes that hangs across and throughout the ceiling is snaking its way forward until she presses a button, and it stops abruptly. She grabs a pole and reaches up to unhook Henry's, my husband's, shirts. "You not sleeping? Because you really no look so good."

I press my lips together and morph my face into something like a smile. I can feel my cheeks digging into themselves, my dimples cratering.

"No," I say, and shake my head. "Not sleeping too much, I guess."

"What wrong?" Mrs. Kwon asks, as she wrestles the shirts down to our level.

"Nothing." I shrug. My face muscles are starting to tremble from the weight of the forced smile. "Nothing at all."

"You not being honest," Mrs. Kwon chastises. "When you no sleep, something is always wrong." She lands the shirts, much like how I imagine a fisherman lands his catch, and splays them across the counter.

I don't answer. Instead, I sift through my purse for my wallet.

"Have you talk to husband about it?" Mrs. Kwon is relentless. "You always picking up his things, but I never meet him. Why? Where is he? Why he never pick up his own shirts?"

"He's working," I say.

"Eh," she responds. "Men always working. They not realizing that the women are working, too." She gestures behind her. "My husband think that because I am wife, I have to clean, cook, and still do dry-clean business. What does he do? Nothing!" She shimmies her hands even more exuberantly than normal.

I smile with what I hope to be sympathy and wait for my change, as she punches the cash register with fervor.

"You know what you need?" she asks, as the drawer to the register bounces open. "More sex." I feel myself turning a hue of purple, which she quickly detects. "Don't you be embarrassed! Every woman need more sex. You sleep better. Your marriage better. Sex make all things better."

"Well, unfortunately," I say, trying to swallow the mortification that comes with your dry cleaner giving you advice on your carnal activities, "Henry is in London. And will be for at least another week." I don't mention that Henry is nearly always in London or San Francisco or Hong Kong or somewhere that isn't our quaint, homey suburb tucked away thirty miles from Manhattan, where people flee from the city life like fugitives who aren't sure what they're outrunning. Henry's constant travel was the price we paid for his success as the youngest partner at his boutique investment bank.

"Oooh, that too bad." Mrs. Kwon's eyes grow small. "You do look like you need some good sex." She shrugs and flashes her teeth again. "Maybe next week you look better!"

Maybe, I think, as I plod out to my sure-to-make-my-life-rosy new car. *But, then again, probably not.*

❧

RIGHT THERE, I nearly moan out load. *Yes, harder right there.*

Garland must have intuited my angst because at that very moment, I feel his fingertips knead into my upper shoulders like a baker might bread.

"You're spasming here," he whispers just loudly enough so I can hear him over the Enya. I feel my muscle involuntarily clench up and resist the very relief that I'm trying to offer it. "This entire section of your back is in deep spasm," he repeats. "We're going to have to do a lot of work on this today."

I grunt and rearrange my face in the donut cushion so that I, ideally, won't look half-alien when Garland is done. Not that he hasn't seen me at my worst before: Once, on my worst day, I devolved into sputtering sobs as his hands worked their way down my torso, releasing what he later told me was "disturbed energy" that came unjiggered through the power of massage. But still. It wasn't a look to which I aspired. Not least because, as my friends from Pilates informed me, Garland, with his sinewy forearms and espresso-colored hair, would occasionally put his hands in places where, perhaps, management wouldn't approve. But where my friends very much did.

But I'd been seeing him every other week for nearly four months, and as of yet, nothing inappropriate at all. Which, in some ways, was a relief. Henry and I had met at twenty-seven, and for the past seven years, there had been no one else. Nor had I truly wanted there to be. I was a wife. I was a *good* wife, and fantasizing about your masseuse, no, fantasizing about *anyone* was outside the bounds of what I characterized a "good" wife to be. I attended the requisite cocktail parties for Henry's firm. I washed our ivory damask sheets every Saturday. I ironed Katie's gingham dresses so that there wasn't a literal thread out of place.

Of course, despite my best and most public efforts, my subconscious occasionally led me down paths that my current consciousness couldn't control. So while Garland worked his delicious finger magic on me, I couldn't help but wonder how it would feel if those fingers wound their way beyond the acceptable parameters of what they teach you in massage school.

I heard him slap some eucalyptus oil between his hands, and my nerves along my spine exploded as he ran his palms over them.

The truth of the matter was that Mrs. Kwon wasn't entirely wrong. Henry and I were going stale, not because we wanted to, but because like a bag of cookies that had inadvertently been left open, the air in our marriage was slowly hardening our crusts.

When was the last time we had sex? I think, forgetting Garland's hands entirely. I filter through my brain until I land on a wedding we'd attended in the Berkshires two months earlier.

"We *have* to do it," I said to Henry, as we lay on the crisp sheets of the inn and both wished that we were asleep instead. "Seriously, Hen, I just read an article in *Redbook* that said that couples who have sex have a much deeper connection and are more likely to stay married."

"What about couples who would rather sleep?" He looked over at me and grinned. "Are they doomed?"

"It didn't say," I said tersely, and rolled to my side.

"I'm kidding, Jill, I'm kidding." I heard the sheets rustle below him as he moved to spoon me, and then, from behind, he slowly unbuttoned my shirt.

Okay, so that was two months, it's not that bad, I tell myself, readjusting my face in the cushion. *Especially because Henry is always away. That has to be taken into account when doing the math. He's always away.*

It didn't used to be like this, of course. When we first met, we ravaged each other like wild beasts, albeit without the wildness and maybe not quite like beasts, as Henry had an aversion to performing oral sex and usually begged off when I had my period, but certainly with the passion that a new relationship brings. And even if the sex wasn't as torrid as it had been in my previous relationship with Jackson, Henry and I clicked together in ways that were unexplainable but instinctual, as if by being with each other, Henry, the

up-and-coming finance guru with a swimmer's build and a mind
like a steel trap, and me, advertising executive, who had coined the
year's biggest jingle, "It's the zizz in the fizz that makes Coke what
it is," with my yoga-hardened abs, somehow illuminated all the de-
ficiencies in my prior boyfriends. I was drawn to him, liberated
with him, and in many ways, saved by him. When we met one night
at a dingy bar in the East Village, I was embroiled in a sinking relationship with Jackson—whom I'd met at graduate school; he was
getting his MFA, I was getting my MBA—that had boulders tied to
it that neither one of us seemed capable of cutting loose.

So it's not like it always used to be this way, I remind myself,
as Enya stopped crooning in the background and another New
Agey singer whom I don't recognize filters out through the speakers
overhead. But still. How could we get back on track? Redbook had
dozens of articles on it, but none of them seemed to help. What was
the one moment where we lost our way? Or was it a series of moments that snowballed into something larger, something intangible,
something careening forward with too much acceleration for us to
stop it now?

What I didn't think about—what I refused to allow myself to
think about—was that Ainsley, another friend from business school
who now lives in a house on my same cul-de-sac and who runs a
ridiculously lucrative eBay business from her garage that sells per-
sonalized baby gifts, had just gotten an invitation to Jackson's wedding. And that, despite the fact that we'd broken up seven years prior
and I'd been the one to finally—firmly and permanently—walk
away from him and on toward Henry, his engagement and upcoming
wedding still ate away at my emotional landscape, as if him avowing
himself to another woman was somehow a blight, a pox on me.

"Are you going to be okay if I tell you the news about Jack?"
Ainsley said two mornings ago when we were power walking with
our aerodynamic strollers in tow.

"Of course!" I said, waving my free hand but not turning to look her in the eye. "Is he still at *Esquire?*"

"Uh-huh," she said, between breaths. *Figures*, I thought. *Figures he'd stay at a job that he didn't love simply because of inertia. Figures that he'd never get that novel off the ground despite his best promises.*

"He's getting married," Ainsley said, shooting the bitterness straight out of me.

I should have responded. I suppose that the ten-second pause before I did respond was what gave me away. It must have been clear that within that ten-second pause—as my brain spun back to *how much I fucking loved him* and then to our first date at a falafel joint stuffed with undergrads where we had to shout above the raucous din but that we had so much to say to each other that it didn't matter, and then to our last and final date at China Fun when we were all talked out, and then to how, even though I'd found complete contentedness with Henry, sometimes I was haunted from the inside out by how much I still craved Jackson, his spontaneity, his zeal, his ability to wander through life without a defined to-do list, and Henry was always, *always* armed with a to-do list—I was in no way okay. Frames from my old life flashed through my brain the way that they do in the movies just before the hero is set to die: the camaraderie that I thrived on at the ad agency, the lazy Saturday mornings when Jack had toted his laptop to the neighborhood diner to work on his stagnant novel and I had forty-five minutes of quiet time just to nurse my coffee and stare out the window dreaming of nothing at all, the Christmas vacation before I ever even met Jack, when Ainsley and I booked a last-minute trip to Paris and kissed random French men on the night before New Year's Eve. There were so many things to miss about my pre-Henry, pre-Katie, pre–this era life; Jack was just one of them.

"Of course I'm okay!" I chirped to Ainsley breathlessly,

partially due to the clip of our pace, partially due to her announcement over his impending nuptials. "I mean, it's been *seven* years for God's sake."

"It's fine if you're not." She shrugged. "It would be totally normal if you're not."

"Well, I am," I answered. "My life with Henry and Katie is exactly where I'm supposed to be. And I have no doubt about that."

We pushed ahead silently, pacing ourselves only by our rapid breaths and the hum of the wheels of our strollers.

Why didn't I just tell her? I think now, with Garland's hands deep into my deltoids. Why didn't I just come out and say, "Ainsley, I think that something's broken between Henry and me. When he goes away for weeks on end, I barely notice the difference, and sometimes, when he's home, I peer over at him, across the living room or over the dining table, and I search his face to try to rediscover what I once found attractive"? Why didn't I just tell her that two Saturdays ago, with Henry in Los Angeles, and a babysitter already booked, I went to see a silly Orlando Bloom–Kate Hudson romantic comedy by myself, and spent the entire remainder of the evening wondering if Orlando Bloom couldn't come rescue me from my spiraling marriage? *Orlando Bloom!* I wrapped myself up in my fantasy and dreamed of bumping into him in TriBeCa or maybe on a vacation to London or just about anywhere other than here. When I trekked to pick up groceries on Monday, I saw his face splashed on a tabloid cover—he was caught canoodling with a supermodel—and felt a tangible, pitiful jolt of jealousy. *Orlando Bloom!* Why didn't I tell Ainsley about Orlando Bloom? She would have found a way to make it funny, to have it all make sense.

But Jack, he wasn't as funny, he didn't make any sort of sense. Or maybe he made too much. Ainsley knew this; I knew this, which is why, I suppose, neither of us dug too deeply as we wound through our neighborhood in a fruitless effort to lose those last eight pregnancy pounds.

And now, lying here with the eucalyptus oils and the hum of spiritual chants and Garland's magical hands, there's no one left to lie to, and I can't help but reconsider.

What if I'd chosen Jackson? What if Henry wasn't supposed to be the one for me? What if I'd never married Henry in the first place? My whole body tenses, and I feel Garland's fingers sink in farther in response. I exhale and push it away. *No. I am happy.* I am a loving wife with a beautiful daughter who speaks, count them, *eighteen whole words*, and whose husband has lit up Wall Street and who can still give me an orgasm, even if it is under duress. (For him, not me.)

I press my eyes shut and will the thoughts away. But they refuse to comply, and instead, they lodge themselves in the crevasses of my brain, poking out just enough that I know they're still with me, like a tiny splinter in your baby toe that gnaws away at you with every step you take.

Garland rolls my glutes like Play-Doh, and I refocus my mind, letting it wander into blank space, into nothingness.

"Your chi is blocked," I hear Garland whisper in my left ear. "I'm going to work to unblock it, but you'll feel some pressure."

"Okay," I grunt.

"Deep breath," he says. "This might hurt."

His hands delve into my temples, then spider down the back of my neck, until his elbows torpedo into the hollow just below my shoulder blades. I let out a gasp that signals that fine line, somewhere between pleasure and pain, and in an instant, I've forgotten all about Henry and Jackson and rotten milk in the car seat and those stupid eighteen fucking words, and all I can do is bite the inside of my lip, breathe, and wish that every moment of my silly insignificant life could feel as good as this one.

Chapter Two

I need to get up. I've been telling myself that I need to get up for at least a good five minutes, and yet I can't move. A jackhammer seems to be beating on my brain, and the inside of my mouth tastes like rotten tangerine. I'm certain that it's light outside, but my sleep mask has blocked out all the offending rays, so I can see only the flashes of yellow that reflect behind my closed eyelids.

"Katie must be awake," I mutter aloud to no one other than myself. *She must be playing in her crib with her stuffed brown doggie that Henry's mother bought her, and she's probably hungry, so get your ass out of bed and go get her.*

Breakfast. The thought makes my stomach leap, and I feel like I might vomit. I raise my seemingly steel-weighted arm to my forehead and run my fingers along my hairline, pulling off a film of old sweat.

Get up. Get up. I repeat to myself again.

With my eyeshade still in place, I swing my knees up and over the side of the bed.

"Ow, crap!" I yell, and frantically fling my sleep mask off my face. My knees have hit a wall, a literal wall, not the type of wall that my spinning instructor refers to when we have ten minutes left in class. I'm now left curled up in the fetal position facing a white plaster wall to which my bed is firmly pressed.

I spin my head to the side.

This is not my room. This is clearly not my room. Yet it's inherently familiar. I know it somehow.

I push myself up and my insides lurch. I'm hungover. Yes, I'm very clearly and certainly hungover. I try to scan my mind for hints of the night before. I can't. I can't remember anything other than my blocked chi and Garland's elbows and how I felt like my body exploded when he pressed me with them.

I propel off the full-sized bed, with its red plaid sheets and the pine headboard that is definitely from IKEA. A memory washes over me of the trip to the store, of bobbing and weaving in the bedding department until we settled on this one. *We.* I'm stricken. I'm ill. I rush toward the bathroom, which I instinctively know is just off to the right of the bedroom. I purge my insides.

We. Jackson and me.

Not possible.

I close my eyes again and reach for the toilet paper to wipe my mouth, then pull up and trip my way to the sink. Under the soft glare of the mirror lights, one of which is burned out, I peer at myself. I pull back my highlighted brown hair that cascades down to the break below my shoulder blades—hair that the last I'd seen had been chopped into a bob that hung just above the nape of my neck and, surely, was at least two shades darker—and I stare. The slight wrinkles around my eyes have yet to seep in; the mole, the one I had removed because it was beginning to bulge, still resides just to the right of my nose; my double ear-pierce, which Jack's mom deemed "slightly déclassé" the last time we had dinner, remains intact.

I am a younger version of myself. Only not.

I spin around, now frantic, and race to the living room, flinging open the walk-in closet door and planting myself inside. It is filled, packed, overloaded with my clothes, my student clothes, not the clothes of my mommy life that conceal the clothes from my business life that are now tucked and organized neatly by color scheme and necessity in my closet in the suburbs of my life.

I stumble into the living room, first stopping to vomit again in the toilet, and see, perched above the fireplace mantel, a picture of Jackson and me celebrating my twenty-seventh birthday—it's nearly impossible to make out the decorations on the cake due to the two dozen plus candles that illuminate it. Another frame holds a shot of Ainsley; Megan, my best friend from high school; and me ringing in the New Year in 1999. Prince instantly fills my head, a flashback to the song that played on a loop in the days leading up to the milestone night, as we ushered in the next decade.

The phone rings, and I jump at least a good two feet in the air. It's only then I notice that I'm naked. *I never sleep naked*, I think. At least not anymore. Now I sleep in silk pajamas that I buy at the Nordstrom half-yearly sale. I stock up on undies and jammies every July. I stopped sleeping naked when Henry and I moved in together because Henry never slept naked, and, well, it just seemed weird to sleep naked by myself.

The machine clicks on.

"Hi, you've reached Jillian and Jackson," I hear myself say. "We can't get to the phone right now, but we'll call you back as soon as we can! Have a good one!"

There's a long beep.

"Jill, it's me. I tried you at work, but you weren't in yet. Calling about our plans. Buzz me."

Megan. Oh my God, it's fucking Megan. I walk over to the machine and stare at it, playing the message again, and then over again once more. *Not possible. Not in any way possible.* Three years ago, Megan drove off the road late one night and collided with a steel pole. She was out in California for business and heading home from dinner and fell asleep at the wheel. At least that was what the police supposed; they never found skid marks and there were no witnesses, so we got a few "Sorry for your losses, ma'am," and her husband, Tyler, got a bloodied wallet, an engagement ring, and a wedding band, and that was it. They said that the best they could tell, she died instantly. I clutched Henry's hand at her funeral on a damp day in October, just before all the leaves plunged from the trees.

I fall onto the cheap beige couch, the one whose fabric scratched your back and that I'd begged and pleaded and whimpered at Jackson to toss out to no avail because, as he told me, "I'm not good with change, babe, and I love this couch and have had it since college, so come on, you can deal," and surveyed the landscape.

I was, unquestionably, back here. Back in the land of my future self's what-ifs. *What if I hadn't tossed aside my former life like it wasn't a life preserver that I might one day need? What if I'd done it all differently when I had a chance? What if, what if, what if?*

The better question is, it seemed, what now?

℮

THE PAPER ON the front hall table says Thursday, July 13, 2000. The headlines trumpet the race for the White House: Is George Bush's record in Texas strong enough to win over voters and can Al Gore select the right vice president to give him a boost? The entertainment section sings about a little movie called *X-Men*, opening the following day, which I knew would skyrocket an Aussie named Hugh Jackman to near superstardom and spawn two sequels. I toss the paper on the floor, run to my desk in the living room, and pick up the cordless.

1-914-555-2973.

I dial my home number. Nancy, my nanny, might pick up.

"Please pick up, please pick up," I whisper fervently as I press the buttons with zealous intensity.

I'm greeted with a high-pitched recording: "The number you requested is not in service. Please check the number you are calling and try again."

I slam down the phone and stare blankly out the window. Shit. I don't know what else to do.

Without warning, my neighbor appears in the window directly opposite and only five feet away, and turns to stare. I offer a frantic wave, and only then realize that I'm still stark nude. I feel my eyebrows dart to my hairline and rush to the bedroom to cover myself.

My closet is crammed and stuffed and bursting, and I wonder how I ever lived like this—in a state of controlled chaos—but then I remember that for years, it provided me comfort: that when my mom left the family, I picked up the literal slack, cleaning up for my little brother, organizing the kitchen so that my dad was never reminded that my mom ditched out, folding and fussing and keeping everything *just so*, as if a linear material life translated to a linear emotional one as well.

When I got to college, when I finally fled the suffocation that I'd built around myself—because, to my father's credit, he'd never asked me to captain our plagued family's ship—it all collapsed. You couldn't walk through my dorm room without stumbling on a week-old pizza box or a marketing textbook from the previous semester or a bra that desperately needed to be washed but was instead peeping out from underneath my twin bed.

So now, trapped in the closet of my former self, nothing is too different from how it used to be. T-shirts drip from shelves, mismatched shoes are stacked atop one another, pashminas, which were everywhere the past few seasons, are balled and tossed into the back left corner.

I pick up a sweatshirt from the floor and fling it over my head. It smells familiar yet distant, and I shake my head, trying to recapture the memory.

Jackson. It smells exactly like Jackson.

I look down and see that, indeed, it's his. Or had been. Or maybe it still is now, if I could just fucking figure out what the hell is going on. But whoever possesses this sweatshirt now in the time-space continuum, it had, at one point, been my favorite. Graying all over and frayed at the wrists and with a stain from chocolate pudding right over the belly button, the front read xxx, and underneath it said U OF M ATHLETICS: It had been Jack's when he played for Michigan's lacrosse team. I run my hands over the lettering and wrap myself up in my arms.

It was hard not to admit that the sweatshirt felt a bit like home.

❧

IN THE LIVING ROOM, the clock glares 10:27 A.M.

So if it is July 13, 2000, that means that, as Megan suggested on her message, I should be at work. I am, at present (or at past), an account manager at Dewey, Morris, and Prince, the leading advertising firm for consumer products.

I notice a Filofax on my desk, and now, more appropriately clad so my neighbors don't get a midmorning peep show, I make my way over and plunk down in the wrought-iron chair that *we'd* bought at Pier 1 when *we* moved in together last December: We'd apartment hunted for three months and finally discovered this modern, yet still-funky-with-prewar-details one-bedroom in the West Village.

"To us," Jack had toasted on Christmas Eve, a week after we'd wrestled a tree into the apartment, a match that left the tree nearly victorious and left both of us with swollen gashes from head (above

Jack's eye) to tip (I couldn't type for three days due to gnarled fingers). "To living together, and to us."

I smiled sweetly and pushed up on my tiptoes, kissing him softly on his too-chapped lips, and agreed. "Yes, to us."

"Jack and Jill," he chuckled, then moved toward the kitchen to refill his wine. "Everyone says that it was fated."

"Everyone does," I agreed, and plopped down on the (itchy, stupid, I-hate-it-so-much) couch and waited for him to do the same so we could zone out to *ER* reruns and pretend that we didn't regret declining my father and his girlfriend's invitation to join them in Belize, even though it was subarctic in New York and we both felt nearly smothered from all the tourists.

Now, I run my fingers through the pages of my date book until they land on today.

Blank. Nada. No helpful reminders at all of what, precisely, I should be doing. I flip a day forward.

Aha. A note to myself that tomorrow, my team at DMP is set to meet with the executives from Coke. I remember that, in my old (or current?) state, I spent hours and days and weeks crafting the perfect pitch, the pitch that would eventually shoot me on a trajectory toward the advertising stratosphere, the same trajectory that I'd abandon at the very hint of Henry's suggestion that, now three months pregnant, we should "trudge" (my word, not his—I believe he said, with glee in his voice, "pack it in for greener pastures") toward the suburbs to find more serenity for our yet-unborn child.

Katie!

I break from my nostalgia-filled mind trip and remember. *Katie! Is she okay without me? Is she hungry? Is she in her crib clutching her doggie and screaming her face off because she hasn't had her morning oatmeal and her daddy is in London and her mommy is stuck in her ex-boyfriend's apartment from 2000? Katie!*

My eyes flood with tears, and I feel my pulse beat through the skin on my moist neck. I reach to call Nancy, my nanny, again, but realize it's to no avail.

It hits me suddenly, brutally and instantly. If I am here, if I am stuck in this wasteland from 2000, then there is no Katie. Not yet. Maybe not ever. She's not rolling around in her crib or working on pushing out her nineteenth word or gazing blankly at the Wiggles while a look that can only be described as lobotomized washes over her face as they sing about their (fucking annoying) Big Red Car over and over and over again. She's nothing but a memory trapped inside of me, an ephemeral, intangible glimpse of where I'm supposed to be headed.

Only now, as I survey the contents of my former life, I'm not sure which direction to go.

Chapter Three

A cell phone is ringing, and I can't find it. I've flipped over the tan fleece blanket that (slightly) covers our (horrid) couch, I've run into the kitchen and cased the counters, and I'm now burying my hands into a purse that I find on one of our wicker chairs (bought on the same outing to Pier 1 as my desk chair) in the dining area. *I remember this purse! I loved this purse!* My father had bought it for me when I got my summer job at DMP after my first year at business school.

What the hell happened to this purse? Did I toss it when we moved? I think, as I finally clasp the vibrating phone that is clanging to the tune of *NSYNC's "Bye Bye Bye."

"It ain't no lie, baby, bye, bye bye," I hum underneath my breath, flipping the phone open and bringing it to my ear.

"Hello?" I pause. "Er, this is Jillian speaking." I freeze, allowing only my eyeballs to move, as if somehow I'm getting caught doing something terribly illicit. I hear air move through my nose as I inhale.

"Uh, Jill? It's Gene. Where are you?" Gene, my intern at DMP who occasionally poses as my assistant, is whispering into the phone.

"I'm here! I'm *here*," I say with emphasis.

"Er, are you okay? You sound . . . strange." I hear a phone ring in the background of the office.

"Fine, fine! I'm fine! What's up? Where are *you*, Gene? Where are *you*?" I open the front door and peek out of it, as if he might appear on the other side. The hallway is empty, so I close the door firmly shut.

"I'm here, Jill. I'm at work!" He speaks very slowly as if I might not understand English. "You're missing the big brainstorming session for Coke, and I was worried. Everyone is asking for you."

"Oh," I answer. "Uh, no, I'm feeling sick today." My brain is spinning. "I, uh, just woke up and forgot to call. Sorry!"

"Okay," he answers with hesitation. "You sure you're okay?"

There are so many questions I want to ask him, drain from him, but just as I'm about to, I hear the front latch click open.

"Yes! Yes," I hiss. "I'll call you later!" I slam the top of the phone closed and toss it onto the pillows of the couch, where it lands with a bounce. Frantically, I spin around, just in time to see Jackson stepping inside.

My spine shoots up straight like I'd been plugged into an eight-volt, and the mere sight of him literally causes my breath to leave my body. I feel my chest tighten.

The humidity from the July air had pasted his wavy blond bangs onto his forehead, so they almost appear painted on, and black circles cloud his naked blue eyes, but he is still handsome in the way that causes girls to turn and look when he walks by, handsome enough that when we met at a campus party two years back, I'd given him, no, I'd pushed on him, my number without hesitation, even though we were both falling-down drunk and I was in no condition to impress anyone. Nor was he.

"Hey," he says, tossing his messenger bag on the floor, and

looking up at me. I am standing with my mouth agape, unable to form audible words. My eyes most certainly bug.

"Hey," he says again, moving closer, eventually close enough to plant a kiss on my forehead. "I called you at work and no one knew where you were, so I tried your cell, but you didn't answer. I wanted to come home to make sure you were okay."

Still, I cannot speak, so I squeak out something that sounds like "eep."

Jack steps back and looks me square in the eye. "Seriously, Jill, what's wrong?"

"Not feeling well," I manage. "Sick." My throat feels like flypaper. I move to one of the (hideous) wicker chairs and sit.

"You look . . ." Jack cocks his head to assess me. "You look high." He furrows his brow with concern. "What's going on?"

"Sick, I'm sick," I repeat. "Took some DayQuil. Maybe that's why I look this way."

"We have that? I thought you were on an antimedication kick." Jack heads to the bathroom to check.

Oh shit, that was true. I was. My team had decided to represent a naturopathic client who claimed that just about everything could be cured by everyday foods found in your pantry, and in one fell swoop, I gutted our medicine cabinet.

"Ooh, no, changed my mind. As is my right! Right?" I bite into the cuticle on my thumb. "I ran out and bought some this morning."

Jack pops back into the living room. "Yeah, you were all sweaty when I woke up this morning. Your pillow was soaked. I guess you had one shot too many last night. Sorry. That was my fault." He laughs and leans over to kiss my forehead.

I have no idea what shot or which party he is referencing—Jack and I were always darting from one event to the next—so I just bob my head like a parrot and hope that I look convincing.

"So . . . I was there when you woke up this morning?" I ask pointedly.

"Sweetie? Go back to bed. You're delirious. You're there every morning when I get up. Dead to the world until the alarm goes off at 7:45, but yes, you're there."

"Interesting," I mutter, more to myself than to him.

"Okay, well, if you're this sick, I'm calling Megan and Tyler to cancel dinner. No way can you make it like this."

Dinner. Dinner with Megan and Tyler. I try to think back to it, and reach for the Filofax, hoping Jack won't notice, to jog my mind. Yes, that's right! Tonight's the night that she's seven weeks pregnant; "too early," they'll say, "to tell anyone, but we couldn't help ourselves with you guys." Six days later, she'll miscarry, and I'll be the one she calls for rescue.

"No, no," I say to Jack, standing to kiss him, as if that's an assurance that I'm well on my way to healthfulness. He recoils at the scent of my rancid breath. "We're going. Where is it again?"

"Café Largo? You picked it. You got pissy when I suggested somewhere else . . ." Jack's voice drifts off. "Are you sure you're okay?"

I try to recall the fight we had over the restaurant. Vaguely, it comes to me. Jack silently seething that I'd chosen a spot that I knew he detested, me screaming into his voiceless void that he should have suggested somewhere else when I asked for his input but that "it was so damn typical of him to cruise along while I did all the work," him responding "that it was only *fucking reservations* and not exactly a big deal" and then slamming the door to our bedroom, and me left wondering how we ever imagined we could coexist under the same roof.

Now—after years of knowing what real problems were, after living with a man who was cautiously loving but no longer fawningly committed, a man who was rational and smart but not quite passionate or spontaneous, after slowly spinning away from the person I vowed to be true to for the rest of my years, after feeling like I lost myself in his shadows and goals—the arguments over restaurants, over who took the trash out last seemed futile, silly, and so much easier than the hurdles that Henry and I would come to face in the road of the future.

"I'm sorry that we're going there," I say softly, cupping his stubbly face in my right hand. "I know that you hate it." I can't remember why I insisted on Café Largo so many years back, but I suspect that it was done to retaliate to some wrong that I thought Jack had inflicted on me. That was how we worked, Jack and me. Do to me what I have done to you; an eye for an eye, and all of that.

"Uh, don't worry about it. We resolved it." His eyes are still searching, awash in confusion and worry. "Okay, I have to get back to work, but get back into bed for a while . . . you look . . . not right."

He takes my arm and ushers me to the bedroom, pulling back the covers with a flourish and watching as I crawl inside. He leans down to kiss me. "Okay, see you tonight. I love you."

I gnaw again on the inside of my cheek. What was I supposed to say in response? I'd spent the past seven years squashing out any reminders of lingering emotional ties to Jackson, ensuring that his fingerprints weren't still marked all over my body, that when I walked away, there were no regrets, no take-backs, and certainly no look-backs.

And now here he was. With his love and his hope and, yes, his imperfections, that, in a few months if everything mirrored the events of my prior life, I'd soon trade in for the love and hope of another man who was equally imperfect, though in far different ways. So, rather than turn the moment into something that it was not, I simply respond as I would have seven years back, back when my younger self did love him, back before my older self stopped allowing myself to wonder if I still *did* love him, and before my masseuse liberated my chi, which seemed to have liberated something else entirely.

And so, I say, "I love you, too," as he makes his way out the door.

It ain't no lie. *NSYNC echoes over and again in my mind. *Baby, bye, bye, bye, bye, bye.*

❧

AN HOUR LATER, I have handed the taxi driver a wad of bills—I always kept a stash in my sock drawer for emergencies and this, certainly, constitutes an emergency, though not the type that I ever saved for—and am holding my hand in front of my face to ward off the glare of the late-morning sun. I stare at my house. My future house. My current house. I don't know.

It looks different, indistinguishably different, but different all the same. Like one of those educational games that I'd do with Katie: All but one element of a picture remains the same, and the trick is pinpointing the teeny, tiny thing that's been swapped out. Maybe a briefcase has been tilted or maybe the leaves on the trees are a different hue of green. Sometimes, she'd see the change before I did—my eighteen-month-old outsmarting me!—and we'd clap our hands and sing aloud and deem her just about the most brilliant creature known to humankind.

I cock my head and search for what's shifted. Maybe the paint on the shutters is fraying a bit more? Maybe the flower beds out front hold irises, not the daffodils I'd nurtured the past two years? I can't tell. "Is this my house? Is it the house of my future?" I mutter to myself as I wind down the brick pathway and burrow into my purse for my keys. It seems futile, insane, to come back here, after what

I've just encountered with Jack. But Katie! I can't just leave Katie! What if she's here? What if I've fallen down some mind-bending rabbit hole, and this is all an LSD trip gone bad? What if I didn't try to come back for her?

Katie! My fingers shake as I push the key into the lock. I jigger it but the latch refuses to turn. I shake it and wrench it in a bit more, furiously pushing and noticeably starting to sweat, when I hear footsteps behind the door. I try to wiggle it out, losing all sense of composure, and realize that my keys are most definitely stuck in the front door to my potential home, when the giant black door swings open to an alarmed-looking late-thirtysomething who appears to be dressed for tennis. I recognize her almost immediately: Lydia Hewitt. And in five years, she and her husband, Donald, would sell us this house when Donald took a promotion in Nashville, and Lydia would blink back tears, urging us to enjoy the home, barely disguising her rancor at being uprooted for her husband's mildly flourishing career in sales at a cell phone distributor.

"Can I help you?" Lydia looks exactly how you'd expect someone to look when you open your door to find a stranger attempting to unlock it. Alarmed, frightened, armed with her racket and a mean forehand.

I take a step back. "I'm . . . I'm sorry," I stutter. "I must be confused. I thought this was my house."

Her grip on her racket noticeably loosens, as she realizes that I'm not here to attack or rob her dry. Just, perhaps, a delirious neighbor who seems to have lost her way.

"Er, no," she says, still somewhat on guard, but softer. "Are you sick? Lost? Should I call someone?"

I peer over her shoulder into the foyer with lavender wallpaper that Henry and I would immediately strip and replace with a coat of cool beige paint, and run my eyes into the kitchen, where Katie would first learn how to crawl. But there are no signs of life here, not signs of *my* life here, anyway. This is Lydia's home, not mine. And not Katie's. Certainly not Katie's.

"I'm sorry to disturb," I say quietly, turning back down the walkway to the cab that lingered by the curb because I'd asked the driver to keep the meter running. "It won't happen again."

"Are you sure?" she shouts to my back. "I'm happy to make a call."

But I don't answer. I only slam the door of the taxi and direct the cabbie back home, back to my *former* home, that is. Because what I can't tell Lydia is that there is no one to call. There is only me, my past, and the holes that I now have to fill in between.

Chapter Four

I arrive early at Café Largo, a characteristic from my old life that I could never shake. Henry, though so fastidious and meticulous in nearly every aspect of his life, ran perpetually late—an anomaly that only pure human quirk can explain. I'd learned to adjust to it—waiting in restaurants, waiting at home for him to come to relieve me so I could finally, desperately, have a girls' night out, waiting for him to get out of the house while Katie and I were already parked in the car—but my personal clock never matched up with his. Most couples do. Most couples acclimate so that a year into the relationship, the early one is almost always constantly running a good twenty minutes behind or vice versa, but Henry and I, well, we just never clicked.

I'm ensconced in a back booth, my fingers keeping time on the citrus-colored tiled table to the saxophone that soared in the background, when I look up and see Jack coming straight toward me.

"Hey," he says, leaning down to brush my lips against his, his lavender tie skimming the tabletop. He surveys me, his brow furrowing. "How do you feel? You look . . ." He tilts his head to the right and pauses. "You look different. Did you do something with your hair?"

I scoot over, and he slides into the sparkly red leather booth beside me. I peer over at him rather than answer. *Jack!* I want to clamp onto his shoulders and shake him to make sure that he is real.

Instead, I press my palm over his sweaty hand.

"No," I say. "I haven't done anything with my hair." I smile. "But it's nice to see you."

He scrunches his face as if I'd just told him that the world was flat.

"But I'm feeling better, much better, so don't worry. Maybe I just needed a good day of rest."

"Maybe," he mumbles, unconvinced, and reaches for a menu, pulling his hand from under mine.

If I looked lighter, different, it might have been because of how I spent my day, because I felt lighter, different, too. After the cab had deposited me back at our apartment and after it became permanently clear that there were no take-backs, that this wasn't some sort of fluke or sick joke or eccentric dream gone bad, and after I plopped on my couch and tried to breathe and breathe and breathe, I made a decision. A shaky one at first, but then I carved it into my soul and swore to abide by it: *This was my second chance, this was what I'd been fervently hoping for.* So I opted to embrace it rather than run. It was, after all, all I could do, anyway. And with my decision planted, I looked up my old number at work, which, after finding it, came rushing back to me. How could I ever have forgotten it?

My career, right up until we packed it in for Westchester, was the one place I slid into the comfort of my skin. There were no reminders of a mother who ditched her family, no hints that I might be mired in a stagnant relationship with a boyfriend who loved me, yes, but who lacked a certain ambition and who might be a tad too worshipful of his own mother, no loneliness that plagued me even when I cuddled with Jackson underneath our IKEA headboard or drank merlot with my equally up-and-coming friends at the latest restaurant written up in *Time Out New York*. At work, I came into my own, as if I were inhabiting another person entirely, thriving on the creative highs and camaraderie of building a campaign from the ground up.

So, with a clearer head, I redialed Gene and assured him I'd be back tomorrow, in time for the meeting with Coke. Only this time, rather than spending the twenty-four hours leading up to the meeting in a frantic flurry trying to nail the quintessential pitch, I spent the afternoon rereading old e-mails, revisiting old photographs, reacquainting myself with my former life. A life, which viewed from wiser, well-worn glasses, didn't look so bad to begin with. Besides, I already had the perfect pitch for Coke, the one that would launch my career like a rocket ship, on a course that even I couldn't have anticipated. A course that would slam into a brick wall when Henry's sperm collided with my egg, and we'd produce the delicious Katie, who was born the color of spring calla lilies and who, though I'd sacrificed just about everything for her, I loved more wholly than anything else I'd ever touched my life through.

"Hellooooo!" I look up to see Megan, *Megan!*, standing by our booth.

"Meg!" I shout, and dig my elbows into Jack to push him out of the booth. "Meg! Oh my God, it's good to see you!" I throw my arms around her neck, and out of the corner of my eye, I can see her shoot a perplexed look at Jack, who just replies with an "I have no idea what the hell is wrong with her" shrug.

"Er, Jill, I saw you three days ago," she says, breaking our embrace, even as I try not to let go. *That's right, we did! God, how I missed my single life, when Jack and I painted the city, out every night, the rush of undiscovered opportunity always beckoning.*

"I know, I know," I say. "But you just look . . . you look

glowing." Her eyebrows dance downward, and my own eyes widen. Have I given anything away? *Crap.* I usher her into the booth, and plop back down on the other side of Jack.

"So . . ." I rub my hands together. "Let's order! And then let's share. What's going on with you? How have you been? Where's Tyler? I've *missed* you." I reach my hands across the table to clutch hers and smile.

"Seriously, Jill, what's going on? You're starting to freak me out."

"How so?" I ask, and take a deep gulp of water: I'm suddenly parched.

"Well, for one, you're talking very, very fast. For two, you're acting like we don't do this every other week. For three . . . ," her voice drifted. "You look different. Did you self-tan or something?"

"I know!" Jack chimes in. "I said the same thing."

"I did nothing," I reply, as my blood rushes to my chest, and I hope that my hives don't run flush the way they're prone to during fits of anxiety. "You guys are ridiculous!" But even as I say this, I can hear my pitch is off a decibel and the words come out like race cars.

"It must be the meds talking then," says Jack, just as Tyler makes his entry, and I bound from my seat to nearly tackle him. After Megan's death, Tyler spiraled downward into an abyss of steely blankness, as if Megan were the only color in his life, and without it, there was only white, black, and gray. He numbed his pain with booze, and slowly, wrenchingly, pulled away from all of us, isolating himself in an angry cocoon where none of us could reach him and he didn't want to be reached.

But now, here he was, so vibrant with his ruddy cheeks and his strawberry hair and his paunch that Megan playfully rubbed when she (re)broke the news about her impending pregnancy, and said, "Pretty soon, I'll actually be bigger than him."

I try to feign surprise at their announcement. I push glee into my voice and ask the waitress for another round of beers ("None for her," I kid, as if the poor struggling actress who bused tables for a living was in on the joke), and I imitate the revelry that imbued our lives that night years ago, even though I knew that it would be so short-lived, too short-lived. *But why not?* I think. *Why not savor this moment and drink it in as it's meant to be swallowed?* Let Megan and Tyler taste this happiness because soon enough, in six short days when she'd find blood in her underwear and cramps that haunted her from the inside out, they'd be stripped of all that. And then, four years later, when Meg is asleep at the wheel, they'd be stripped of so much more.

So I drink like there is literally no tomorrow, as if I don't know what that tomorrow would bring, and I bask in the glow of finding my second chance. I slip my hand under the table, and I weave my fingers into Jack's, and I try to forget that what happens next might already be fated, that we might all be fated to make the same mistakes over and back and over again, and that my coming back, my second chance might not be a second chance at all.

@

Five hours later, I stare at the ceiling, long after Jack has passed out beside me, and listen to his gentle wheeze of air—in out, in out, in out. I roll my thumb over my ring finger, an unconscious habit, and am struck by its nakedness. My rings, my signs of devotion to Henry and to my family, are no longer there, taken, gone, just like everything else from my future self.

I watch light bounce off the walls from the cars on the street below. Henry. Where was he now? There was no way of knowing. We weren't set to meet for another three months, *if I choose to meet him again,* I remind myself. Jack rolls to his side, lets out a sigh, and flings an arm around me.

It had only been a day, but still, I didn't miss Henry. I should; I
knew that I should, but what I felt wasn't the ache of a wife who
might have lost her husband. What I felt instead was relief. Relief
from the mundanity of our lives. Henry provided so many things—
security, warmth, a round, solid partner—but zeal, fire, no, not
them, and now, free from the suffocation of my seemingly claustrophobic relationship, I only felt free.

Maybe this is why my mother left. The thought startles me,
shaking something inside. Maybe she couldn't take the passive familiarity that comes from sharing a bathroom or swapping the
same stories night after night over dinner or scraping bird shit off
the Range Rover that was supposed to give you that shiny, pic-
turesque life. Maybe it was all too much, or really, all too little for
her. Maybe she dreamed of something more, and when I came
along, and then Andy, my brother, came along, she couldn't take
one more fucking minute of the Stepfordian existence that she'd
built with my father.

Not that my life with Henry was Stepfordian. My life with
Henry was perfectly placid. Ours was the marriage that people
looked at and said, "They'll make it. They're not going to be the
ones to split because he chased around his secretary or she slowly
drank herself to death." We *were* that couple in the Range Rover
ad, only ours was the picture taken after five years of marriage,
after we'd stopped noticing the other's intricacies, after we'd already wooed each other and pledged ourselves to each other, and
had, thus, in many ways, surrendered to complacency.

I'd read about this in *Redbook*—that scientists have discovered
that in the first year or so of marriage, your brain receptors still register chemicals that make you want to dry hump your spouse on
every flat surface that you can find. Then slowly, these chemicals
abate, and eventually, if you don't find ways to jump-start them—I
remember that the doctor who was interviewed suggested exhilarat-

ing experiences such as skydiving—then you're stuck waddling around the vestiges of your younger libidos and memories of what you once had.

I'd mentioned this to Henry one night when he was calling from San Francisco to say good night to Katie before her 7:30 (sharp!) bedtime.

"Maybe we should go skydiving together," I said, chopping a cucumber in our granite-countered, white-tiled kitchen. My head was angled to hold the phone between my ear and shoulder, and somewhere within one of my vertebrae, a cramp was beginning to form.

"Where's this coming from?" He laughed. "Besides, you're scared of flying."

"I know," I sort of whined. "But we need to relight the spark. And I read that this might do it."

"Our spark is just fine," he answered. "Stop worrying about our spark. Can you put Katie on before I run to a meeting?"

"Sure." I set down the knife and wandered into Katie's perky pink playroom, where she was pulling out the hair of a now nearly bald blond doll she'd insisted that I buy her during a two-minute trip to Toys "R" Us for a neighbor child's birthday present. Henry blew her kisses over the phone, then rattled off a quick "love you" (to me), before he dashed toward his waiting clients.

So now, with our spark nearly extinguished, I hardly feel bad about not missing him. *It's not like I didn't warn him*, I think. It's not like I didn't leave that goddamn *Redbook* article on his nightstand when he got home from his trip and asked him to read it so that he, too, could see the stupid signs that our marriage was a plundered ship that was slowly sinking under its own weight.

"Hey," Jackson says softly, rousing me from the memory. "Why are you still up?" His voice is creaky from sleep.

I shrug, though he can't see it in the darkness of the bedroom.

"Come here." He pulls toward me, and I inhale his scent of sandalwood and vanilla that even seven years later always reminded me of him, even when I was still close enough to remember why we'd come undone. As the years went on, those reasons, as they tend to do, became murkier, like a pond after a rainstorm, and after I got home from my power walk with Ainsley on which she broke the news of his upcoming wedding, I locked myself in the bathroom and heaved out purging tears for nearly thirty minutes. Then I splashed my face with water, dotted concealer under my eyes, and headed toward the market. I had dinner to plan, a family to feed, after all.

Jack shifts himself on top of me and tugs down the strap of my tank top, fluttering kisses on my shoulder and across my collarbone. In response, my hips rise to his without question, and he presses back down on mine. Quickly, too quickly, I'm tossing my shirt over my head, and he's making his way over my breasts, down to my belly button, then back up again, until the wait is almost unbearable, and I pull him inside of me.

Jesus Christ! I'd forgotten all about sex with Jack, I think. *Jesus, Jesus, Jesus! Holy Lord, Jesus!*

Jack and I find our rhythm easily, like it hadn't been more than a half decade since I'd done this with him, like I hadn't given myself to another man exclusively over the course of those years.

Shit, Henry. I hope for a fleeting second that this isn't considered adultery, but realize that I haven't technically *met* Henry, so I push the silly, inconsequential thought from my mind. It's not hard to do.

Jack flips me on top of him, and I feel like my insides might explode.

It's never like this with Henry, I think. *Hasn't really ever been like this with Henry.* And then, that's all I think about my soon-to-be or maybe-might-not-be husband because a few seconds later, I am awash in white heat and I can't think of anything at all.

We collapse on top of each other, silent and sweaty. Enveloped in the security of his arms, his measured breath on my neck, I wonder if I really can do it all over again; if this time, I can do it right, and if so, what that might mean for my old past and, thus, for my new future.

❧

SLEEP REFUSED ME. I try every trick I can think of, humming Katie's favorite lullabies to myself, mimicking Jack's breathing with my own, but nothing can slow down the racing in my mind.

It is clear, I realize once again with force, that there is no turning back from here. There is no trail of Katie's Cheerios to chase around the house, none of Henry's orange juice glasses to place in the dishwasher come morning. It is only me, this new life, and wherever it takes me.

I push myself up from the bed, rattling off any lingering grogginess, and wind my way into the spare bedroom, the one that Jack pretended was an office for his writing, but both of us knew was essentially a waste of square footage.

What if my other life was the one that I'd imagined? What if I never met Henry, never birthed Katie? What if this is all some sort of nauseating dream?

I feel my pulse tangibly speed up at the base of my neck. Because, true, I didn't miss Henry all that much and, more true, this small taste of freedom, of reprieve, was so glorious it was like inhaling barrelfuls of sunshine on an arctic day, but still. I don't want to forget. I don't want to forsake the memories of who I'd come to be, even though I realize, fully, that my regrets were both enormous and plentiful. But still.

And so, with a lucid mind and a shaking hand, I grab a pen from Jack's Michigan cup and a notepad tucked away by his printer.

And then, I begin to put it all down, on record, in case I can never get it back, in case, really, this isn't all a dream. Because whatever laments I might have, they're still worth holding on to, even as I'm trying to let them go.

☙ H E N R Y

I met Henry at a bar in the East Village called The Tetons, which was both asinine (there was no hint of mountainous decor) and fortuitous, as it served as excellent small-talk conversation fodder upon meeting.

I scurried into the dive and glanced around for Ainsley, who was training it in from Westchester at my behest. Jack and I were coming more than a little undone, and I needed a literal shoulder. Now, in retrospect, it's hard to remember all the reasons we were unraveling, but I do remember the initial panic that nearly choked me upon the thought of walking away from him.

Ainsley was late, so I slid onto a bar stool, ordered a cosmo, and wove my fingers through my hair, untangling knots brought on by the early-October wind and rain. The ends of my hair shook, and tiny droplets belly flopped to the floor, where they sank into beer-stained tiles. From the look of it, they were doing the floor a favor, really.

Beside me, a man with a slim nose and a smooth complexion was cracking peanuts with elegant fingers and piling up the shells into a neat, concise tower. I surveyed him as inconspicuously as I could and decided he must be an architect. A snap judgment, and I had no plan to investigate further, until he turned to me and said, "Have you ever been to the Tetons? I mean, besides this bar, which, obviously, isn't much like the real Tetons."

He laughed with no self-consciousness at all, fully aware, yet entirely unembarrassed, at the forwardness of his pickup line. I hadn't even noticed that he'd noticed me.

"No." I shook my head and smiled back, bigger, grander, than I'd meant to, but something about him made me not stop myself. "Camping isn't really my thing."

"Me neither." He shrugged. "Camping, that is. I did go to the Tetons in eleventh grade, though. Part of a wilderness trip. The mountains are beautiful. But that's pretty much when I learned that camping wasn't my thing."

We grinned at each other like this was some sort of secret, like some sort of inside joke that only the two of us got, even though, really, looking back on it seven years later, it seems almost insignificant, silly even.

They say that you can tell everything you need to know about a person in the first few minutes that you meet them. In retrospect, I suppose that this is true. Henry was in control and meticulous even then, but warm, too, welcoming in his way. And we easily fell into each other.

Ainsley called to say that her train had broken down, and a few minutes later, his friend also buzzed to say that he was stuck at work. But neither Henry nor I budged from our bar stools; instead, I ordered another cosmo, and he another beer, and we sat and sat and talked and talked, feeling like the luckiest people in the world, or at least, in The Tetons and the near vicinity.

☺

Chapter Five

Nice work," my boss, Josie, says on my first morning back in my old office, after our meeting with Coke management, and after I'd debuted my "It's the zizz in the fizz that makes Coke what it is" tagline, complete with storyboards of regular folk rapping to their made-up tunes with bubbles floating above them. Just like I knew Josie would say when she'd swing by my desk fifteen minutes after huddling in the conference room, in which the Coke team would agree to hire our agency for their monster marketing push.

"It was nothing," I say, slugging back my second coffee of the day.

My workstation, not unlike my closet, is in various degrees of disassembly and disarray. Post-it notes frame my computer screen, and tumbling stacks of paper cascade over one another and on top of pens, pencils, and stock photography, all of which neck their way close to my keyboard, which sits atop the only free space on my desk. Josie delicately displaces two tote bags that are clogged with freebies from potential clients from the chair opposite my desk and sits.

She looks as I remember her to look: sallow, worn, like someone who was once striking and who still had the potential for pure beauty but who lacked both the adequate sleep and necessary time to transform herself. Her dull brown hair is pulled into a messy bun at the nape of her neck, and the wrinkles around her eyes age her at least five years. On first glance, you'd easily mistake her for midforties even though she is one month shy of thirty-nine.

"So," she sighs. "Your idea was fantastic, obviously. I'm impressed with how well you pulled it all together as one cohesive idea."

I press my lips together and smile. It was easy, after all. I started with my catchphrase—the one I'd conceptualized all on my own seven years ago—then I poached the ideas that we later incorporated once Coke had signed on. Ben, an account executive, was the one who devised the "people on the street" backdrop, while Susan, our whiz over in graphics, dotted in the floating bubbles that bopped from person to person. Originally, I'd thrown out the tagline like a blindfolded person might a dart: I'd hoped that it would hit something in the vicinity. This time, I wrapped up those darts and handed them over with a bow.

"The plan is this," Josie continues, rubbing her eyes. "Coke wants the completed storyboards ready next week. Which means that if you have weekend plans, you have to cancel. Pass it along to the team. And obviously, I'll be here, too."

She stares at a stress ball that peeks out from under yesterday's paper on the corner of my desk. I knew she was thinking about her kids. How she'd have to tell them that Mom couldn't make it to their soccer match or play rehearsal or whatever eight- and ten-year-olds did on their weekends from which parents were supposed to reap complete joy. Josie's husband, Art, was a set designer for opera houses, which basically meant that he was mostly unemployed and home with the children. And which also meant that she didn't have a choice: that she sacrificed the opportunity to quit her job or take extended leave because, as she once told me after a happy hour filled with two too many chardonnays, "Someone has to pay the bills, and in my household, that person is me. Me! ME!"

"No, no, no," I say today. "You stay home. I have it under control."

"Don't be ridiculous, I'm the boss. Of course I'll be here."

I hear the resignation in her voice and wonder if she worries that her kids hate her. I want to tell her that they mostly came out fine. Yes, that at sixteen, her daughter, Amanda, would break into her high school, falling-down drunk, and get suspended for three days, but that as of now, armed with my glimpse into their future, they weren't in rehab and they weren't wearing armbands to symbolize their hatred for their mother, and that mostly, her family unit was intact, even if still, when she e-mailed me, I detected that simmering tone of resentment for the time that she'd lost because she'd spent so much of it at work.

"Josie, I insist." I lean toward her. "Look, really, I have this all mapped out in my mind. One hundred percent. This is second nature to me, and I absolutely don't need hand-holding this weekend." Relief washes over her face. "Spend the time with your kids. I'll call you if we run into a problem."

"You sure?" she says, standing to leave.

"Positive," I reiterate.

"Okay," she says. "I'll make you a deal. You deliver on this account, and I'll single-handedly prime you for my job."

"Deal." I nod.

I wait until she's shuffled out of my office to break into a Cheshire grin. Because Josie's crown, gold and shiny and so within my reach, feels like just the first of the riches that I'm here now to reap.

☙

FIVE DAYS LATER, a near eternity in my then-is-now-is-then warped world, my phone rings at work. I'm wrapping up the finishing touches on the storyboards, which, my bosses raved, had never been done more cleanly or efficiently, when the yellow light flashes on the phone and the ring bleats through my earpiece. I motion to my team to take a break and press "Talk."

"Jillian Westfield."

"Oh Jesus, Jill, I need help!" Megan sobs on the other end. I look at the calendar: I'd completely forgotten. Today is the day she miscarried. "Tyler is out of town, and no one else knows, and I can't stop bleeding!" Her voice spins its way into hysterics.

"Okay, Meg, calm down. I'm on my way. Will be there in ten." I whip my headset off and go to hang up, when I hear her screaming through it.

"You don't know where I am!"

Oh crap. I did, actually. We'd done this before. It hadn't gone well the first time, either.

"Where are you?" I say, just to placate her.

"I'm in the bathroom of the Pierre! And there's just blood . . . everywhere." She hiccups as she tries to take a breath. "I was in a lunch meeting . . . and it's just *everywhere!*" She dissolves into sputters, and I race off to save her.

I find her crumpled in a corner stall on the first floor of the hotel. Her skin is pasty and moist, her hands trembling, and her pants are bunched next to the toilet, ruddied and soiled and drenched. I'd already thought to call 911 on the way: Last time, I hadn't known the extent of the catastrophe and she'd lost enough blood to require a transfusion. This time, maybe I could change the wreckage that the miscarriage was about to wreak.

After the paramedics burst in and after I held her clammy hand in the ambulance and she wailed and begged the EMTs not to let her baby die, we sat in the solitude of her hospital room and waited for the doctors to come and explain what had gone so wrong that caused her body to purge its own flesh and blood.

"It's not your fault," I say to her softly, with only the beeping of her heart monitor as our backdrop, just like I said seven years ago.

"How can you know that?" she answers. Fat tears streak her cheeks.

"Because it's just not. Miscarriages aren't anyone's fault. They just happen." She doesn't reply and instead turns her face to stare out the window.

"I wanted this so badly," she says, finally, her voice breaking again. "Tyler and I have been trying for over a year."

"I'm sorry, Meg." I reach to touch her free arm, the one that's not hooked up to the IV.

A sturdy-looking African American doctor with kind green eyes finally breaks our mourning.

"The good news," he announces, looking at her chart, "is that we've stopped your bleeding, and there are no signs of infection."

"Oh thank God," I exhale loudly, even though I'd meant to keep it in. *I'd gotten there fast enough. Last time I hadn't. Maybe this time I had.* Meg glances over with a look of surprise, but I just smile. Last time, the damage was more severe, so this doctor had delivered far worse news. Last time, he'd muttered things about possible internal scarring, heavy blood loss, unclear prognosis on future fertility.

"But the bad news is," he continues and I feel my face drop, because this, I had indeed heard before, "that we don't know why you hemorrhaged. A normal miscarriage shouldn't bring anywhere near this amount of blood, but because you were so early in your pregnancy, it's very difficult for us to examine the embryo and assess what happened."

Megan's face curls up at the word *embryo*, and tears trickle out all over again.

"So what now?" she manages.

"Well, you'll bleed for another few weeks, and once your

obstetrician has given you the green light, you can certainly start trying again." Megan ekes out a smile, and the doctor clears his throat, ready to leave.

"But what about what happened today?" I press shrilly, even though I know Megan had gotten the answer she needed to hear— *you can certainly start trying again.* "Can't you get any answers from it? I mean, there has to be something we can take from this so it doesn't happen again!"

They both furrow their brows and look perplexedly at me, springing up from the faux-red leather chair like a carnival-issue jack-in-the-box.

"It's okay, Jill," Megan says. "He told me we can try again soon."

"Yes," the doctor chimes in. "Most miscarriages are simply a result of a genetic abnormality, and there's no reason that she'll have another because she had one already."

I watch Meg sigh, and I nod.

What I want to say, what I'm absolutely bursting to say, is that this isn't a genetic abnormality, at least it wasn't the last time I sat in the hospital and held her hand. That Megan's body would expel these tiny beings over and over again, and that maybe if we'd taken a closer look when we first rammed up against this gut-purging wall, things might have turned out differently.

But I got there sooner this time, I tell myself now. And even though the doctor's words echoed in the same manner as they did before and even though the sum of his prognosis was the same, I got there sooner. And maybe, just maybe, that would be enough to rewrite the future.

Chapter Six

It is 1:30 on a Saturday afternoon, and I am running late, frantically, hopelessly late. Which would be bad enough to begin with. But I am tearing through Grand Central Station, which is congested with wayward tourists and suburban dwellers in for the night and well over two dozen homeless men who have taken refuge inside from the sweltering, choking late-July air. My train is scheduled to pull out at 1:32, and though I am darting and bobbing through the clusters of people, there is little hope that I'll burst onto the platform in less than one hundred and twenty seconds.

Especially because I've yet to buy my ticket.

I skid to a stop in front of the counter, thrust forward twelve bucks, and ask for a round-trip ticket to Rye.

The giant electronic clock ticks above me, and that's it. I'm officially going to miss the opening festivities of Jackson's niece's birthday party. They start with a piñata, and then quickly move on to a treasure hunt before breaking for snacks.

This wasn't how it was supposed to go. I was supposed to arrive precisely at the appointed hour, where upon I'd spend the rest of the afternoon posturing and preening for Jack's three siblings, manning the bob-for-apples barrel, and most important, proving to his mother that I was smart enough/beautiful enough/savvy enough/ just enough to be dating her son.

And now I was late.

Just freaking great, I think, as I park on a bench and wipe off the beads of sweat that are launching from my cheekbones onto the parquet floor.

I'd spent the morning at the office: It turns out that even though I thought I had the literal foresight to know even the tiniest details of the Coke campaign, the actual work still required manpower, and since, unlike the last time around, I now helmed this ship, a good portion of that manpower came from me.

"But you'll be there, right?" Jack asked this morning, as I stuffed down a stale bagel and impatiently waited for the coffee to brew. "Because it will really help things."

I chewed on the dry dough and swallowed roughly to dislodge it from my throat.

"Of course I'll be there," I snapped. "There is nothing I'd rather do than spend the day attempting to impress your mother. Which, I should know, is a near impossibility."

"Come on, Jill," Jack said. "She had a right to be annoyed last month."

Though it had theoretically been over half a decade, I knew exactly to what he was referring. "The debacle" is what he would eventually call it, complete with the requisite finger quotes, and it was "the debacle" that would slowly heave our tilting relationship into a full-on nosedive, not unlike the *Titanic* before it broke in half and plunged under the icy waters of the Atlantic.

It was the sixtieth birthday party of Vivian, Jack's mom, in June 2000, and they'd come into the city to celebrate at a friend's apartment—one of those sprawling, full-floor apartments that would smell like money if it didn't smell like Murphy's oil and roses, thanks to the live-in housekeeper and on-call florist.

When we arrived, Jack, in a crisp gray suit, kissed his mother's cheek, and she pulled him in so tight I thought she might not let go. Then she held out a cool hand to me, said, "Jillian," with a cocked eyebrow, and I wondered if my nose would freeze off from her chill.

"Did you see that?" I whispered, as we made our way to the bar.

"Don't be ridiculous," Jack answered, motioning to the bartender for two scotches. "That's just her way. She's not one for affection for people other than family."

"Would it be too much for her to *change* her way for your girl-friend of two years?"

"Not now," Jack said. "I don't want to get into this now."

"It's always 'not now,' " I hissed, just as Jack's three older sisters approached.

"Drop it," he said with finality.

I grabbed my scotch and headed to the library to calm myself, emerging only for a refill, and then another. When Jack finally found me an hour later, I was twenty blurry pages into *Great Expectations.*

"It's toast time," he said. "Come out. Mother wants us all there."

"She won't miss me," I replied and flipped a page.

"Come out, Jillian. This isn't the time or the place to rehash this."

"When *is* the time or the place, Jack? Because every single time your mother pulls this shit, you either ignore it or act like it's not up for discussion!" I slammed the book closed and threw it back on the shelf. I tried to stand for emphasis but my knees wobbled below me. Three scotches might do that.

"Just deal with it!" he said, his voice now raised to match mine. "It is how she is. She's not changing! Why don't you get that?"

"And why don't *you* get that if she won't change, maybe *you're* the one who needs to?" I was so irate (or perhaps it was those three scotches), my vision blurred.

"So now this is about me?"

"It's always been about you!"

"And what about you? None of this has anything to do with you?"

"She's your goddamn mother, Jack!" I yelled. "And I'm your goddamn girlfriend. Why can't you just tell her that I'm a priority to you? Why can't you just say, 'Accept her, Mother!' Is that so fucking hard?"

"And why can't you just say, 'Jack loves her,' and get over it!" His voice resonated so loudly that the books shook on the walls.

I stared him down—suddenly and instantly sober—too furious to speak, until I noticed an eerie silence humming from the rest of the apartment, the kind of silence that comes when people are pretending not to have overheard something they shouldn't have overheard, but are too astonished to start talking to cover up their eavesdropping. Jack heard it, too, and I saw his eyes widen.

"Shit," he muttered underneath his breath, then spun on his heels, and disappeared out the door.

He came to get me thirty minutes later.

"We should leave," he said.

"Fine by me." I threw my hands up in the air.

"She heard everything," he answered flatly, as we stepped onto the elevator with eyes on our backs. "What a total and complete fucking debacle."

So this morning, when Jack demanded to know if I'd be on time to his niece's party, I certainly knew why he was more than a little concerned, more than a tad bit overwrought about Vivian's and my reunion. I didn't blame him. Last time, yes, I did. Most certainly, I did. But armed with hindsight, I'd resolved to try a different tactic:

In my previous life, I'd quietly and desperately fought for Jack to cut the figurative umbilical cord; this time, I'd lose the self-indignation and focus more on the long-term strategy, less on the short-term gratification. After all, swallowing my anger and my ego and, yes, a tiny morsel of my self-respect was a small price for a second shot at my future, or so I considered over my stale bagel and brewing coffee.

And now, at the train station, at the pinnacle moment in which I was truly ready to prove myself, I was running late. What was an honest oversight—a conference call that lingered longer than anticipated—would turn into a full sandstorm of trouble.

The ticker at Grand Central finally indicates that my train (to hell) is boarding, and I lug my heavy feet toward it, pausing briefly at the newsstand to pick up the latest copy of *Esquire*, where Jack is now a senior editor.

"He's going to be a famous novelist someday," Vivian told me over scallops at Chanterelle the first time we met. "All of his high school teachers and college professors have said so."

I nodded with the sort of enthusiasm that only a new girlfriend can muster.

"I know," I said. "I've read his short stories. They're so good."

"Not good, my dear," she corrected me. Vivian smelled of a woman who was rarely corrected herself. "They're magical." She took a long sip of Pellegrino and fingered the pearls on her giraffe-like neck, while Jack stared at his fork tines and tried to pretend that he cared as much about his writing as she did.

I flip through the July issue of *Esquire* as the train pulls away from New York. I'd read all of these pieces before, of course, but they are distant enough—like a memory of a story that happened to someone else—that they still feel somewhat fresh. The train barrels forward and eventually spits me out in Rye, only five miles from my future home with Henry, only a stone's throw from my other life, which now seems not like just another life but like another world entirely.

A mother and young daughter exit the train hand in hand in front of me. The little girl wears a peach smocked dress with white lacy socks and shiny black patent leather shoes. Her curls jingle as she walks. I watch the pair disappear in a patterned rhythm down the platform steps. *Katie.* A surge rushes up inside of me, and then, just as quickly, is gone.

I move my own feet forward and down the same steps. As the person behind me looks on, surely, I, too, disappear as I go on my way.

☙

ALLIE, JACKSON'S NOW six-year-old niece and star of the party, was having a meltdown. A meltdown of epic proportions. The magician her mother, Leigh, had hired had magically not appeared as promised, and thus olive-colored snot was flying down Allie's chin, sticky fists were being thrown around with abandon and fury, tears were flowing, angry and unstoppable. Parents huddled around the pool and feigned sympathy (with just a small dose of judgment and disdain) while Leigh, Jack's sister, older by four years, attempted to forge peace. But Allie offered no such white flag.

I survey the scene from behind the sliding door just off the patio. Jack and Vivian are hovering near the bar set up for "grownups," and Bentley, Jack's father, is nursing what I imagine to be a very, *very* stiff martini and wishing that he were on the golf course, much like he was almost every other Saturday. I smirk: I could almost detect him trying to calculate a getaway; he usually was. Nearly all of the time, I didn't blame him.

Take me! I invariably wanted to cry out, just after he'd hop up from the dinner table or the breakfast buffet, citing an emergency in the office or a crisis at one of his plants. Most times, he'd then catch my eye and wink, a sly recognition that if anyone wanted to be the hell away from there more than him, he knew it was me. Bentley and I had a tacit understanding—he placated Vivian because he had to, but he didn't want me to hold their forty-year marriage against him.

The bartender refills Bentley's glass, and still, Allie wails.

It's time for action. I've seen this tantrum before, only today, I've come prepared, complete with the requisite supplies. I push the glass door to my side, my sweaty palms leaving imprints as I do.

"Allie!" I say, skipping over to her. "Guess what?"

"Whaaaat?" she sputters.

"Turns out that you don't need that lousy magician! Because I went to magic school, and I can show you a few tricks." I raise my eyebrows knowingly, and Allie's screeches stop so abruptly, everyone turns to stare. It is as if all the noise in the world has been sucked into a dry vacuum.

"I don't believe you," she says with mixed doubt in her voice.

"Fine, don't believe me. I can go do my magic tricks inside." I turn to go and notice Jack now watching me with curiosity. Even Vivian is looking at me with something less than derision, which I suppose is something.

"WAIT!" Allie shouts. "I want to see magic!" She pauses and crosses her arms. "Prove it."

"Well, before I do, I think you have something stuck in your belly button."

"Do not!"

"Do too!" I reach down to the waist of her shirt and tuck my hand in. "Told you!"

I pull out a gleaming silver dollar, and Allie squeals. The gaggle of other first graders quickly rush around us, and I turn toward a towheaded boy who had just lost his front tooth. "And you! What do you have behind your ear?" I produce another coin to thundering applause and deafening shrieks of joy that can only emanate from humans under the age of seven.

"Okay, so, birthday girl, pick a card, any card." I take a deck of cards from my back pocket and shuffle them. Allie purses her lips and meticulously plucks one smack from the middle. "Now put it back." She does as instructed. I reshuffle the deck two more times, and then cut it in half.

"Is *this* your card?" I ask dramatically.

"YES!" Allie screams, jumping up and down with saucer eyes and nearly frothing at the mouth. "DO IT AGAIN!!!"

And so I did. I did it again and again, and I made little doggies out of balloons, and pulled more coins from their ears, and then I even went to my bag and whipped out a clown makeup kit, painting their faces with strawberry red cheeks and black button noses until the sun slowly faded into the Westchester sky, and fireflies began to flicker around the cavernous grounds of Jackson's childhood home.

Eventually, Jack and I said our good-byes. Allie wrapped herself around my legs and told me I was the best magician they'd all seen at any party all year. Bentley pulled me into a bear hug, so tight that I could taste the scent of his Cohibas, and even Vivian managed to break her icy facade for more than a glancing second.

"Thank you, dear," she said, not warmly, but not too coolly, either. "You were quite something today." She kissed me on each cheek, and I saw the family beaming behind her.

"Anytime, Mrs. Turnhill," I answered, pulling back to meet both her eyes and her approval.

"Vivian, dear. Feel free to call me Vivian." She offered an (almost) genuine smile, then tugged her cashmere sweater over her waist to iron out any nonexistent wrinkles and retreated into the house.

"The next time we're in the city, can we call you?" Leigh asked. Her hands rested on Allie's shoulders, who was parked at her feet and who gazed up at me, her new hero, with huge, hopeful eyes.

"Of course!" I said with honest surprise and leaning down to kiss Allie one last time. "It would be the highlight of my week."

Then Jack flung his arm around my shoulder, having forgotten entirely that just hours earlier, when I burst through the door fifty minutes late, he was too annoyed to even spit out a hello. None of that mattered now. Now, we were headed home.

❧

"I DIDN'T KNOW that you knew magic," Jack says, after we'd climbed out of the bathtub, where he'd scrubbed the clown paint off my fingers and the remaining dirt from playing in the grass from underneath my nails. We are splayed on top of our plaid comforter, and he is rubbing my feet.

"There are a lot of things you don't know about me, I suppose." I shrug.

"But magic? Seriously?" He laughs. "I mean, normally, I'd call you lame, but you did save the day."

"I did indeed." I smile. "And you best be careful. I'm skilled enough to make you disappear." *That's only the half of it,* I think.

"Just don't saw me in half," he says, sticking out his tongue, then crawling up toward the head of the bed and placing himself on top of me.

The truth is that Jack didn't realize that I knew magic because, in fact, the me he knew *didn't*. The me he knew couldn't have been more removed from kids and their exploits, mostly because they reminded me of my discolored childhood and the scars it had laid into me.

And then came Katie. She wasn't planned. She wasn't un-planned. She just was. Henry and I spoke in vague terms about children before we got married; he agreed for both of us that we wanted them, and I didn't disagree enough to argue. I did want children; I was just terrified of the damage that I might do to them. So the easier solution was not to have them at all. But then I fell in love with Henry, an only child who felt lonely like me most of his life, though for different reasons, and it seemed like it was an easy compromise to give him.

After two years of marriage, he urged me to go off the pill. I looked at them with bittersweet fondness and tossed them in the trash. While we weren't actively trying to shoot his sperm straight toward my egg, three months later, I was pregnant. Nine months later, my life would change in all conceivable (literal and not) ways. Ready or not. Here she comes.

During my pregnancy, I read every last morsel of information that was available to the literate public. If there was a book or an article or a website on gestation (At ten weeks in utero: fingernails develop! At eighteen weeks: your child will suck his thumb!), I de-voured it. And after I pushed Katie out, I subscribed to all the mag-azines, too: *Parents, Parenting, Baby Talk, American Baby, Your Baby, Mothers and Babies, Babies and Mothers.* Our mailbox was clogged with them the month through. And in my desperation, I would memorize far more than just the age-appropriate tips or stage-of-life information that applied to Katie and me. ("Silly Solids! How to Start Your Baby on Fun Food!") No, I read articles for mothers of eight-year-olds, for divorced fathers who saw their kids only on weekends, for adoptive mothers who worried about bonding issues with their new African children. I hungrily ate them up because, really, what else did I have to do (Pilates class only met three times a week); and boredom aside, I read them with the frantic hope that Katie might turn our differently than I did. Or maybe that I would turn out differently than my mother. It was a blurry line, and one that I didn't consider too much.

Which is exactly how I became an expert magician. Read enough magazines, and you can do just about anything. Because inevitably, on any given month, tucked inside the pages of these bastions of knowledge, there are articles on pulling rabbits out of hats and pulling coins out of noses and pulling off the perfect birthday party, as if that might ensure, or perhaps even prove, that you are the mommy dearest. The mommy best.

"It was sexy," Jackson says tonight, slowly lifting my tank top over my head. "Seeing you with the kids today."

"Yeah, even your mom managed a grin." I giggle as he kisses my neck. "Not quite a smile, but a toothless grin."

"Don't bring her up right now," he grunts.

"Duly noted." I feel his mouth work its way down my collarbone.

"So, Ms. Magician," Jack says, his voice husky and low, "how about you show me some of those new tricks?"

"How about you show me some of yours first?"

"Happy to," he says, reaching down to unbuckle my belt.

I press my eyes closed and try to remember why I'd ever jumped off this track to begin with. Because these tiny accommodations, like placating his mother with magic tricks or sidestepping arguments about her in the first place—these small shifts—didn't seem so seismic now that I understood the consequences of forgoing them. Last time, I asked Jack to make changes; this time, it seemed so much easier if I just made them in myself. *It doesn't feel like so much,* I think. *No, these compromises definitely don't feel like too much.*

Jack tugs off my pants.

What matters, I tell myself just before clearing my mind, is that I'm here, now, making new memories while the old ones are fading into dust.

Chapter Seven

T his came for you."

I look up from my loupe, with which I was poring over story-boards, at the sound of Josie's voice, and see that her head has been replaced with a Herculean-sized gift basket.

"Ooh, goodies!" I set the loupe aside and rub my hands to-gether. "What have you got?"

The monstrosity lands on my desk with a thud, and my pencil cup rattles.

"Well, you've made it," Josie says, easing herself into a chair and shaking out her arms. "This is the official invitation to the an-nual Coke friends and family event, which basically means they in-vite all of their investors to Cipriani and pour top-shelf liquor down their throats to convince them that management is doing right by their money."

I start to unpeel the layers of pink plastic that envelop the basket.

"Have you ever been?" I ask.

"Five years ago," she answers. "Before they left us for BBDO. It's legendary. And they don't hand these invites out lightly. When I got invited, I'd already been promoted to director."

I stand on my tiptoes and try to peer into the depths of the silo-sized gift.

"So," Josie continues, "as I said, you've made it. Really knocked the hell out of this campaign."

"Thanks," I say with a shrug. "It's been pretty easy."

"So I've noticed." Josie tucks a loose strand of hair behind her ear. "You've juggled the responsibility well, and just so you know, I've put in a word for a promotion." I meet her eyes and she smiles. "Seriously, Jill, my job could be yours in a few years."

I force a grin but feel my pulse beating in my neck, rising in panic. I'm not supposed to get a promotion. I'm supposed to cruise along comfortably at this level until I meet Henry and eventually quit when my belly bulges out to the point at which it can no longer be disguised.

But all of that's different now, I remind myself and exhale. Your future is what you make of it, and so what if you don't exactly envision a life like Josie's: one in which you feel like you're leaving half of you behind every morning when you kiss your kids good-bye, and then leaving the other half of you behind each dusk when the hum of your computer whirs to a stop and you click off the light to go home and fall asleep on the couch next to your husband who has flipped the TV to ESPN.

Her life doesn't have to be mine, I tell myself. *My* life, my new life, is yet unwritten.

"That's amazing, Josie. Thank you," I say, my voice weighted in appreciation. I reach into the basket and pull out some bounty. "Seriously? They make Coke-flavored Jelly Bellys? And Coke-flavored licorice?"

"Oh yeah, you'd be amazed. My daughter lives for this stuff."

Tentatively, I take a bite, and it tastes like processed cola with six shots of sugar blended in.

I can't remember the last time I had jelly beans. And then it hits me with a rush: Easter 2007, just a few months back, when Katie, at fifteen months, had finally stopped lumbering like a drunken seaman and was rushing around my father's backyard in Connecticut with the freewheeling bravado that nearly defines toddlerhood, before you're old enough to remember that falling hurts and that stumbling leaves bruises that won't fade for days.

I'd spent the previous night dyeing hard-boiled eggs various shades of lavender, pink, yellow, and baby blue, and then, after greeting my dad and Linda, his girlfriend of nearly a decade but whom he refused to wed, I tucked the pastel-hued creations behind trees and logs and flower beds to create our very own Easter egg hunt. (I'd read about it in *Parents.*) From my perch on the porch, I watched Henry chase Katie around the grass—she'd lost interest in uncovering the eggs after four minutes, tops. Linda came out with a brimming bag of candy, and even though my trainer at the gym had sworn me off refined sugar, I reached for the Jelly Bellys and popped five (only twenty-two calories, I reminded myself!) in my mouth, savoring the tang of the tartness and the hint of crunchiness that comes with dissolving granulated sugar between your molars.

"These actually aren't bad," I say now to Josie. I stuff down a whole handful. "God, I never eat this crap."

"Yeah right, me neither!" She laughs and throws me a wink. "And with that, I'm sure that I'll see you at the vending machines at 4:00. I'll fight you for the Red Vines."

Oops. Indeed, back before Katie granted me a muffin top and eight stubborn pounds that wouldn't budge despite my virtuous cross-training and weight-lifting routine (as read about in *Self*), I abused sugar much like someone might abuse crack.

"Oh," Josie said, popping her head back into the door opening. "You should buy a new dress for this. And bring that boyfriend of yours. He's a keeper."

"He is, isn't he?" I grin.

Maybe this time, he'll actually stick.

❧

"How about this one?" Megan holds up a red, white, and blue empire-waist gown that looks like it would be more appropriate for a Fourth of July float than a classy candelabra-lit affair with a swing band playing in the background while various canapés are offered by tuxedo-clad waiters.

I scrunch my face up like I'd just eaten a sour pickle and shake my head no. I still hadn't adjusted to the fashion of half a decade past. In 2007, I was the embodiment of the Lilly Pulitzer catalog: crisp dark jeans, linen blouses, floral-printed sundresses.

"It's the look that makes the woman," I'd tell myself each morning after dragging myself from bed, dreading the oncoming day, the tedium and the poop-filled diapers and the plastic smile that would eventually cause my cheeks to cramp if I didn't let it fall at least three times during one of Katie's playdates. So I'd reach into the depths of my closet and pull out a splashy pink and green tank top with ironed khaki capris to match, and I'd slide on deep choco-late leather sandals, and pull my highlighted hair into a clean low ponytail, and wash just a touch of cream blush across my cheeks and onto my lips, and then I'd stare into the mirror and convince myself that indeed, "it's the look that makes the woman," and now, this woman was me. Then I'd nod at the embodiment of mommyhood perfection and turn to climb the stairs to whisk Katie from her crib.

"Come on," Megan whines. "I never thought I'd say this, but Jill, I'm sick of shopping. We've been at this for nearly two hours, and you haven't liked anything you've seen!"

Is it my fault that designers in 2000 seemed to think it was a brilliant idea to bring back the hideous fashions from the '80s? Is it my fault that I have good enough taste to just say no to prints that look like they belong on the curtains of my Westchester home and shoulder pads that couldn't flatter a linebacker?

"Here," I say, pulling a strapless silver cocktail dress from the back rack. "This might work."

"Finally," Megan sighs, and plops down on a beige leather chair that they put out for drained husbands who are forced to trudge after their wives for a rash of weekend shopping. Nearly a month after her miscarriage, Meg's looking vibrant, healthy even, and I can't help but stare just before I duck into the dressing room.

Last time around, I hadn't stopped to notice. Jack and I were starting to wind our way free of each other, like a ball of yarn in which just one thread had come loose, and the Coke project was drowning my free time, and I'd started dreaming about my mother again, so somehow, Meg got lost in the shuffle. Lost in the innocuous way that happens when life simply piles up. You grab a friend on her cell for two minutes, then promise to call each other back later, but later becomes tomorrow, and tomorrow ebbs into a week, and before you've even realized it, a month has flown by, and you've disengaged yourself from each other's worlds. Which doesn't mean that you don't adore each other, and certainly doesn't mean that when you do catch up that you don't pour out all of the missing details. You do. But for that month or those weeks, you're blind to the nuances that change a person over the course of time, that stack up like dominoes until she's a different person entirely. This time out, I'd vowed to keep a closer eye on Megan, to perhaps protect her from the spiral that would suck her downward into emotional depths that, at least in my previous life, I'd failed to understand. Or perhaps more honestly, I failed to understand because I didn't see the spiral in the first place.

"How's work?" I ask Megan over coffee, after I admired my

naked body in the dressing room mirror (No stretch marks from Katie! No stomach that perpetually looks three months pregnant! No shaking jello under the curve of my butt!) and purchased the silver dress (two sizes smaller!).

"Eh," she says. "I don't really give a shit." Meg's an associate at Bartlett and Jones, one of the top law firms in the city, where they process their lawyers in the way that cuts of beef might be at a slaughterhouse. They string you up, put you through your paces, and just like those poor cows, you rarely get out alive.

"That bad?" I say. She never wanted to be a lawyer in the first place, and just went to law school because she couldn't think of anything better to do, a holding pattern for those first few postcollege years and her early twenties.

"Just a lot of filing papers and reading over fine print in documents and blah, blah, blah." She rolls her eyes, then blurts out, "So Tyler and I are ready to try again."

"Has your doctor given you the okay?" I attempt to offer enough support in my voice to conceal my alarm at her announcement.

She nods, her mouth full of raisin scone.

"And you feel ready to do this?" I pause. "Not physically. Emotionally."

"You sound like my doctor," she laughs, though there's no joy behind it. "She told me that since I've stopped bleeding, we can try again as soon as I get my period. But that maybe I should take some time to cope with the loss of the first baby."

"And you disagree?" I raise my mug to my lips, careful not to spill the steaming coffee on my fingers. My eyes watch her steadily over the rim.

"I don't know." She shrugs. "But why put it off? What's the point in delaying it? The longer we wait, the longer it is until I get pregnant again." Her face falls, and I don't know what to say, so I say nothing.

"You know what's funny," she continues, not really asking a question.

"No," I say. "What?"

"You spend your whole life frantically trying not to get pregnant. I mean, I've been on the pill since I was sixteen! Eleven fucking years of being on the pill until I went off it last year. So you spend your whole life trying to prevent this thing—condoms, pills, gels, creams, whatever—and then, it turns out that guess what? It's not so easy to do, to get pregnant in the first place!"

"I was certain that I was pregnant back in high school once," I say. "With Daniel. God, remember him? Did I ever tell you this story, how our condom broke, and I was two days late, and I was *freaking out?*" I stop, unsure why I'm telling the story. I think of Daniel, his black curls and his cherry cheeks, and how we split soon after I got my period, in that awkward, stilted way when you still see each other in the hallways and still wonder whether or not you broke up because the other person thought you didn't know how to kiss or because your boobs were too small.

"Oh, God, yeah, I know." Megan's words are accelerating. "I can't tell you how many times I thought I was pregnant. Crying on the toilet because my period hadn't come or because I'd forgotten to take a pill *exactly* on the dot—because you know, that's what the stupid package warns you about—or because of whatever." She stops to gather her breath. "And Jesus, I remember being so filled with goddamn fear because, well, what the hell do you do if you're eighteen and pregnant or twenty and pregnant, and now, I'm twenty-eight, and I can't get fucking pregnant, and then when I do, I lose the baby!"

I think she's going to start crying, so I reach over to touch her hand, but instead, she peers up with a wistful smile.

"Jesus," she says. "If I knew that it would be so hard to get pregnant, I'd have had a lot more sex."

I snort out some coffee and nod.

I raise my mug. "To more sex," I say, and startlingly, Mrs. Kwon, my dry cleaner, echoes in my ear.

"To more sex," Meg replies, matching her mug to mine and clinking them together.

"And to a baby," I say, fervently, feverishly hoping that this time, Meg is more blessed.

"To a baby," she answers. "To babies for both of us. And to whatever those babies might bring." She catches the panic in my eye. "Not now." She smiles and waves a free hand. "But, you know, in the future. To the babies of our future."

"I'll drink to that," I say. "To the babies of our future."

I feel my chest tighten like a clamp's been placed around my heart. *Katie*, I think. *Katie*. The baby of my future. What happens to Katie now that the future is nothing more than a foggy memory, one that might fade when the sun rises and the morning mist lifts?

Chapter Eight

There is a perpetual and bewildering sense of déjà vu when you desert the future and reinsert yourself into the past. Like a rat, spinning on its wheel, who keeps running by the same scenery over and over again, only each time, the scientist changes just enough of the backdrop so the rodent wonders if he's merely imagining the sameness or if, indeed, everything is exactly as it's always been.

Part of this is amusing: I can catch up on old episodes of *Buffy the Vampire Slayer* and can render Jackson speechless when I insist that we place bets, which I subsequently win, on who will get the boot each week on *Survivor.*

"What the hell?" he says with his hands in the air, just after that button-cute Colleen gets her torch extinguished. "What freaky voodoo signs did you pick up on to figure it out this time?"

I grin and bite into the gooey cheese pizza that we order every Thursday night for our *Survivor* viewings.

"Just good perception," I say. "Either you can read people or you can't."

"Uh-uh," he answers, unconvinced. "Have you been reading spoilers again?"

"Hand to God, I haven't." I laugh.

"Fine. I owe you a twenty-minute back massage before bed." He gets up to grab me some more Diet Coke (we have an endless supply thanks to work) and pecks my lips as he goes. "But I swear, I better win one of these days or else I'm searching your computer for incriminating evidence of rule-breaking!"

"Search all you want," I practically sing. "Some things are just a gift, and you either have it or you don't."

But these moments of bemusement aside, there are other things about revisiting the life you've already trodden that are so disconcerting that you feel as if you're being tailed, watched by someone hidden in the shadows who might leap out at any moment, until, of course, you realize that this person is you. There is a constant sense that I am playing a dangerous game of tug-of-war with fate, and I find myself continually wondering if everything I do throughout my day is predestined. If, as I stop into Starbucks for my morning coffee, I did this exact same thing at the exact same time half a decade earlier or, as I stop by Gene's desk to gossip, if I'm rehashing information that's already been filtered through my sensorial landscape. I've discovered that I can't remember all the mundane details of my day-to-day life, so while there's a vague sense of familiarity, little of it seems nailed down or tangible. Which leaves me feeling like I'm swimming in quicksand, at once wanting it to suck me in and do with me what it might, and alternatively, grasping and clawing my way out because the thought of going under, of essentially leaving fate to have its way with me, is too spine-chillingly terrifying to allow.

I also live in continual fear of giving myself away.

Never once do I consider blurting out my secrets, even to Megan, who has entrusted me with hers, or even to Jackson, who has proven a kinder boyfriend than I remembered.

So I catch myself from spilling the endings of movies or snapping at Jack that he's already told me the story about discovering that his boss was sleeping with a coeditor or lacking patience with my team at work because I'd long ago memorized the steps to creating a masterful Coke campaign, whereas this is their first time at this circus.

I am contemplating fate, and the role that I might play in it, one Tuesday morning on the bus on the way into work. It is an oppressively muggy day in late August, one in which the swampy air clings to your sticky skin and a bolt of air-conditioning from a store that you pass by feels like salvation. A water main has broken in the bowels of the subway line, and thus, swarms of New Yorkers are huddled on the corners at bus stops and are fanning themselves with their newspapers while waiting for their rides.

My CD player hums in my ear (no iPods! I've made a mental note to invest in Apple), and I'm reconnecting with music that ties me to memories of former days, only those days are now. When I was thirty-four, in my future life, "If You're Gone" by Matchbox Twenty would occasionally filter over the airwaves of my Range Rover, and I'd stare out the window, watching the graying buildings coast by, haunted by the reminder of Jack, and how I played the song over and over and over again when we split. But now, it's nothing more than a song that jolts a memory of something yet to happen, something that *might not even* happen if I can grab the gears and shift them away from my destiny.

I am listening to Matchbox Twenty, and I am mulling over that very destiny, when the doors of the bus open at Twenty-eighth Street, and a wave of passengers presses forward. Bodies clog the car, which wafts with a mixed scent of fresh cologne, hot coffee, and body odor, and I tuck my legs underneath my seat to make way for the tangle of people. A heavyset woman who has sweat pooling behind her ears elbows me on the side of my head, then glares when I don't apologize.

After watching her move beyond me, I shift my eyes back

toward the front and brace my weight for the lurch of the engine as we start again. Looking forward, I see masses of bobbing heads, swaying in rhythmic time to the clanking and churning of the bus's wheels. I'm examining a tight French braid on a girl who appears no older than thirteen, and flushing away thoughts of the mornings I'd spent parked on Katie's floor braiding her hair meticulously over and again until she and I would concur that she was the embodiment of follicular perfection, when I feel someone's eyes, heavy and direct, gunning toward me like a spotlight.

I refocus my attention to return the gaze, and right as the jolt of shock and recognition runs through me, the bus careens to an abrupt stop, and the masses are hurled off balance. Everyone reaches for a pole, a neighbor's arm, or a hardened blue plastic seat to steady themselves. The doors squeak open, and just as quickly as the wave pushed forward, it now ebbs; the hurrying people rush on toward their offices, their days, their lives. Though it's not my stop, I stand urgently and follow them, getting caught in the flow, so I'm ushered down the steps of the bus before even realizing that I've consciously moved. I turn and look, perplexedly at first, then frantically and more fervidly. Halfway down the block, I spot a sky blue shirt and hair the color of damp sand, and I weave through the foot traffic to try to reach him in time.

But when I finally land at the corner, breathless with both anxiety and anticipation, he is gone. I spin around and then around again, staring up the avenue and down the perpendicular streets, but there is nothing. So, reluctantly, I head uptown toward my office, toward the route that I was carving out for myself, for my future.

Henry, I think. *It was Henry.*

Had we done this before? I wonder. *Had a water main break steered us on to a bus on which we'd noticed each other in passing, only to let the tides of commuters pull us away? Were we fated to meet, regardless of this map that I was intent on following?*

Another bus roars by me and blows a hot blast of exhaust as it goes. With heavy feet and a racing heart, I plod on, turning back one more time, though I know that there is nothing there left to see. *Henry*, I say to myself once again.

But then I realize that if he isn't my destiny, there isn't much use in saying his name at all. I wash it from my mind and watch the buses barrel up Madison Avenue until they reach the horizon line, and then, it is as if they were never there at all.

ℰ H E N R Y

Henry proposed almost a year to the day after we met. And like just about everything else about him up until that point, his proposal was perfect. So quintessentially him, and still entirely perfect. Planned but not rushed, poignant but not effusive. Unexpected but not a surprise. Perfect.

We were on vacation in Paris and everyone—Megan, Ainsley, Josie—was certain he'd do it then. "Right under the Eiffel Tower," Gene suggested one day when we were splitting turkey sandwiches at my desk. "Or at twilight along the Seine," Josie sang out from the hall when she overheard the conversation.

I was so swollen with anticipation that I'd nearly ruined the vacation—every meal, every site was a potential landmark to highlight the culmination of our love. And yet, there was nothing. Because, of course, I understood in retrospect, Henry realized that I'd already envisioned the entire Parisian proposal in my mind, and that there was little he could do to catapult his efforts above my imaginary ones. That's how well he knew me.

On the plane ride home, just as I was stewing in disgruntled bitterness and thinking of excuses to offer Gene and Josie and the entire office crowd who had nearly started a pool on how Henry would propose in the City of Lights, Henry pointed out the window into the dark, starry sky and said, "I know that we can't see the moon from here, but I feel like I can."

"I don't follow," I answered.

"What I mean to say," he flustered on, "is that wherever we are, it's as if I'm blessed with the moon and the stars on my heels because I'm with you." His cheeks reddened. "I know it's cheesy, and I know it sounds like a Hallmark card, but it's true."

"Thank you," I said, brushing my lips to his, and reaching for his hand beneath our blankets. It was as close to soul-searching posturing that he'd ever come.

"So this, my moon and stars, is the only way I can think to repay you." He slid something velvety and hard into my hand, and when I popped the box open, there it was: the ring that ensured that we'd be happily ever after for the rest of our days.

The flight attendant brought us champagne, and I raised the armrest between our seats and tucked myself so close to him that not even a sliver of space divided us, and I was, for a moment at least, so soaked in contentedness that I could have pocketed up that feeling and coasted on it for years to come.

Chapter Nine

I stare out my office window, peering at the view, but mostly seeing the images of Henry and my former life. I try to shake them from my brain but they're stuck, refusing to budge, and they've been firmly planted there for the three hours since Henry unknowingly met my eyes on the bus and subsequently sent me tripping, spiraling down memory lane.

"Sorry to disturb," Gene says as he knocks lightly on the door and pushes it open. "Mail's here."

"Thanks," I say distractedly, swiveling around in my chair and reaching for the pile.

"Bad morning?" he asks.

I like Gene. Liked him last time around, and like him this time around, too. He's a twenty-five-year-old high school graduate who discovered that being the best graphic artist in your senior class doesn't guarantee that the art world will fling open its doors for you at graduation, and so, after six years of making espressos at a West Village coffee bar, he enrolled in college at night and interns with us during the day. I'll occasionally ask him to peruse my storyboards, and almost inevitably, he'll hone in on tiny details that I overlooked. While Henry excelled at the fine print, I did not, at least not until I swirled myself into an unrelenting perfect housewife in which I mastered the art of the finest print, and thus, I was always surprised at how much Gene could highlight what I'd missed.

"It's nothing," I reply to him now, standing to close my blinds.

"If you don't mind me saying so, you've looked better."

"Thanks, Gene." I smile. "I always appreciate the backhanded compliment."

"Problems with the Coke account?" He sits, even though I haven't invited him to do so.

"No, no problems with the Coke account at all."

"Yeah, I hear you're kicking ass on that, actually." He folds his hands underneath his chin and rests them there.

"You do? Spill."

"You know, people talk when the interns are around because they think that we don't have ears. Or exist. Or whatever." He shrugs and reaches up to scratch a piercing on his left upper lobe. "But word on the street is that you're being groomed as the next big thing."

"Ooh la la," I say, popping a Coke-flavored Jelly Belly in my mouth. "Sounds fancy."

"So if it's not work, what is it?" he presses.

I sigh. "I saw . . ." I pause, mulling over how to define this. "I saw an ex on the bus this morning, that's all. Threw me off a bit, I guess."

"Ah, gotcha. Made you feel all nauseous and nervous and all of that?"

I nod and feel queasy just at the thought of it.

"Well, it might mean something, and it might mean nothing," he continues. "How are things with your current man?"

"Good," I say firmly, because they are.

In fact, things with Jack are smoother, more fluid than I remembered them to be. Unlike in my life with Henry, there are no niggling demands, no dinners to prepare, no obligatory company cocktail parties to attend, no expectations to cater to. There is no push to make amends with my mother, Henry's favorite way to prod, no pull from Katie to give more of myself. Simply, now, I feel liberated, unburdened. If I work late, Jack, free-spirited and game, treks uptown to a Yankees game or gathers coworkers to attend a restaurant opening. And when I find a moment to break away from the chains that now bind me to my desk, I join him: no guilt that I work too often, no reprimands that we've ordered pizza or Chinese four nights running, no problem if he's the one who has to haul our laundry to the basement when it's piled so high that it resembles a foothill, not a hamper.

No, I think, today with Gene, *things are humming along as smoothly as anticipated, no potholes, no land mines to throw us off course.* Maybe it's because I'm able to anticipate those land mines before they go off. In our previous life, I'd hoped that with some encouragement, Jack would discover the inner writer that Vivian so believed lay hidden in his depths. I nagged and I nudged and I elbowed him into his fiction, despite his flat interest and nearly obvious lethargy at the subject. In my previous life, I eventually wrote him off as lazy and unambitious, a trust-fund kid who kicked up his heels and coasted on the wave he'd had the good fortune to ride in on. But with hindsight, I let all that go: Jack's enthusiasm for life was infectious, and damned if I didn't want to catch his fever.

With Henry, I knew ambition, I knew the straight and narrow, and seven years later, it felt choking, claustrophobic almost. So this time around, I pushed aside those lingering doubts about Jack, which, in days past, would spiral into needling nit-picking, which would escalate into full-blown arguments, which would culminate in one of us sighing in sarcastic relief at the fact that we weren't in this relationship permanently. And then we'd apologize, and wash, rinse, repeat at least once a week.

But now, yes, thanks to a slight adjustment in my expectations, a tactic on which I was certain *Redbook* would surely frown, things were indeed going well. *It doesn't feel like too much,* I'd tell myself every time I made one of these tiny tweaks. *One day soon, it might, but for now, it doesn't feel like too much.*

"Okay, so if things are cruising with your man, then why worry?" Gene says now.

"I'm not worried," I point out. "You're the one who told *me* that I looked worried."

He crunches his brow. "You do though. You do look worried. Which means one of two things." He reaches over some papers on my desk to grab a piece of Coke-flavored licorice, then gnaws on it ponderingly. "That either things aren't going as well as you think with your guy—and you're just kidding yourself—or else this ex has left such a mark on you that you and your man could be in high heaven and it wouldn't matter. He'd still rattle you."

I feel the color drain from my face and rather than offer a firm answer, I say, "What are you, my shrink?"

"I wish," he says, rising to leave. "Then at least someone would pay me around here."

"Ha ha," I answer. "You know that I've put in a good word for you to be my executive assistant. I'm hoping it will happen any day now."

"To God's ears," he replies, already halfway down the hall. "Enjoy the mail."

I laugh to myself, as I reach for the stack of letters that he's placed on top of even more stacks of letters and files and folders. Three envelopes slide from the pile and coast off my desk, bouncing off the wastebasket and nose-diving to the blue rug that came straight from Corporate Rugs "R" Us.

The first envelope contains a coupon pack from my neighborhood's Better Business Bureau, and the second is just my cell phone bill. The third is cream colored with an Elvis stamp, and fills me with that sense again, the sense that I've held this envelope before, that it's fallen into my life in some way though not exactly in *this* way at one point prior, and as I flip it over to slide my fingers underneath the flap, a surge of adrenaline courses through me.

I unfold the lined paper and recognize the handwriting with a start. The words are eerily familiar but only like a mirage might be: I remember them from long ago, but they were never committed to memory—years ago, after reading this same note, I fled the office for a gasp of air, then balled up the monogrammed stationery and angrily threw it into the garbage on Seventh Avenue. And then I pushed the words from my mind and vowed that I wouldn't retrace either them or the meaning behind them again.

Child-sized beads of sweat form on my brow, and I allow myself to read, knowing that I'd both hate myself for doing so and regret it with a full heart if I didn't. Her handwriting curves and loops just like an elementary-school teacher's might. It is flawless, as if her penmanship might be a testimonial for her character.

Dear Jillian,

I hope that this letter finds its way to you. I have been holding on to it for many years, trying to find the right time to send it, but failing to do so each time. But now, the time feels right. So I hope that this finds you, and I more hope that you accept the intrusion.

I realize that it has been nearly eighteen years, and that I left your father and your brother and you without explanation, and that—I realize this more than ever now—was terribly unfair.

I would like to find a way to explain myself. I'd like to be able to tell my side of the story, though I do know that this is a lot to ask of the daughter who has been without me for most of her life.

But I am writing nevertheless to ask this of you: If you could find it within yourself to meet me, to, perhaps, listen to my apologies.

Because I would like to be able to offer them to you. And I'd like even more so to get to know you.

If you'd be amenable to this, please do call me at 212-525-3418.

> *All of my love,*
> *Your mother, Ilene*

I reread the letter three times; each time, it brings something new back to me from when I read it the first time—seven years ago. Calling my father and listening to the heartbroken shock of a man whose ghost just came back to haunt him. Trying to contact my brother, trekking through some godforsaken manure-filled pasture in the remote regions of Asia to let him know that our mother had resurfaced. Coping with the boiling, furious shards of rage that her audacity inspired in the angry circles of my mind.

Today, with a quick jerk, I push my chair back and rise to tear out of the building. To circle Seventh Avenue until I find the quasi serenity I need in that moment, serenity that would be so fleeting, so temporary that I'd remain incensed at my mother's actions for the next half decade plus. To curl up her letter in the balls of my hands until it is solid enough to be used as a weapon, and to hurl it into the trash so I can't call her, even if I am tempted.

But instead I sit as quickly as I stand.

I press the paper against my desk and smooth the creases in it, over and again, until they are nearly invisible. My pulse drums loudly in my neck, and I exhale, trying to push it all, so much, away. Then I open my desk drawer and tuck the letter inside. It might be, I decide, something worth hanging on to for the future.

Chapter Ten

The upper tier of advertising's elite is sandwiched together at the Coke extravaganza, and true to Josie's word, it is quickly evident that my invite might catapult me to the hallowed halls of our industry's high society. The taxi pulls up to the looming stone structure that housed Cipriani, and as I step out, I barely avoid a pigeon that is grazing on a stray crumb from an abandoned bagel. The skies had opened up that afternoon, turning the color of steel, and furiously unloaded on the city, so the air, still bursting with heavy humidity, blew over us, and felt more like early October than late August.

Jack swoops around from the other side of the cab and grabs my hand, a tacit symbol to move beyond the argument we'd been having on the ride down. The same argument we'd had seven years back, only last time, it had been over pasta at our favorite local Italian restaurant.

I hadn't meant it to happen, of course. I'd been so adept at dancing around our hot coals that when it slipped out, my unintentional comment, I didn't even realize what I'd said. I literally had to mentally rewind the conversation, like a VCR, to see where we might have jutted off course.

"Let's get out of here," Jack was saying, while I was reading our cab driver's license, flattened against the plastic partition that separated the front from the back, and wondering if the driver had left his family behind in whatever country he hailed from to come here and make a better world for them. His taxi reeked of evergreen air freshener, and I hoped the scent wouldn't attach itself to my pores and stay with me once we had vacated the vehicle.

"Out of the cab?" I asked, turning toward Jack. "We still have fifteen blocks to go."

"No. Out of *here* here." He waved his hands. "Let's plan a trip."

"That's not going to resolve everything with my mother," I sighed. I'd told Jack about my mom's note earlier that afternoon, and he'd reacted as he had the last time I'd been through this—with his cocksure nonchalance, which I sometimes found irritating, but which I now envied.

"Of course it's not going to resolve everything with your mother," Jack said, folding his hand over mine. "But it could still be a hell of a lot of fun. And that's the point." He squeezed my fingers and smiled. "October, maybe? Miami?"

"I thought you had a writer's retreat in October. To work on your novel."

Jack's eyebrows darted downward.

"I mentioned that to you?" His voice was flat, and I did my mental rewind to see where I'd gone wrong.

Er, no, come to think of it, you hadn't mentioned it to me. I only know about it because when we broke up, you cocooned yourself in the Adirondacks under the guise of writing, when what you were really doing was nurturing festering wounds that our split had left on both of us.

"Um." My brain raced. "I saw something you'd gotten in the mail about it . . . figured you would go."

But it wasn't just my slipup that sucked the enthusiasm from his tone. It was the mentioning of that-of-which-we-shall-not-speak. His novel. I'd pushed him on it last time. At Vivian's behest that, indeed, her son was the next coming of Hemingway, I'd pushed him. Never considering that Jack's talent wasn't anything grander than any other average MFA student or that his passion for supposed skill was significantly outweighed by his mother's. I pushed him and cajoled him and hammered out hours in which I insisted that he write, and he would—I'd hear the spatter of the computer keyboard rattling out like machine-gun fire—but the more he wrote, the less shiny he became, as if the work itself drained out all of his joy. So this time around, I nudged less and intuited more and realized that perhaps Jack wasn't destined to be the next great writer, which, of course, was entirely fine with me. As long as he cared about being the next great *something.* Whatever that might be.

"Oh," Jack said toward the glass taxi partition, with a sharpness that could puncture a balloon, but hesitatingly accepting the explanation. "No, I'd rather go to Miami."

"Sounds like heaven to me," I said hurriedly, brushing past the indiscretion and hopeful that we could move beyond it entirely. *Let Vivian be the one to prod him,* I thought. *I'll just be here to ride along and inhale the wind as we go.* Because that's what I enjoyed most about Jack now: the ride, how smooth and seamless and easy it all felt when I jumped onboard.

"So where is your mom now?" Jack said, switching back to a seemingly less dodgy subject, though, I think, it's only less *dodgy* for him. For me, it awoke reams of dormant emotions that I thought might nearly strangle me.

"Here, I think, I mean, at least from her area code. She must be here." I looked out the streaked window of the cab and wondered how often I've walked by her apartment, how many times I've just barely missed her at the grocery store or the gym or the dry cleaner. How long she's known where I've been and that I was so close to her grasp. I shook my head.

"It's been almost eighteen years," I stated, more to myself than to Jack. "I don't think I have much to say to her. I didn't even know if she was alive. I sort of figured that she wasn't, since she'd never popped back up."

The truth was that when my mother hightailed it out of the family, when she left us a flimsy note that literally read good-bye, and when Andy, my brother, and I ran to her closets to find them barren, I never really looked for her. I prayed for her return, yes, but I was nine, and after I hand-scrawled signs that I'd planned to stick up on telephone poles around the neighborhood, and after my father gently suggested that she wasn't "missing" in the way that the signs implied, I simply gave up. After six months, I even stopped praying that she'd come back. She'd run away, and far be it from me to try to rein her back in, like a kite tangled in a tree. Instead of asking God to return her to us, I littered my prepubescent mind with various reasons that she'd left us: I hadn't been grateful enough for my ninth birthday party; I'd gotten a B in geography; she was always asking me to clean up my room, and I rarely, if ever, tidied to her satisfaction. And soon enough, I bathed myself with sadness and guilt, and knew that she wasn't coming back because I'd pushed her away, and why would she want to return to such a spoiled, rotten kid who wasn't thankful enough for her parties and couldn't be bothered to put back her My Little Ponies? My father promised me that this wasn't so; he called me into our molasses-colored den after dinner one night and kindly and firmly told me that *this wasn't so*, but mostly he, too, squirreled into his pain, and his silences offered little reassurance.

But eventually, as my preteen years gave way to more deductive teenage ones, I grew hostile, bitter, resentful at her departure, and I vowed to erase her from my space entirely. Which, most days, when I wasn't letting her betrayal define me, I managed to do quite well.

So no, I didn't realize that she lived within miles of me and that conceivably, she'd never really gone that far to begin with.

"Well, maybe you should call her. I don't know. It's up to you," Jack said to me tonight, as the taxi pulls to an abrupt stop at a yellow light.

Of course it's up to me! I almost snapped, then realize that it wasn't him that I'm mad at. It was just my initial inclination, to mount an overwhelming defense of my actions because I'd spent so many years doing so with Henry, who never understood, who, in his own words, *couldn't understand,* how I could let my mother slip away after decades of not knowing her.

"You're crazy not to track her down," he'd say, over pasta or when I'd finally soothed Katie to bed or when I was stretching after a power walk, ambushing me with the subject when I was least prepared.

"How would I be crazy not to?" I'd always retort back, once I'd caught my breath at the surprise attack. "Here is a woman who has wanted no part of my life, who decided that I'd be better off without a mother than with her *as* my mother, and gave me no say in the matter, and now, she wants back in? I think I'd be crazy *to* give her that chance."

"She's your mother!" Henry would say, his voice boiling with judgment. "Isn't that worth something?"

I'd seethe silently and exit the room, fleeing both my husband who didn't know what was best for me and the skeletons that he'd insist on digging back up.

So tonight, with Jack, it's hard not to rage at his innocuous reply, even though I know that he doesn't fault me for my choice. Hell, I'm not even sure how much my choice registers with him. He was so tied to his mother that, I think in the cab, *he just doesn't get it*, would never get the fury and the devastation that comes from abandonment. But he didn't get it in an entirely different way from Henry. Henry got it—he got how she scarred me—and yet he still chose to tirelessly push me to make different choices. Jack just breezed right by it because the pain was so beyond his scope of recognition, and now, in the cab, I am relieved, *grateful* for this, because it absolves me of the anguish of rehashing a dead situation.

Before I can think any further, we're at Cipriani, and I step past the pigeon, and Jack takes my hand, and we pretend that the tiny fissures that were microscopically exposed in the cab—my mother, his ambition—aren't part of a larger problem between two people who fail to understand the intricacies of the other.

With nothing else to do, we step forward, onward, and away we go.

ℰ

A WAITER GREETS US with drinks (rum and Coke!) and pushes open the grand, gilded doors. The cavernous space, which could easily hold a thousand guests, had been overhauled to resemble a botanical garden. Hundreds upon hundreds of rose petals had been strung from each chandelier, so the room not only smells like the first rites of spring but it also looks like perhaps Dali's interpretation of an arboretum: blossoming stems cascading down from the ceiling, jutting into themselves and over us, illuminated by twinkling white lights that glisten like polka-dotting stars through the branches. Towering statues composed entirely of fruits of the season—pineapples, peaches, pears, and oranges—adorn each cocktail table, and the splatter of color, coupled with the crisp burnt-orange tablecloths, bounces off the stark rose petals, and truly, I feel as if I've stepped into the Garden of Eden.

"Who do you know here?" Jack shouts in my ear, trying to make conversation above the din of the swing band at the back of the room and the clatter of hundreds of other voices, all equally elevated in an attempt to be heard.

"No one, really," I shout back.

We both stare blankly at the buzzing hive of partygoers until, miraculously, I spy Josie through a wall of people. I grab Jack's hand and push my way past gesturing limbs, wafts of perfume, and hoards of jewels until we land smack in front of her.

"Oh good! Jillian! Perfect timing," she exclaims. "The Coke team is right over there, and I want to introduce you."

"I'll be at the bar," Jack says, winking and flashing a grin. He'd befriend more people there by the time he'd ordered his drink than I would at this entire party.

Josie pulls me by the crook of my arm to a group of forty-something-looking men who appear nearly interchangeable, with their navy pin-striped suits and their freshly shaven cheeks that glow with a hint of Hampton's summer sun and their cackle of laughter that implies that someone just told an entirely inappropriate joke.

"Gentlemen, excuse us," Josie says. "I want you to meet the brains behind your new ad campaign. Jillian, meet the men for whom you're about to make a lot of money."

She smiles, and I notice for the first time how pretty she looks tonight. Less washed out, with just enough blush to illuminate her cheekbones and a smattering of lipstick to fashion a pout. Her hair, normally tied back into a floppy bun, cascades below her shoulders

and over her red A-line dress that's staid enough for an executive
but flashy enough for a still-under-forty woman who wants to be
noticed.

I hold out my hand and grasp the bear claw grips of the senior
Coke managers, regaling them with my ideas and delightful small
talk and filling the silences with witty double entendres that easily
outmatch their macho humor that was being batted around before
Josie and I burst their boys-only bubble.

They finally beg an exit to hit the bar, and Josie and I watch
them go.

"You know Bart, the one you just met with the purple tie?" she
asks. "I dated him in college. We broke up when he moved to San
Francisco after we graduated."

"Oh," I reply because I have nothing else to say. Then I add,
"He's cute."

"He is, isn't he?" Her voice is too wistful for a woman who
doesn't have regrets.

"Where's Art tonight? Home with the kids?" I ask.

"No." She shakes her head. "He got a last-minute gig in San
Jose." She half snorts but the anger behind it belies her mock
amusement. "Emergency on an opera set out there."

I raise my eyebrows.

"No, really," she says. "You know: faulty candelabras and curtains that just won't behave themselves." She starts to laugh,
slowly, sadly at first, then accelerating until she's curled over her
left side, holding up her rum and Coke in her right hand so it won't
topple on the floor, shaking, shuddering uncontrollably until she finally rights herself and wipes away her tears. "A fucking opera set
emergency! Can you imagine?" she sputters again, but pulls herself
in and tucks away any remnants of laughter with a firm sigh. "So
yeah, there's Bart—here, now, reminding me of . . . *so much* . . . and
then . . ." she pauses, "there's Art."

"Separated by only a 'B,' " I offer, trying a little levity.

"If only," she responds dejectedly while scanning the crowd in hopes of catching Bart's eye all over again. "So what about you and Jack? Engagement anytime soon?"

No, I think, then remind myself that this future is yet untold.

"Maybe," I say instead. "We'll see. I guess it's up to him."

"Why would you say that?" Josie tenses and turns toward me. "It's up to both of you."

Not really, I want to burst. *Last time I gave myself to him for two fucking years and yet nothing, just more of the same old Jack, coasting along comfortably at cruising altitude. No ring, no hints, no squat, so when it finally became apparent that we were treading water rather than swimming toward something, I bolted. Because that was my only choice, my only say. I left him before he could leave me or at least until I wasted the better part of my misspent adult years, because I had no reason to believe that there was anything more he was willing to swim toward anyway.*

Tonight, I shrug. "I just meant that he's the one who proposes, that's all."

Josie shrugs back, a tacit admission that indeed I might be stuck, and then surveys the scene looking for her own lost ghosts. I glance around, swiveling my head in search of a familiar face, and then I see one.

We lock eyes, and he moves toward me, hacking through the thicket of partygoers, he moves right toward me.

It's Henry, of course. Here and now, present and past. Why did I ever believe that I could stop the collision of time?

@

MY FEET ARE seemingly made of lead. I want to move them. I so urgently want to raise them and flee, and yet, I cannot.

He is getting closer, and I'm starting to panic. *I'm not ready for this! I am supposed to have my sweet time with Jackson, figuring out the Henry question when I'm ready to figure it out!* I feel a flare of hives snare itself around my neck, marring my collarbone like a Jackson Pollock painting and clashing with the starkness of my silver strapless dress.

He is moving in slow motion, and I see the flop of his deep-sandy hair ride over his forehead, and he reaches up to push it back out of his eyes. As I learn to love him, I discover that this is his tell: the sign that he's nervous or bluffing or, occasionally, lying. Not that I'd catch him lying all that often, but yes, sometimes, I'd trap him in one. That he had to stay late for work, when, in fact, he was golfing at our club; I'd hear about it two days later when Ainsley and I would take the kids for a toddler swim, and the valet might mention it in passing. Or that he hand-selected my ruby anniversary bracelet, which he'd present to me over merlot and candles at the finest restaurant in Rye, only to have his secretary ask, with her tongue so planted in her cheek it's remarkable that she can speak at all, how I enjoyed the gift that *Henry* picked out. Wink, wink. Nudge, nudge. She'd emphasize the "Henry," just in case I hadn't picked up on the insinuation.

Tonight, he is nearly in front of me, again, swatting at his hair, attempting to tuck a strand that's too long to hang properly yet too short to reach his ear, into place, when my brain finally connects to my legs. I turn to go, desperately, urgently, but there is literally no place to run. Around me, clusters of hobnobbers block my way, like brick walls on all sides, and the only viable exit is directly where he is coming from. I look to Josie beside me for help, but she has long since faded on me, wistfully sipping her rum and dreaming of her youth while scanning—still scanning—for Bart.

Too soon, and finally, he is here.

"You're the girl from the bus, right?" he says, smiling and extending his free hand. The band has stopped playing, and a buzz of electric silence fills the dead space.

"What are you doing here?" I reply. It's out too fast for me to take it back. But of course, Henry's not supposed to be here. This isn't where we meet. This isn't how it all plays out. In a flash, I wonder how many near misses I've had with Henry in my former life . . . if he were someone whom I'd see around my neighborhood, at the grocery store, in the gym, *on the bus*, who just went unnoticed or to whom I'd occasionally nod, but who wasn't meant to play any significant role in my life other than a familiar face with whom I would exchange glances from time to time in passing.

"Uh, excuse me?" He tries to take a step back, but instead, just elbow jousts with someone behind him, and finds himself on the losing end.

"I . . . just . . ." I find that I'm unable to speak. Henry. *Henry! This is what he looked like when we met*, I think. His eyes are still drowned with hope. His teeth seem whiter, his posture taller. No fine lines creaking into his forehead or around his eyes. Everything about his veneer seems glossier, more vibrant. *Was I the reason you lost that?* I wonder. *Or do I simply not notice anymore?*

"Should I not be here?" he asks, perplexed.

"Er, no. I'm sorry." My tongue feels scrambled. "It came out wrong." *It came out exactly right! What are you doing here?*

"Well, to answer your question, my company is a major shareholder in Coke, so, that's why I'm here. And you?"

It occurs to me suddenly that Henry has every right to be here. He might have even been here seven years ago. It's *me*; I'm the one who has changed things, who has inserted herself into places I haven't previously been. *I'm* the one who is new here.

"I, uh, I do their advertising." I stare at my hands rather than into his eyes, which feel like phantoms bearing down on me.

At this exact moment, Jack reappears, squeezing his way between two women who appear to be as bored as I am frantic.

"Finally!" he says. "I've been circling this place forever looking for you." He pauses to assess the situation. "Oh, sorry to interrupt. Introductions are in order."

"This is Henry," I say before I realize my mistake.

Confusion floods his face. "How did you know my name?"

Shit. "You told me a few minutes ago!" I bleat, my voice ringing like a siren. I feel sweat pool underneath my arms, and my blood pressure is exploding like a firework. "When you walked up! How can you not remember? And I said, 'Yes, I'm Jillian, from the bus the other day.' "

He brushes back his hair and tries to rattle his brain. I can see him thinking, because I know him too well, *how could I have forgotten a moment from just a few minutes earlier*, but then deciding that he doesn't want to be rude and acknowledge that he's already misplaced my name, so he goes with it, just as I knew that he would because Henry is too proper to create a minimelee with a new acquaintance.

"It must be these drinks!" he answers, raising his martini and spilling it on his wrist. "I should obviously lay off—"

"I say that too much is never enough," Jackson interrupts, shaking Henry's free hand with vigor, as a way of introduction.

"It's true," I say. "He does say that." Jack's nights out with his editorial crew are legendary and, most often, regretted the morning following.

"Well, with that, I should get back to my friends." Henry

smiles, though it looks more like a wince. "Nice to meet you, Jillian. Or nice to *remeet* you, I should say. And I hope to see you around again soon."

He nods, then pushes past through the cluster of the crowd.

Not if I can help it, I think, ignoring the palpable longing that sits like a bruise over me. But then I realize, *what if I can't?*

ℰ H E N R Y

Henry and I married at a white-shuttered, black-shingled church in Connecticut, ten minutes from my childhood home, which my father now shares with Linda. My florist dotted the pews with gardenias, and when we swapped vows, with just forty-five of our friends and family behind us, you could almost taste the floral-scented sweetness that cloaked both the church and our union.

We celebrated in my father's backyard, the same backyard in which Henry, at least in my memories of what I thought to be true, chased Katie in their failed quest for (those stupid took-me-hours-to-dye, my-fingers-were-pastel-hued-for-days) Easter eggs. Torches lit the lawn, and bouquets of more gardenias drenched each table, and mirth and conversation filled the dusk air. It was a private, quaint, nearly perfect evening.

When you looked at us, when you watched our first dance or when you noticed Henry kiss the top of my head before standing to give his speech, you'd think that we were many times blessed. And, best as I can remember, I thought we were, too.

"Please forgive me," Henry said in front of the crowd on the wood dance floor that my florist had laid down the day before. "Because I'm about to get sentimental, which, for those of you who know me, is quite an aberration."

Our guests tittered with amusement at the truth of his statement. Of the many things that Henry was—logical, precise, loyal—overly emotive was not one of them.

"As most of you know, I am an only child," Henry continued. "Which has its perks, certainly—all the toys you can hope for as a kid—but also has its downsides—no siblings at the ready for constant companionship or a younger brother to beat up on." He paused for laughter. "But the one real downside is that you do spend your life looking for someone who is on your side, who has your back. I spent a lot of my life looking for that." He cleared his throat and looked over to me, and I tried to dislodge the tangible ball of emotion clogging my throat.

"And then, I met Jillian, who, when work explodes or I need someone to lean on, well, she's there. She's just always *there*, and for me, as someone who has lived his life without someone else always being there—no offense, Mom and Dad—it is everything. *She* is everything." He wiped away tears that flowed down his tan cheeks. "So I raise my glass to *you*, Jill, who has filled that space for me that I've searched for for thirty-one years. To my Jillian, I love you more than the moon and the stars."

Our guests roared out thunderous applause and held their champagne glasses high, and Henry wove his way back to me, kissing me hard and lovingly until I finally pulled away.

So yes, you would think that we were many times blessed. You'd think that you were so damn happy that we'd found each other, and even though this was our life, not yours, your eyes would well with tears at the thought of such happiness because we, you told yourself, were what you strived for. And seeing us now, you knew that this love, this bond between two people who started out as nothing more than strangers but who grew to discover that each was the other's half, wasn't unattainable, and if we could have it, so too could you.

Chapter Eleven

Slowly, the assured grip with which I once held my future is coming unraveled. When this endeavor began, I could foresee most, though certainly not all, of the events that were to rear their heads, like daffodils bursting out of spring soil. True, the little things—who would pop into my office, where Jack and I would eat for dinner—had long since fled my memory, but the bigger, more impacting things—an earsplitting argument over a dreaded and demoralizing weekend at Jack's parents' weekend home (this time, rather than endure the hysteria and the withering commentary that spouted from each of us, I simply agreed to the figurative jail time), a flare-up at work over misplaced film from the photo shoot (try calling the cab company, I suggested now)—have been easy enough to dodge. There is a reason, I suppose, that the cliché is a cliché: Hindsight truly is twenty-twenty.

But now, things have started to radiate like waves. Like a nearly imperceptible drop in a puddle that sets off a tiny ripple that shakes the entire pool of water. Eventually, these subtle shifts alter everything about what you've come to anticipate.

I know this because come Labor Day weekend, I'm sitting on the back deck of Megan and Tyler's beach house on the Jersey shore, rolling the nutty taste of an Amstel over my tongue, and rocking on her wooden white porch swing while watching Jack and Tyler toss the football through the thundering ocean waves. I know this because six years ago, while I was here, Jack wasn't. He was invited, yes, but I drove down without him when we'd become embroiled in yet another fight over his writing, or perhaps more accurately, his future.

"Stop trying to push me!" he screamed loud enough for the neighbors to hear. "I get it from my mom, I get it from you, I'm getting it from both ends. Jesus Christ! I'm writing when I can, and just *stop*!"

"So now you're lumping me with your mother?" I yelled back. "Because I thought that your stupid fucking novel made you happy! I thought I was doing you a *favor* by suggesting that maybe you blow off a night out with your friends to stay home and work on it!" I paced the living room floor behind our (goddamn) couch.

"It *does* make me happy. It's the pressure that doesn't! So stop! Just fucking stop!"

"Fine," I said flatly. "Send a memo to your mother because I was just trying to please you both." Which maybe wasn't true, when I thought about it now. I never tried to please Vivian, really, but I figured that saying that I did might score me points. What I truly hoped for, much more than pleasing Vivian, was that Jack might come into his own, stop muddling around at a job he took only because it was offered to him, stop wading around his late twenties like he was still in his early twenties.

And then Jack slammed the door and walked out, and I, relieved at both the silence and his absence, escaped to Meg's summer house in the rental car.

This time, when Jack muttered that *he really probably maybe should get some writing done soon*, I merely smiled and curled my hand around his cheek, assuring him that he would write when he was inspired to and not to force something that wasn't yet ready to come. He nodded, kissed my forehead, and soon enough, we were roaring down the highway to the shore. *Does it feel like too much? Not yet, no not yet. Jack was still so easy,* I told myself. *It's better than the alternative, surely, it is better than that.*

This afternoon, Meg brought me another beer, but skipped one for herself.

"Not drinking?" I ask.

"Don't get your hopes up," she says. "It's a precautionary measure. I won't know for another week. I can't risk doing any damage right now." I saw her visibly shudder, as if exorcising some sort of shadow that nevertheless slithered within her.

"Meg," I say and place my hand on her arm, "you know that the miscarriage wasn't about anything that you did. The doctor couldn't have been more clear about this."

"Can't be too cautious." She shrugs and sucks down a sip of lemonade.

"You sure you don't need to talk about this? About what you're dealing with?" I ask her again, just like I've asked her a dozen times since our emergency trip to the hospital. Just like I ask her every time I hear that tiny sliver of hope fill her voice.

"No," she shakes her head. "I'm fine. It happens. It sucks. But I'm fine."

I start to say something else, but chew the inside of my lip instead. I still haven't quite adjusted to having Meg here, alive and thriving, even if emotionally, she's wilting, curling at the edges like a piece of lettuce left in the fridge too long. So I tread lightly, not wanting to mar the incredible good fortune that comes with rediscovering a friend whom you had once lost. Permanently so.

A family of five and their golden retriever walk by, plopping down in the sand just to the right of the deck and spreading their blanket for an early-dinner picnic. The wind keeps sailing the blanket aloft, so the youngest, a redhead who couldn't have been more than eight, runs around to each side and traps it into submission by placing flip-flops on each corner.

"So anyway," Meg says, watching the family unload their cooler. "You and Jack seem good. Should I be on proposal watch?" She flashes a huge grin that's devoid of happiness, one that I recognize from my old life, when I was the one topped off with plastic enthusiasm.

"Maybe," I say. "Let me ask you . . . do you ever have any regrets with Tyler? I mean, you guys married so young, and not that you're not perfect for each other, but . . . I dunno." I swig my beer. "I'm not sure what I'm trying to say here."

"I know what you're saying," Meg answers. "And not really. I mean, I don't have many regrets. I guess I never in a million years imagined that we wouldn't have a kid by now, but other than that, no. He makes being married pretty easy."

I nod and stare back out at the family—the mom is now distributing sandwiches, and the older brother has the youngest in a headlock. Megan follows my gaze.

"I just know that I'll be such a great mom," she says. "It's, like, all I can think about these days. How much a mother must love her child, and how it must feel to have that love returned. Like you're finally not alone."

I look at her with a start. "Meg, you're *not* alone. You have me. You have Tyler. I hope that you don't feel alone."

"No, that came out wrong," she says as she waves her hand. I notice bright splashes of pink along her cuticles where she's gnawed them down to fresh skin. "I just mean, like, your child is tied to you forever, and nothing that anyone does can take that from you."

I think of Katie and how, now, even when I try not to miss her, it's impossible: Missing her is like a film over my skin that can't be washed away. Then I try to think of my fondest memory of my own mother. A sign that at some point, she must have ferociously, uninhibitedly, ardently loved me in the way that Megan is so sure that mothers are bound, the way that I grew to love Katie, even if I wasn't struck with it from the very second she was born.

The memory comes to me quickly, without too much effort. I was nine, and my dad was out of town on business, like he often was, running an import company that took him across the globe in search of new partnerships. Andy had been tucked into bed early—the summer heat had beaten him down, so he quickly spiraled into slumber after our grilled cheese and tomato dinner—and my mom had just finished tending to her garden in our backyard. It was only minutes after dusk, so the skies weren't yet black, but there was only a faint glow of light, and fireflies were blinking on and off throughout the yard, begging to be caught. I grabbed two jelly jars from the cabinet and ran down the porch, tossing one in my mother's hand and tugging her onto the grass. She giggled and followed me, and for the next hour—long after the sun had officially sunk beyond the horizon—we ran through the yard, capturing the fireflies then setting them free, over and over again. Finally, with dirt on our hands and sweat on our necks, we spilled into the kitchen and scooped out hulking heaps of ice cream, building sundaes larger than my nine-year-old self had ever imagined, and then devouring them in nearly one breath. When my eyelids grew too heavy for themselves, my mother carried me up to my bedroom, buried me under my sheets, and kissed me good night. Grime and all, which, for my mother, was a remarkable exception.

I've returned to that scene so often, too often, that I'm not even sure if I've concocted some of the details. Maybe they weren't sundaes, maybe they were just scoops of ice cream. Maybe it wasn't an hour in the yard, more like fifteen minutes. I really couldn't say. Because it's the one memory I have that reminds me that perhaps my mother wasn't the monster I later crafted her to be; that yes, indeed,

I was loved, and that her leaving, her abandonment had nothing to do with me, and so much more to do with herself.

"My mother sent me a note," I say to Megan today, as we remain transfixed on the picnicking family on the beach. "Eighteen years of nothing, and now, she sends me a note. Wants to reconnect."

Meg turns to me, her face a mix of hope and astonishment but also, because she knows the details that Jack doesn't, and that maybe, even later, Henry doesn't either, that I've never regurgitated wholly to him, I see pity. Meg was there at my high-school graduation, when my father sat by himself amid all the couples who, even if divorced, came to support their graduates. She was there on my twenty-first birthday when, because I was so drunk at a bar, I announced that earlier in the day, I'd trotted to my mailbox in hopes of a card from my mother, but got, I said at the time, *"Shit, nada, zilch, zero from that bitch!"* She knows the wounds my mother carved into me that have taken years to heal, and how hard I worked at healing them.

"Oh Jesus, Jill, I'm sorry." She reaches over and holds my hand. "You okay?"

I nod and, for the first time since receiving the letter, find tears slowly leaking out. I wipe away a drop that's weaseled its way down to my chin.

"I just don't know what to do. Call her. Not call her. I've asked Jack but he's not much help—"

"Well, who cares what Jack would do," Megan interrupts.

"Oh, well, I mean, I guess I do." I surprise myself in saying it.

"Aw, Jill, this has nothing to do with Jack and what he would do." Meg stands and kisses the top of my head. "This has to do with you and what *you* need. Don't confuse the two." She pauses to nurse out the last sip of her lemonade. "If you *do* decide to call her—which you might—then let it be because it's your needs, not because of what he thinks . . . or doesn't think," she adds in.

She walks into the kitchen, and I hear the screen door slam.

"So let me ask you," I call over my shoulder. "Do you still think that a mother's love trumps all?" I think of Katie, and how, though I love her enough to make my heart explode, splattering out of my chest like a smashed pumpkin, sometimes the burden of it, of motherhood, felt too much.

"I do," Meg says, returning with a fresh beer and a refilled glass of lemonade. "Call me an eternal optimist, but I do."

℮

IN MY OLD LIFE, I often dreamed of Jack. He'd intrude at unsuspecting times—popping in occasionally to remind me of the life I'd left behind, or perhaps more honestly, the life I was leading now, the one plagued with what-ifs and self-doubt and festering resentment and sippy cups and bald-headed dolls and spoiled milk dumped in the back of my Range Rover. Invariably, in these dreams, Jack and I were always happy, with no gnawing, looming concerns that would eat us from the inside out.

These dreams were set against backdrops of fictitious realities—trips we'd never taken, stories we'd never told. I'd wake up and feel haunted from my very core, like a tick had wheedled its way into the pit of my stomach and was spreading a virus on out, and I would inevitably spend the rest of the day lingering in memories of our burned relationship, wondering where he was, how he was, and if he ever dreamed of me in return.

Tonight, wrapped beneath a quilted blanket at Megan and Tyler's beach house, with the lapping sounds of the ocean filtering through the open window, and with Jack's measured breath beside me, I am dreaming of Henry.

It is an early Saturday morning, no Saturday morning in particular, and Henry is still flooded with sleep, whimpering to himself every few minutes as he slumbers. We appear to be on a ship, and I peer out of a tiny sliver of a porthole to see dark blue, nearly black, water, and a cloudless crisp sky. I slip out of the bed, steadying myself under the rocking floor, and retreat to the bathroom, then emerge to shake him awake.

"I'm pregnant," I whisper, my lips pressed to his ear. He grunts and snorts but doesn't move. "Hen, *I'm pregnant.*"

His eyes whip open and in one quick movement, he pulls me down to him, throwing me over the bed, then looping on top of me. The boat rolls beneath us, and we're nearly tossed onto the slats of stained oak beneath us. Quick as lightning, we both reach for the headboard like a life vest, until the crest below passes.

"Come here, my fertile and knocked-up wife," he says breathlessly, and brings me closer. I tuck myself underneath his shoulder, and we lie in silence, our chests rising and falling in time with the other and with the waves beneath. I stare at Henry's toes which, in my dream, are abnormally long, disproportioned such that they consume nearly his entire foot. The air smells like sausage, and I hear frying from the galley, and I wonder who is making us breakfast.

I flop my arm over Henry's stomach, fingering the gentle loft of hair that floats just below his belly button, and then a foghorn sounds loudly, bleating like a laboring cow, in the distance. The cacophony stirs me, and I shudder, then glance down to discover that my belly has already expanded, that it is morphing even before my eyes, growing like an alien puffer fish, like a balloon filled with a rush of helium. I try to raise myself up, but I'm flattened, paralyzed in the bed, and I can only watch in agonizing horror until my body is so ripe that I'm nearly bursting with child, and that at any moment, I am poised to explode.

"Henry!" I scream with a shrillness that could puncture our

miniature glass window. "It isn't time! I only just found out! It isn't yet time!"

I reach for him, but my hand grasps nothing but air. Frantically, I will myself to move, pushing frozen, unheeding muscles, commanding them until they relent, and nearly sitting up and lumbering under the new weight of my stomach, I scream again. "Henry! Get over here *now*, Henry!"

But he doesn't answer. There is nothing but silence, even the horns from the passing boats and the sizzle of the sausage have fallen away, and just before I shake myself awake, in the last few gasping seconds of my dream, I find myself weighted to the bed, bulging and terrified, and realize that I am utterly alone. Henry is gone, vanishing into the blackened waters that push against us at every turn, as if he were never there in the first place, as if he were never there at all.

❧

EVENTUALLY, AFTER STARING at the ceiling fan and listening to gulls on the beach, I fall back asleep. I dream of nothing, or at least nothing that I choose to remember. I am wasted in slumber when a ringing phone jolts me awake.

Jack's hand flashes toward the nightstand, and he gropes for his cell.

"Urg," he manages, before he pushes out, "hello."

I look at the bedside clock. It's 5:15 A.M.

"Is she okay?" I hear Jack saying. He reaches for the lamp and clicks it on.

"Oh, come on!" I hiss and throw myself under the covers.

"Why didn't you call me earlier?" His voice is giving way to increasing urgency. "No, of course not. I would have been there in a second. I'm just here with Jill! No, no, it's just a weekend vacation. It's not a problem."

I pull the blanket back and shoot him a look to let him know that while I have no idea what his comment was in reference to, I'm considering being deeply offended.

"No, no, I'm leaving now. I'll be there in a few hours. Okay. Yes. See you then." Jack stands and pulls his jeans off a wicker chair in the corner of the room.

"What's going on?" I ask. My voice croaks with sleep, and I can taste my sour breath.

"My mom," he answers, tossing a T-shirt over his head. I've never seen him dress so quickly. Clothes are flying through the air at superhuman rates.

"Is she okay?" I prop up on my elbows and scan my brain. I have no recollection of any heart attacks, car accidents, or other brutalities that might cause such panic.

"She broke her hip," he says. "Last night, trying to string lights on the tree out back for their Labor Day party. Fell off the ladder."

Ah yes, that's right.

"I have to head to the hospital. I'm sorry, babe, to cut the weekend short." He is shimmying his feet into his sneakers, trying to weasel them in without untying the laces.

"Well, I'll come," I say. "I'm happy to come with you." I swing my legs off the bed and feel my back crack in two places. My body is begging for a few more hours to be dead to the world.

"No." He shakes his head. "No, no. It's fine. You stay here and enjoy the next few days."

"Jack, don't be silly. I want to come. Keep you company. It's what girlfriends do."

"Really, baby, don't worry about it. I'm fine on my own. I'm just trying to get out of here as fast as possible so I'm there when she wakes up this morning." He moves over to kiss me, as if that will blunt the fact that my company isn't warranted for a family emergency, *his* family emergency. "My dad said that she was asking for me last night. My sisters have their hands full with their kids, so, I'm the only one who can come."

"But, Jack . . ." I start, then pause, biting back any shards of offense that I might have taken in my old life with him, blunting them instead with openhearted, concerned girlfriend overtones. "I'd really like to go—"

"Jill, please, really, I appreciate it," he interrupts. "But my dad and I can handle this."

"Of course you can handle it," I say mutedly. "I didn't want to come to *handle* it, I wanted to come to show my support."

"Oh, well, that's very sweet," he says, too distracted to put any meaning behind it. "But I'm good." He pecks me again on the lips and runs his fingertips over my cheeks and down my collarbone, then grabs his overnight bag and bolts out the door. "I'll call you this afternoon," he says, just before I hear the thud of his footsteps plodding down the stairs, and then the slam of the front door.

I ease my way back into bed and flip off the light, clamping a lid on any disappointment, the way that my mother might have jarred up jam fresh from her garden, sealing it tightly so it could last the winter through.

Well, you weren't there last time, either, I remind myself. *So really, nothing to worry about. Nothing's changed.*

Slowly, I slip into sleep, dreaming of neither Henry nor Jack, not realizing that I seem to have missed the point entirely.

Chapter Twelve

On Labor Day, my office is quiet. Everyone else has fled the city and their desks for literal greener pastures. Meg and Tyler asked me to stay on at their beach house, but after Jack's departure, I couldn't muster the spirit for the sandy walks or the margarita mixes or anything that would come along with what was supposed to be the quintessential weekend with my rehabilitated relationship. So instead, I begged off their offers of homemade pancakes and sank into the rental car that reeked of stale cigarettes and floral air freshener, and headed back to the deadened enclave of my office. Storyboards, print layouts, copyedits I could do. I'd already done, in fact, half a decade back. There were no worries that, despite my best efforts, I'd still be spurned.

It was like it always was at work, both before and now, and today, I meditated over my loupe and the sketches and tried to forget that even though I was a chameleon with Jack, changing tiny parts of myself until I blended in completely with his environment, somehow it might not be enough. And I tried not to consider that even though I've been in my new life for nearly two months, still, at times, it feels like I'm shoving puzzle pieces into slots that are too narrow or too jagged for a proper fit. *It should be seamless this time*, I stop to think before flushing my mind clear. *That's the whole point. You have the game plan already; you know the moves. You simply have to follow them. It should be seamless,* I reiterate to no one but myself. And yet in so many ways, it is not.

I am huddled over my desk, peering at a "woman on the street" frame, when I hear my cell phone buzzing from the depths of my bag. A nerve in my neck flares ruefully as I hurl my torso over the arm of my chair to reach the phone in time.

"Hello?" I tuck the phone underneath my ear and stand to stretch. I've been cocked over the images for two hours, and my shoulders are palpably pulsing.

"Jillian? Er. Hi, it's Leigh." She pauses. "Jack's sister."

"Oh, hi!" My voice molds into some sort of squeal, and I try to ratchet it back, hoping I don't sound desperate both for the interruption and for the fact that she, *Jack's sister,* is calling. She never called me in my old life.

"I hope it's okay that I'm calling. . . . Jack told me that you're on your own this weekend because of my mother's accident."

"Oh, well, yeah, you know. Things happen. Jack told me that she's recuperating just fine, though." I coo with understanding. *Even though I don't fucking understand at all! Yes, you do,* I reassure myself. *Yes, you do.*

"She is," Leigh affirmed. "Though you know my mother. She might be recuperating, but it's the rest of us who suffer."

I allow a nervous laugh, unsure about Leigh's motivations, more unsure because I've never heard a child of Vivian's deign to say something less than revelatory about her. I grab a Coke-flavored stick of gum and fold it under my tongue.

"Anyway, I was calling because Allie and I are headed to the city in a few minutes, and she was hoping we might see you. Would you be interested in meeting us at the zoo in an hour or so?"

"Of course!" I say without hesitation and worry if I might come off as needy, or worse, pathetic. *Lonely girl sitting in deserted office waiting for phone to ring so she can prove herself to aloof boyfriend.* Not exactly a classified ad to woo Jack's family.

"Allie, get down from the windowsill right now!" Leigh shrieks, and I hold the phone away from my ear. "Sorry," she sighs. "Okay, great. She'll be thrilled. We'll see you at the front gate of the zoo in an hour."

Leigh clicks off but, as I turn back out toward the window and stare down at the sidewalk at the strolling pedestrians and moms and dads and families and people who have lost their way, her voice sticks like taffy in my ear. It's hard not to recognize it, of course. Her quiet and frantic desperation, fleeting though it may have been, sounds exactly like me, back in my old life, back before I was granted a chance to know better and a chance to wash myself clean of that desperation for good.

THOUGH THE CITY has emptied for the long holiday weekend, the Central Park Zoo teems with families who weren't lucky enough to escape the filmy air and the blaring horns of taxis. I see Allie before she sees me. Her white-blond hair is pulled back into low pigtails, her yellow capris are dotted with imprints of watermelons, and her ivory tank top is splashed with a giant icon of the fruit. She is clutching Leigh's hand and half picking her nose, and I can't help but stare: Though Katie inherited my own deep mahogany locks, she would be, I intuit, the very vision of Allie come four and a half years.

Before I can examine these implications, Allie spots me.

"JILLIAAAAANNNNN!" She rushes over at me in a frothing

frenzy, and torpedoes her body at my legs, then attempts to climb up me like a spider on a vine, until I lean over to heave her up in an encompassing hug.

"Allie! Come on, get off her." Over Allie's shoulder, I see Leigh jogging to catch up with us. "Jillian doesn't need you all over her."

"I don't mind." I place Allie on her own two feet and grab hold of her hand. "That's as good a welcome as I've ever gotten."

We amble through the iron gates and, tugged by Allie, make our way into the penguin house. In the darkened exhibit, which smells like damp seaweed and kosher salt, Allie presses her face against the partition that separates us from the birds, close enough that we can see her breath fogging up the glass, and gazes in rapture as two penguins dive below the surface of the frigid water, pushing their bodies through as if they were merely moving through air, and swimming together until finally, after what feels like an eternity, they glide toward the other end of the rocks and scurry back to the pack.

Leigh and I watch from the back wall, silent and equally mesmerized, as various penguins continue to plunge in, for seemingly no reason at all, other than to submerge themselves in the waiting water and to, I imagine, taste the relief or even the joy that this moment—that of taking the leap—brings. I watch the birds dive over and over again, and somewhere inside of me, I feel the heat of jealousy. To be that free. To take that plunge. Until, at the very moment I realize how overwhelmingly silly it is to envy a penguin, *a penguin trapped at a zoo no less*, Allie whips out of the exhibit, bored in a flash, in the way that six-year-olds can be, and Leigh and I are left to chase her wake.

Once outside in the sharp glare of the midday sun, I squint to adjust my eyes and, for a second, am struck with a sharp pang of vertigo, which leaves as quickly as it comes.

"Hey, Allie," I say to her back, as she heads toward the polar bears. "Did you know that penguins mate for life? That makes them pretty unusual for animals."

She stops and turns my way. "So you mean that it's like they get married? Like Mommy and Daddy?"

"Something like that," Leigh answers.

"Though I don't know if there are actually weddings!" I grin. I find myself unconsciously playing with the bare space on my ring finger. Though it has been empty for two months, I'm still always surprised when my thumb reaches over and finds the rings gone.

"Well, they're already wearing tuxedos if they need them!" Allie says, and we all laugh, though I pause before doing so, so astonished at what a little person she has evolved into. *Katie.* The pang lingers this time rather than fleeing my body like an unwanted chill. I watch Allie rush toward the polar bears, and I'm nearly drowned in nostalgia of my own precious girl.

"They grow up fast," I hear Leigh saying, as if she had a map of my brain. "Sometimes I can't believe that she's as wise as she is. I mean, shouldn't she still be in diapers?" She sighs, but it's not a sigh of lament or remorse. Just a sigh of a mother who can't pin down time, who can't shake it to a stop and say, Don't let my baby get old, don't let it all get away from me before I have a chance to inhale it all in.

"Thanks for inviting me today," I say, trying to dust off the memory of Katie. "It was a welcome surprise." I pause, unsure of what else to add. Jack's family had excavated such an emotional moat that I find myself off balance when a bridge has finally been lowered.

"Well, Allie fell a little bit in love with you at her birthday," Leigh says. "And Jack mentioned that he left you halfway through your weekend, so . . ." She stops, too. New territory for both of us, I suppose, as I watch her consider how to continue. "Look, Jill, I know that my family isn't always the easiest lot. My mother alone is enough to make you bananas . . ."

"So you see that, right? It's not just me?" I hear the relief flood my voice, in the knowledge that finally, someone, *anyone*, might be an ally.

"No, it's not just you," Leigh laughs. "She never quite learned how to find the balance between being a mother and having her own life outside of us. I was the youngest of the girls, so I got the least attention, which, I suppose, was a blessing—I survived the smothering. But Jack, well . . ."

"Behold the prodigal son," I inject.

"Something like that," she answers, as we sit on a bench and watch Allie stand rapt at the polar bears who remind me of over-sized marshmallows.

"Do you ever worry? You know, that you'll turn into her?" My breath accelerates, and I hope that I haven't crossed the line, cracking the new, fragile foundation that we're tenuously erecting.

"Sometimes, I guess, sure," Leigh answers, unfazed. "You know, motherhood is the best thing that can happen to you, but it can also be the thing that can drain you completely. I mean, I know that sounds weird, and I hope it doesn't sound awful, especially to someone who doesn't have kids, but it's the truth."

"It doesn't sound weird to me at all," I say, and I think of how many pieces of myself I lost when Katie was born, how much I missed having a purpose other than pressing my breast into her mouth and singing her to sleep and swapping out dirty diapers for new ones. All of which were wonderful, *truly wonderful*, but there were other pieces I left behind that were abandoned too quickly and too thoroughly; it almost felt like they had been physically cut from my being.

Six months after Katie was born, Henry, who perhaps sensed my listlessness, or perhaps had just grown bored with a wife who had nothing else to contribute to nightly dinner discussions other than reports on poop-filled diapers or sales at BabyGap, suggested that I consider volunteering somewhere. Getting out there and away from the stifling routine I'd fallen into.

"Why don't you call one of the homeless shelters or a cancer organization or something and see if they could use some help with their marketing?"

"I don't think we have homeless shelters in Rye," I answered, blowing on my postdinner tea.

"I was speaking metaphorically," he said.

"Why would I do that? I'm perfectly happy taking care of Katie." I hoped that my voice sounded less hollow than the truth behind it.

"I just thought that you might want to do something else, too, you know, with your free time." He rose from the dinner table to clear the plates.

"Free time! I don't have any free time! Do you think that this mommy thing is a vacation?" I plunked my cup down harder than I'd intended, and the tea swirled near the top, then over the edges and onto the table. I mopped it up with the ribbing from my sweatshirt sleeve and hoped that Henry didn't notice. "I'm nursing her or changing her or bathing her or entertaining her, and when the nanny comes, I have errands to run! I don't have a single second of freaking *free time*! Thank you very much."

"Jesus, Jill, I was just making a suggestion. Sometimes space away from the baby can be healthy."

"So now I'm unhealthy?" I could feel tears perching themselves on the ledges of my eyes.

"Oh good God, calm down. It was just a thought." He plodded into the living room and grabbed the remote.

"If it's so important to you that I *get space*, then why did you make me quit work?"

"What are you talking about?" Henry said, returning to the door frame to face me. "You *wanted* to quit work! I didn't make you!"

"How can you say that? You packed me up and shipped me off to the suburbs, and now you're telling me that I'm unhealthy and need space and that I should get out of the house, blah, blah, fucking, blah!"

"All of which you agreed to! Happily!" Henry was now shouting. "Jesus Christ, the thanks I get for making a simple suggestion that you take up volunteering!"

"Be quiet!" I hissed. "You'll wake Katie."

But it was too late. Seconds later, I heard her wail, and I could feel Henry's eyes boring into me from behind as I rushed to my crying daughter, though I don't know who was more disturbed, her or me.

Today, on our bench at the zoo, it wasn't hard to grasp the connotations of what Leigh said: that motherhood could both fill you up and, if you let it, and maybe only if you let it, suck you dry.

"Will you have more?" I ask her, after Allie runs over to us and begs for ice cream money.

"Maybe," Leigh says. "We'll see." She shrugs, then laughs. "I feel like I've finally figured this mom thing out. Adding another one might throw the whole balance down the tubes."

"Well, I'm an untrained expert, but it looks like you're doing pretty well to me." Allie hands the ice cream vendor three dollars and struggles, as if it were of grave, consequential world importance, to make a decision on flavors.

"I hope so," Leigh says. "But you know, you just try to do the best you can. No one ever tells you that the best you can should be enough."

Allie settles on strawberry and heads back toward us, her cone tipping perilously toward the ground like an unbalanced seesaw until she rights it at the last second. Soon, we hug our good-byes and Leigh smiles a kind smile, saying we should do this again and not too far in the future.

I watch them amble down the brick path of the park, surrounded by a tunnel of lush trees that will soon be shedding their leaves, then renewing them, and I play Leigh's words over again in my mind. *My best should have been enough,* I think. *So why didn't enough ever feel like enough for me?*

℮ HENRY

We moved to Westchester when I was nearly five months pregnant, six weeks after I quit my job at DMP and right around when my abdomen had blossomed into a perfect curve and my breasts were full and ripe like cantaloupes. Henry promised that I glowed, and the truth is that I tried my very hardest to do just that: to appear lit from within in anticipation of this new being. As if I could will my skin to be a bit rosier, my veneer to be a bit shinier, my aura to be a bit more illuminated. And a lot of the time, it worked; I convinced not only Henry, but myself as well—duped myself into believing that I wasn't wholly terrified of passing on the damage of my own mother to my new child, that I wasn't predestined to carve out permanent, penetrating scars.

Henry was more prepared for the change than I was. Or maybe it's just that for Henry, so little changed—the only difference in his life now was the square footage of our living space and a longer commute—but for me, nearly everything changed. Or was changing. Looking back on it now, maybe our move was when everything really did start to *move,* to shift, like sand ebbing beneath our toes. The ground was still there, surely, we were still standing, but it was being pulled out from beneath us while we stood atop it, barely noticing. Only later, we'd look down and see that the shore had completely eroded.

Our new house felt big, too big, for little—though not that little anymore—old me. I'd wander from room to room, plodding and bored, checking my watch far too often and wondering how soon Henry would be home to help absorb some of the air, to help fill some of the space. In hindsight, I see now that I should have told him how hollow I felt, how demolished by loneliness I was. But back then, I figured, what's the point? We'd made the move and we certainly weren't moving back. Not now. So I flitted about our looming house, and I called Ainsley for power walks, and I decorated vigorously to turn the barren walls and floors and rooms into what I hoped would be a *home*. Besides, I'd remind myself, soon enough, Katie would be here, and she'd be all the company I'd need. At least that's what I told myself on my better days.

As the evenings grew cool and the crimson leaves fell around us and when Henry was home early enough, we'd stroll through the quiet streets of our neighborhood, hand in hand, and spill forth our picture of the future—the peach-toned nursery, the looping scent of baby powder, the sounds of tottering, padded footsteps as our little bean learned to navigate her way in the world. Other times, we'd rest on the love seat on the back porch, feet tangled into each other, with Henry's hand palming my stomach, wordlessly absorbing the new life that kicked inside of me.

Somehow, I learned to put my isolation aside. I'd read all about it in a magazine—which one, now, I can't remember. But I'd imagine myself heaving my loneliness upward and setting it down, leaving it on the side of the road by the gro-

cery store or at the mall by Pottery Barn. After mentally un-
furling it, I'd drive away, skidding out of the parking lot, ex-
haling with relief, but too afraid to look in the rearview
mirror in case I discovered that I hadn't left it there at all,
that, in fact, it had weaseled its way back into the car, back
into me, and dumping it on the side of the road, dumping it
anywhere, was nothing short of impossible.

Chapter Thirteen

When Jack returns from his mother's sickbed, he also returns with new gusto for his novel, the one that has floundered like a graying, flopping fish since we met. At graduate school, prodded by Vivian and her aspirations, Jack wrote and rewrote and re-rewrote drafts upon drafts, many of which his professors admired well enough, but none of which earned him publication or garnered awards like some of his peers.

Occasionally, after a glass of red wine, and ample assurances that I wouldn't judge him, we'd sit on his futon, reading together— he'd jot down notes or mutter something to himself, then hand me a page, and so it would go, passing the pages back and forth as if we were a fluid entity. Upon graduation, he was offered his much-sought-after position at *Esquire*, and he tuned back into his "novel," if it could be called that because, to the best of my knowledge, it was really only sputtering starts of disconnecting chapters, only when guilt overtook or when Vivian injected him with an IV of ambition.

"Seeing her there, you know, stuck in bed, and looking so frail," Jack says tonight between sips of a Heineken, "you know, I just realized. It's time to shit or get off the pot."

"That sounds fantastic," I answer, only mildly engaged; I've heard this false start before. Many, many times before. I lace up my sneakers to head out for a late run.

"Oh, by the way," he says, "Leigh told me you guys had a great time at the zoo yesterday. I've officially been given my family's seal of approval."

"You needed a seal of approval?" I stand upright and try to sound less offended than I am. "You're twenty-seven years old, Jack. You seriously need their approval?"

I think of Henry and how after he proposed, he told me that he'd taken my father for drinks before our Paris trip, not so much to ask for his permission, but to assure my dad that he'd watch over me for the rest of my days. It wasn't approval that he sought, and I admired him, always, for that confidence, of never second-guessing, of being sure of his choices because for him, his choices were sensical, like a math problem resolving itself as it was intended to be solved.

"Well, of course I need their approval," Jack says, as if it were the most obvious thing in the world. "Family comes first, and if you're going to be a part of my family, I'd just want to be sure that we all jelled."

"We've been dating for two years. And only now you're worried about jelling?" I say tersely. The lace on my left shoe feels too loose, and I wiggle my heel to secure my foothold.

"Well, maybe now," he says, moving toward me and placing his hands on my hips, "I'm ready to make it more than two years."

I open my mouth to say more but I'm so stunned by his innuendo—*that was innuendo, right?* I think—that I opt to overlook my irritation at his need for familial approval. I'd grown so accustomed to turning a blind eye that it wasn't hard to do.

"Okay, get going on your run," he continues. "I want to fire up the computer and get writing. I figure if I crank every night after work for the next month, I might be able to get this to agents by Thanksgiving."

"Sounds great," I answer. "Dive back in there. Just like you always say."

"What's that supposed to mean?" he says, cocking his head in question.

"Nothing." I shrug, too late. The tiny slip of judgment flew out of me before I could clamp down on it.

"Nice try. What did you mean by that?" he says.

"Forget it," I answer, heading toward the door to squeeze in the jog before the sun disappears completely.

"No, seriously, Jill, what the hell was that supposed to mean?"

Oh fuck it, I think. His earlier comments about Leigh are still sticking under my skin like a wayward flea, but more so, I'm still broiling with resentment at his refusal to take me along to aid his mother the previous weekend. I can feel my anger pulsing through my blood, even as I try to pretend that I've washed it clean. His inability to acknowledge any wrongdoing riles me further.

So why don't you just say that? I ask myself. *Why don't you just launch in and tell him the goddamn truth?*

"It's just that this is a pattern, you know; you stop, you start, you flounder, you get back up, but it never amounts to anything." I pause, considering. "I guess I just wonder why you bother, when it doesn't seem like you're really that interested in writing in the first place." I exhale, relieved to nick his armor in the same way that he nicked mine, even while knowing that this is the very thing, these whittling arguments, that I've been dodging—like tiptoeing around broken glass—since my return.

"Well, that's awfully below the belt," he says, his voice elevated, his eyebrows askew. "And for the record, you couldn't be more wrong."

"Fine," I sigh. "I'm wrong." I'm struck with an odd sensation of not caring too much either way, a passivity that feels unfamiliar, like I might have actually neutered myself.

"No," he escalates. "I can't even *believe* that you have *that little faith in me*! That you think I'm some sort of *lazy dilettante* who can barely wipe his own fucking ass!"

"Oh Jesus Christ," I say. "Calm down. I never said anything of the sort."

I could already see this spinning into a fight from our earlier days, the kind that ended with bitter silences and halfhearted apologies and residual blame that would nip and ding and gnaw their way into our relationship until one day, we woke up and saw scars, real scars, and then I'd flee to a bar and meet Henry, who was supposed to be my salvation.

"Look, I'm sorry; what I said came out wrong." I backtrack though I'm not sure how sorry I am. "All I was saying is that just because your mom might want you to become the next great writer doesn't mean that you have to take it up as your calling. *You* should figure out what your passion is, not her."

"So now you're telling me that I'm doing this just because of my mom?" Jack sits flatly on the windowsill, and I can see the sun quickly slipping behind the horizon. Echoes of my fights with Henry bounce around my mind; how quickly one can misinterpret and skew and let it all get away, like an eel from a fishing line.

"No," I say, so anxious to put this behind us, just like I always am. "I'm just saying that you're responsible for your own life, that's all. Not her, not me. You."

He purses his lips. "As if I didn't know that," he says.

"Good," I answer, kissing him lightly but avoiding his eyes, then heading out the door, running, running, running as if Jack is the only one who needs to take a closer look at responsibility and ownership and what role we each have in claiming our own.

❧

FOUR DAYS LATER, it is a rainy Friday afternoon, one that has ushered in a temperature nosedive, such that in the office, we're all caught off guard in our tank tops and still-summery dresses, and we spend the duration of the day shivering and rubbing our arms or clutching chalky hot chocolate that someone dug up in the back of the office pantry. The weather forecast warns of flooding, which people use as an excuse to head out early, and by 4:30, my office hums in near silence, the walls bouncing with gray from the clouds perched impossibly low just outside my window.

My mother's note, though tucked away in my top drawer under pens and Post-it notes and DMP letterhead, cries out to me daily, as if it is emitting some sort of sonar alarm that only I can hear. Finally, I relent.

I dig underneath the paper clips and the uncapped highlighters and the month-old invitation to the Coke party, and wrestle her letter to the surface.

Could she really have been here this whole time? I think, as I stare down at the handwriting, which is as familiar to me as my own. I'd asked my father this very question when I called to tell him about her correspondence, but he had no answers. He just hung mutely on the phone, stuttering his responses, as surprised as I was, I suppose, that my mother hadn't needed a true escape; she just needed an escape from us. Growing up, when I'd thought of her, which I had tried to do as infrequently as my psyche would allow, I'd always assumed that she'd gallivanted to Paris or had set up a seaside shop in St. Lucia or had owned a restaurant in Madrid. Never once did it occur to me that she'd hover so close. If you wanted to flee your life, after all, why wouldn't you run as far as possible, so there was no chance of ever looking back?

Tenuously, I type her name into my browser. I feel my heart quicken as I push "Enter," knowing that what I turn up will open new doors, doors that I've slammed shut for nearly two decades, doors that my first time around, I was perfectly okay with—no, more than okay; I was completely at peace with keeping them locked for good. I remember explaining all of this to Henry on our third date over spaghetti Bolognese in a tiny Italian joint decorated with colored Christmas lights in Little Italy, right before we went home and slept together for the first time. And how he seemed to absorb my angst, how he deflected my bitterness and didn't judge me for it, how it felt like I finally purged myself and in doing so, I could lay these wounds to rest. But I never did, of course. Wounds like this don't just seal themselves overnight and disappear into the ether. Because even after they've healed, even after the scars are entirely undetectable, the memories of the damage are still seared into your brain, like posttraumatic stress from a mugging. You tell everyone that you're fine and you even convince yourself that this is so, until one day, a man leers a little too close to you on the street, and you find yourself dissolving into fear and panic and sweat all over again. This was what it was like to live with the memory of my mother's abandonment. Even when I pushed it good-bye, it lingered, like a stench that you'd grown so used to, you couldn't smell it any longer. And then, later, after we'd married, Henry wouldn't let me forget it, anyway, as if he thought that reclaiming my maternal bond with her would somehow cure me of all my ills.

Google returns no hits on my mother's name. I lean back into my chair, almost relieved, and reach for my hot chocolate. It's only then that I notice that my hands are shaking.

How could someone's life be so invisible that even Google can't find them? I wonder.

"You're still here?" Josie pops her head in the door frame, then wanders in and plunks down in a chair opposite my desk. "I thought I was the only one left."

"Keeping the midnight oil burning," I say, turning my head from the computer screen but keeping my eyes on it until they're forced to look away.

"I hear you," she says, removing one of her heels to rub the arch of her foot. "Speaking of which, I just got off the phone with the Coke guys—"

"What happened with Bart?" I interrupt.

"Oh, Jesus, nothing." She waves her free hand and turns crimson. "That was just one too many drinks talking." She shakes her head and her voice drifts off. "Or something."

"Or something," I agree.

"Well, anyway, more important, good news. Coke's decided to hire us not just for this campaign, but for all their advertising: print, radio, TV."

"Wow!" I say. "That's amazing! Congratulations, Jo."

"Don't congratulate me . . . you're the one who did this. And so . . ." she pauses for effect, "as of Monday, consider yourself an account director."

"Seriously?" *This definitely didn't happen in my old life.* Back then, my back was patted and I heard "job well done," but never was I heralded as an advertising genius, which is more or less what this promotion—two years early—trumpeted. "Thank you, Jo!" I rock back in my chair, as some sort of exclamation, and it creaks in reply.

"My pleasure," she says, slipping her shoe back on. "You've earned it. Now go grab that boyfriend of yours and celebrate."

"Oh, well, he's actually at his parents' house this weekend. His mother broke her hip, and he likes to be at her beck and call and all of that." I feel the enthusiasm sucked from my body much like a punctured tire. "But you should head home yourself. Hang with the kids and all that."

She shrugs. "They're actually visiting Art in San Jose. Their last gasp of summer before school starts next week."

We both stare at the floor, embarrassed to acknowledge the obvious: that neither of us has any other place to be, that neither of us has anyone who needs us badly enough to vacate our hushed, melancholy offices.

"Well, I guess that's it," she says finally to break the silence. She stands to leave. "Don't work all weekend, okay?"

"Promise." I smile but drop it as soon as she rounds out of my office. I reach for the phone to call Jack and tell him about the promotion, then think otherwise. Whenever Jack is with his mother, I feel like my calls are an intrusion, like he's humoring me until he can click off and return to his first priority.

I shuffle papers around on my desk, hunting for busywork, until I realize that my mother's search results, or lack thereof, still blare out from my screen. I grab her letter and reread it once again, like I haven't already committed every word and every hint of meaning behind them to memory. Biting my bottom lip, I reconsider my search tactics, and then type her phone number into the Google bar. One entry pops up.

Ilene Porter. 120 Fifth Avenue. New York, NY 10011.

I stare at the information so long that it becomes fuzzy and spins on itself.

Porter. 120. Ilene. 10011. New York. Fifth Avenue.

I try to make sense of it, but I cannot. Porter isn't her maiden name, and it's certainly not her married name. And then it hits me so clearly that I can't believe that it didn't dawn on me to begin with: My mother has remarried. She has rebuilt her life, and perhaps her family, with someone new, someone who is not my father, children who are not me or Andy; it wasn't *a* family she didn't want, it was *our family* she didn't want.

I gasp for a breath of air, like that might cleanse me or erase the knowledge of my new discovery, but it does nothing, other than leave me heaving deeply for more. Feeling queasy, I push my chair back abruptly, and it tips on itself and rattles to the ground. Then I hurl myself out of the office, down the elevator, and into the storm-swept streets. It's raining so hard that I think I might suffocate from the unrelenting sheets, which, I suppose as I fly down the block, is all the better, because then, no one will be able to see my tears.

Chapter Fourteen

The weather refuses to relent. All weekend I hear the *tap-tapping* of drops on my air conditioner, which juts out of my living room window, a window I spent an inordinate amount of time gazing out. This slow time, this time with no one to satisfy but myself—no husband to foster, no toddler to clean—still feels off, even two months after I've returned to my old life, like a slippery skin that doesn't quite fit. I consider darting into the office but worry that I might run into Josie, and I'd be too embarrassed to face her and admit that I might be evolving into a second version of her: all work, no life.

In Westchester, in our grandiose house, there was no such thing as downtime. There was always laundry to be done or diapers to be restocked or Cheerios to wrestle from under the couch. At nights, when Henry would travel, which was almost all the time, I'd try to sink into bed with a new book, after I'd bathed Katie *(bubble bath!)* and tucked her in for the night *(Goodnight Moon)*. But I never quite figured out how to turn it off, the button that said "full-time mom," so mostly, I flipped through magazines or sped over websites, concocting new recipes to be tested or new art projects for upcoming playdates or worrying about hosting the best birthday party in the neighborhood, even if her birthday was four months out.

And now, there is literally no one to answer to. A quiet so profound that it is almost tangible. Jack is tending to his mother; Meg and Tyler have retreated to their beach house for, as she whispers from her cell phone, "baby-making sex." Ainsley has already moved north to Rye. I realize, as I stare out at the expanses of water tumbling from the sky, loneliness isn't something that materialized when Henry and I married or when Katie was born. It's followed me my whole life, like a shadow I'm unwilling to shake.

A therapist might tell me that this stems from my mother's abandonment, but I'm not so sure. Aren't there traits that we're simply innately born with? When Katie arrived, she was feisty from the start. Her screams were enough to pierce glass, and her colic was seemingly endless. For weeks, I operated on autopilot in a revolving haze of utterly exhausted delirium, in which I'd wake to her shrieks, attempt to comfort her with my breast, then clutch her close and rock her to stop the crying. When that wouldn't work, we'd walk through the neighborhood, me, desperate with the hope that the hum of her stroller would calm her; her, utterly refusing to be calmed. Henry tried to help; it wasn't that he didn't offer. But he wasn't the one nursing her. He wasn't the one who had grown her for the past nine months. "He's not her mother," I'd mutter when he would try to soothe her and fail or change her and put the diaper on backward or make any tiny misstep that I so prided myself on avoiding. It would have been a miracle, I supposed now from my perch in my shared apartment with Jack and seven years earlier, not for me to resent him.

The days when Katie was a newborn dragged on endlessly. I would sit on our front porch and try to urge the sun to go down; *the sooner that nightfall came, the sooner we would be putting this wretched day behind us*, I'd think, ignoring the obvious fact that I'd have to wake up and do it all over again. I would rock on our porch swing and think, *No one tells you that it's going to be like this. No one says that this will be the hardest thing you've ever done. That it's not just puffs of pink and baby coos and sweet rosy cheeks. Why didn't anyone warn me?* But then, when Katie would quiet herself, and I'd rub her back while she dozed in her crib, I'd palpably feel it—the absence of loneliness that too often plagued me—and my face would flare with shame, as if crawling with tiny fire ants, that I ever had moments of regret. And then I'd push all of it aside and wrap myself into the package of a perfect mother. Above everything, that is what I did best.

So now, whether or not a therapist would blame my own mom for my feelings of alienation, part of me just knows that this is how I came out. That the damage she did to me had its impact, sure, but that wasn't the beginning, and now, I'm not sure where it ends. How it ends.

It ends here! I want to tell myself. *With your second shot. Get out there and do something about it, with this good fortune and this second chance and the knowledge that you have to repair yourself and Jack.*

I stare out into the monsoon and will this to be the truth.

Finally, for a brief moment, the skies shift from angry gunmetal gray to a whitewash, and energized by the turn, I frantically lace up my sneakers and head for a run. It will be, I realize with surprise, the first time I've left the apartment all weekend.

I amble out into the downtown streets, unsure of a particular destination. Though I normally head straight to a running path near the river, today, inexplicably, I head east, winding through the sloshy city streets, nodding at the lone passerby who has also seized this rainless window to rush from his or her apartment and gasp in some fresh air. I fly past dilapidated delis and hipster boutiques and coast over puddles that threaten to break my stride but never do. My legs are crying out for pumping blood and coursing adrenaline, like a baby colt who needs to break free, and refuse to be thrown off their rhythm. I tread through the East Village and up the avenues, until it becomes clear where I'm headed, where my body was leading me this whole time, even if my brain pretended that it wasn't so. Denial. No one ever accused me of being anything less than an expert.

I stop suddenly on the street opposite the building, *her* building.

The awning reads 120 FIFTH AVENUE. It's a looming white limestone structure that, even just peering in from the outside, reeks of wealth, the sort of building that you can't move into without lofty tax returns and a cushy job on Wall Street. At the entrance, a uniformed doorman sweeps aside some leaves that have fallen in the storm, then snaps to attention and tips his hat as a blond woman, elegant in an olive overcoat and knee-high boots, exits the glass doors. I watch her turn the corner of the street and wonder, even though I know that my mother is raven haired, if it could have been her. If, perhaps, her hair color is just one of many things that she'd changed about herself. I watch the doorman as another song cycles through my earphones but then am literally jolted from my stance by a loud clap of thunder. With seemingly no warning, the skies unfold themselves, and within seconds, I'm soaked all the way through.

"Shit," I say under my breath, as I flick drops off my forehead and pick up my pace to a near sprint. Three blocks down, I spot a Starbucks and throw myself inside, my shoes slopping and my clothes ready to be wrung dry. I am standing in the entrance, shaking water off my arms, like a dog after a dip in a lake, when I hear my name being called from behind me.

Of course, I think, as I turn to greet him.

And there he is, Henry. Following me nearly as closely as my own shadow of loneliness.

           ☙

"We have to stop meeting like this," he says, grinning.

I force my face into something of a smile, but I fear, with my smeared mascara and my matted hair, that I look more akin to a grotesque slasher film character than the best version of myself.

"Can I get you a drink?" he asks, then hands me some napkins as if they might be of any use in drying off. I dab at myself but realize it's futile: It's like I've just gotten out of the shower and am wiping away the water with nonabsorbent toilet paper.

"N-no, thank you," I stutter. "I can't stay."

That's right, you can't! I tell myself. *You have a boyfriend who, though he is currently more enamored with his mother than with you, still seems relatively enamored with you. And you already KNOW what happens next with Henry! Give yourself the chance to find your new path! Do. Not. Stay.* Three beads of water trickle down my nose, then dive to the floor. I feel my blood race, and I'm not sure if these beads are remnants from the storm or are now from the rapidly increasing flow of sweat that I feel overtaking me.

"You're going back out there?" Henry says. "Just to get away from me?" I stare at him a second too long before I realize that he hasn't read my mind and is, in fact, joking, *flirting*, even. I can't remember the last time Henry flirted with me.

"No, no, nothing like that," I say. "I just, you know, have things to get done."

At this exact moment, a clap of thunder booms so loudly that several people behind us scream and I jump six inches in the air, clutching my chest in fear. When I land, my shoes make an audible squirt.

"Jesus Christ!" I shout.

"Well, good luck to you," Henry says. "Though it sure seems to me that you might be better off here than out there." *More flirting!*

I look him straight in the eye and feel like I'm trapped in one of Katie's episodes of *Sesame Street.* The one where Big Bird keeps running into a wall over and over again because he can't seem to figure out that he needs to go over, not through it. Only, this time, I'm Big Bird, and the walls have closed in on all sides.

"Fine," I say reluctantly, just before another ear-shattering crack echoes outside. "I guess my to-dos can wait." *No!* I hear my brain screaming. *Flee! Flee as fast as you can, thunder be dashed, lightning be damned! Let me repeat,* I tell myself. *Do. Not. Stay.*

But when Henry sizes me up and says, "Don't tell me, let me guess what you want." And then follows up with "I got it, you're a chai tea sort of gal." It unnerves me to the point where I can't even consider leaving. Because he's right: He's nailed me; without even knowing anything about me, it already feels like he does.

We settle on a table in the front. Henry folds his *New York Times,* running his fingers over the creases until the pages lay perfectly and seamlessly flat, the way that he would every weekend for the next seven years of our lives, and I try to ignore the sense of panicked familiarity that it brings. Then he runs his hands through his hair, like he always does when he's nervous, and a tiny part of me slowly opens up, a part that feels like it had been hibernating and is ready to face the spring anew.

And still, I remind myself, this could not, in any way, be a good idea. *Do! Not! Stay!*

"So Jillian, this is what I know about you," Henry says, sipping his double espresso. "You do advertising for Coke. You ride the bus. You have a boyfriend, who, best as I can tell, is now nowhere to be found. You appear to like jogging. And . . ." He cocks his head and pauses, mulling over what to say next. "You look adorable, even when you resemble a drowned rat." He smiles triumphantly, and I chew on my inner cheek to avoid doing the same.

"All correct," I say, then add on second thought, "though the boyfriend is very much still in the picture."

"Duly noted," he answers. "So what else is there to know about you?"

"That's about it." I laugh. "That's the exciting version of me, all wrapped up in a ten-second summary." And it's true, I realize. The me of my past isn't all that different from the me of my future: patterned, boring lives that, if necessary, can be wrapped up with a tidy bow, tucked under the bed, and forgotten about entirely unless someone mistakenly stumbles on them while cleaning for dust.

He holds my gaze, then says much more seriously. "There's no way that this is all you've got."

"It feels like it is," I say with a shrug, then remember where I'd landed at the end of my run. Before I can even think to retreat, I say, "Well, then there's the fact that my mother abandoned me when I was nine, and now she wants to reconcile."

My eyes widen in surprise at the statement, and I immediately wish that I could reel it back in. *Who are you, the crazy girl who overreveals on the first date? The girl who guys share horror stories about because she can't shut up!* I scream internally. *But this isn't a date!* I remind myself, then grow irritated that I'd even consider the notion. I swig my tea to compensate and hope that he doesn't notice. A tiny dribble leaks out the left corner of my mouth, and I mat it with the back of my hand.

Rather than recoil at my far-too-intimate disclosure, or act repulsed by my less-than-meticulous table manners, however, Henry furrows his eyebrows and looks at me with sympathy.

"I'm sorry," he says. "That must be scary."

I want to leap across the plush burgundy sofa and clutch him, hug him so closely that I can feel his whiskered cheek against mine.

Because through all of this, no one, not Jack, not Megan, not my father, not even me, has tapped into what is truly the most excruciating part of this entire ordeal: that my mother's reentry into my life isn't just nerve-racking or emotionally uprooting, it's horrifically terrifying in a way that I've never tasted before. That discovering the true reason that she left us might be worse than never knowing, and now that I have the chance to uncover these truths, the fear is nearly paralyzing.

And so suddenly, I spill out the story of my mother, of my history, of how she left us on a cool fall morning, and how she came back in the same manner, and how I feel as if I'm the infantry who was hit by mortal shells with no warning. The words rush out of me, tumbling on themselves, and when I'm done, I feel purged. And while I'm sure that Henry made me feel this way more times than I can count back before we grew stale, I sit on the couch in Starbucks and try to remember when *anyone*, either in this life or my other one, made me feel so reborn.

Finally, as if on cue, the thunder stops and the rain tapers to a dull trickle, and my senses jolt, reminding me that Henry is a slippery slope and one that I've already tumbled down before.

"I should go," I say and stand abruptly.

"Oh, okay." His face floods with disappointment. "Well . . ." He lingers. "I would like to hear how this ends. With your mom, I mean."

"I have a boyfriend, Henry." *Yes! You! Do!*

"I know," he says without a trace of regret, without missing a beat. "It's just that it's not often I find someone I can talk to. And with you, it's like . . . something that I can't explain." There isn't even a hint of embarrassment as he says it.

I nod because I feel it, too.

"Friends," I say, and extend my hand to shake his. "How about if we settle on friends."

"Friends," he echoes. He grasps my palm, and I hope he doesn't notice me flinch as a tug of electric familiarity courses through me.

I turn to leave and push open the dripping glass door.

"So I'll see you around," he calls after me.

"Well, you've been following me pretty well these days."

"Then there's no doubt I'll catch you soon." He smiles.

"Catch me if you can," I answer before I realize that I probably shouldn't put myself out as Henry's bait.

℮ KATIE

Henry was promoted to "youngest partner ever at the firm" when I was seven months pregnant. Thirty-one weeks, to be exact. I remember because I had my first internal exam earlier that day. He came home with a bottle of champagne and convinced me that a few sips wouldn't cause permanent damage, and I was so grateful for a literal taste of prepregnancy life that I had an entire glass. Though, truth told, I was so fraught with panic of the damage I might have done that I couldn't sleep at all that night.

"This won't change anything—a little more work for a much bigger bonus," Henry assured me, after we'd made love for only the third time since conceiving Katie. He ran his fingers over my basketball-sized stomach. I nodded, awash in postsex chemicals that can convince even the most rueful of spouses that her relationship isn't plunging into doomed waters.

Two weeks later, when I was thirty-three weeks along, Henry shipped off for what would evolve into an unending business trip: They stacked on top of one another like playing cards, and his little time at home would be cluttered with sleeping, laundry, and repacking. Ainsley, whose due date was eight weeks ahead of mine, gave birth while Henry was in Hong Kong, so I filled my days pitching in at her house, watching her carefully and hoping that what appeared to be innate mothering skills would somehow transfer to me via osmosis. Or something. Ainsley's competence was surely compounded by the fact that her husband was home; he'd happily cashed in his paternity leave to dote on both mother and son.

"Paternity leave?" Henry scoffed when I mentioned it after he returned. He still smelled of stale airplane air. "Seriously? That's just about the lamest thing I've ever heard of. *No one* would do that at my firm."

I shrugged and wondered why I'd bothered to bring it up in the first place. It's not like I really believed that Henry could—or would—be able to set aside three weeks to stay with us. Maybe I should have just asked for three days. Probably. Yes. I should have asked for that, at least. Three days to help me adjust to my fear and my nerves and the excruciating shadows that stayed with me, hinting in the background that I'd screw this mothering thing up. But instead, I said nothing. It seemed easier that way, I suppose.

As my due date slowly, *slowly* crept up, my ankles ballooned, and my heartburn flared, and Henry's pace grew no less leisurely. He bought me gift certificates for massages and remembered to tote home flowers on occasion and even withstood an all-afternoon trip to Pea in the Pod, but still, these were the plugs to fill in the wider gap, and it was hard not to admit, though I pushed my smile up as far as it could go and rubbed my belly with gusto, that this gap had a larger crevasse that snaked its way through us.

When my water broke in the kitchen as I prepared

homemade lasagna *(Gourmet!)*, Henry was in a car to the airport. I was one week early and had assured him that no, *no chance* would I deliver while he was on his one-day trip to Chicago. I'd read about it, after all; first-time moms are likely to go late.

Contractions followed like tidal waves, so I frantically phoned him, desperate to reach him before he literally jetted off, and then I called a cab, which arrived twelve minutes and three contraction cycles later and reeked like fading curry and Old Spice. And this is how I ended up admitting myself into the labor and delivery ward at Westchester Medical Center.

Henry burst through the door ten minutes later, frantic and sweaty, and when I saw him, apologetic and also full of hope, I forgot the gap and the crevasses and the changes that had nudged their way into our marriage that we'd been unable to adapt to. If I'd ever recognized them at all. Instead, I concentrated on my breathing, and Henry counted with me, and later, held up my legs and screamed with me. And after eleven hours of excruciating labor, Katie made her way into our world.

Chapter Fifteen

Gene and I are splitting buttered bagels in celebration of both of our promotions—he's now my official assistant—on Monday morning when reception buzzes my line, informing me of a delivery that's been deposited at the front desk.

"I'll grab it," Gene says, licking his fingers and springing to.

"You're not my errand boy," I say. But just as I stand, Josie swings into my office with a look that says "stick around," so Gene heads off to retrieve it.

"Well, I know it's your first day in your new position, but we've already run into a snag," she says, then tosses a pile of headshots on my desk, which land on top of softened packaged pats of butter that I normally deny myself but made an exception for in light of the celebration. "Coke's not happy with our choice of the kid model for the 'zizz' print ads." She plops into the chair, still warm from Gene, and squeezes the bridge of her nose. "As if this is just what I need right now."

"You okay?" I ask, because clearly, this doesn't seem like the sort of monumental crisis that Josie seems to think that it might be.

"Fine." She waves her hands. "Look, I've run through all of

those headshots and none of them really stands out to me, so can you take a flip through and see if you can find the next big star?"

She said this with a foreign, unfamiliar sarcasm. Whether or not we were creating high art, Josie was the first to believe that what we did *mattered*. That the hours we spent holed up in our airless offices changed commerce and the marketplace, and that leaving our clients satisfied was as important as any job in any industry.

"No problem," I answer, perplexed. "How hard can it be to find a cute kid?"

"Harder than you think," she says. "I was here all weekend digging through piles of headshots and faxing them to Bart, but none of them worked for him."

"To Bart?" I say.

"It's nothing," she reiterates with a finality that seems either true or depressing, and I don't pursue it to find out. "The shoot is in two days, which means that we have to find someone they agree to, get the kid fitted, get test shots done, get him the script . . ." She sighs. "Anyway, can you just take a look and see if any of them jumps out at you?"

"Yeah, of course," I say.

"Good," she answers with no enthusiasm and turns to leave.

Shaking my head, I scoot my chair close to my desk and begin sifting through the pile of photos. Though the children are varied in skin color and hairstyle, in height and in weight, they all possess a similar look: that of frozen smiles and trying-too-hard eyes and plasticky expressions that do little to swoon me, and more important, would do little to swoon the consumer. I flip through the stack again, and it's not hard to see why Bart was unimpressed.

Just as I'm doubling back to rethink an adorable, if cookie-cutter, Afroed six-year-old, Gene waddles through my door, weighed down by a ballooning vase of flowers, big enough that it might be fair to compare the bouquet to a tree. A minitree, perhaps.

"Move some crap on your desk," he cries frantically. "Quickly, before I drop this load!"

I shove some old mail onto the floor, and he lurches forward, aiming for the now-empty spot and landing the vase with a thud. The stems shudder with reverb.

"Wow, someone adores you!" Gene says, stepping back to observe the floral jungle.

I grab the card that abuts an orange tiger lily and run my finger under the seal of the envelope.

Jill—

I am so proud of your promotion and am sorry that I've been so distracted of late.

Dinner tonight at "our place"?

> *I love you,*
> *Jack*

My face expands into an unweighted smile, and I shake my head in wonder.

I'd left two messages on Jack's phone after I returned home from my interlude with Henry at Starbucks. In the first, I told him about my promotion, and in the second, alarmed by the fact that I couldn't dislodge Henry from my head, I told him how much I missed him, how much I loved him, and how I wish that he'd come home that night, rather than taking the early train in the morning, even though the sun had long since tucked itself beneath the horizon and my eyelids drooped with fatigue and I knew that there was little chance of him doing so.

I fell into a listless sleep an hour later and woke at midnight to no messages. But now, there was this. *And on a Monday, too!* I knew that Monday mornings were Jack's busiest, clogged with editorial meetings and copy deadlines and delinquent excuses from his freelance writers, so when this mass of floral obscenity landed on my desk in the midst of all of this, well, it felt like something. Not everything, but something to be sure, and for me, so desperate to rid Henry from my system, to expel him like rotting waste, it certainly felt like enough.

"So I take it the boyfriend problems have been resolved," Gene asks, nearly blinded by the glare from my beaming grin.

"You can take that correctly," I say, bending over to smell the literal roses.

"Well, that's good news," he says. "Because I didn't want to say it back then, but I can say it now. Ex-boyfriends are always trouble."

"Not always," I answer. "Just most of the time."

"Always," he says firmly. "Always since the beginning of time. Don't go thinking otherwise."

"I wasn't," I say, as Gene heads out the door with a perfunctory glance. Until I realize that I was thinking that exactly, but that indeed ex-boyfriends *are* always trouble, and a wave of gratefulness passes over me, as I recognize how closely I'd been tiptoeing to throwing it all away. And now, with Jack present and accounted for, how I wouldn't have to think of Henry again. Trouble he was, and trouble he would be no longer.

℮

"CONSIDER YOUR CRISIS solved," I say, walking into Josie's office.

She holds up a finger and mouths "hang on," while pressing the phone into her ear, so I busy myself perusing her bookcases, which are sunken down with shiny plaques of industry awards and dozens of books on marketing, branding, and consumerism.

Josie's isn't quite a corner office but more of a junior suite. She was the most recent partner, and this was the only space they had

left. Unlike my own office, which resembles the shambles of unde-
termined wreckages, Josie's is angular, tidy, and virtually spotless. I
run my hand over her pine shelving and wonder if she stays late,
just to make sure that everything is in its place as it should be,
rather than heading home to her kids. But then I remember my own
life, my own *old* life, where my house was the embodiment of perfection, as if starched linens and bursting, bright flower beds somehow symbolized a robust soul, and it creeps over me that Josie and
I might share more than just a knack for advertising.

"I'm sorry," she says, setting the phone back in its cradle.
"Art." She shakes her head, and I'm unsure if she's referring to a
problem with the art for the Coke campaign or to her husband. She
runs her hands over her face and smooths her fingers over her eyebrows and exhales. "He's been offered a full-time position in San
Jose."

"Oh . . . that's great" is all I can think to say, though she
doesn't seem to hear me.

"So what? So what now?" she says, and I realize that, in fact,
she hasn't heard me. "Am I supposed to resign from this fucking job
so that Art can be the full-time art director of the *San Jose fucking
Opera*? Are you kidding me?"

"I . . ."

"No, seriously, I mean, do I sound like a horrible wife? That
my husband has finally gotten a permanent job, after, I don't know,
two goddamn decades, and I'm not even happy about it?"

"I don't know, Josie," I say softly. "But I'm pretty sure that
doesn't make you a horrible wife."

"I don't know, either," she sighs. "I've sacrificed so much for
my family, and now, after years of working my ass off so my kids
wouldn't have to worry or so that we could send them to college
without scraping by, he lands this, and it's like, 'Well, thank you very
much, I appreciate you putting in your time, but now I can handle

it, so pack up and move to San Jose!'" Her voice singsongs. "San *fucking* Jose!"

I think of Henry and my pangs of isolation—how he whisked me off to the suburbs without much of a second thought to what I might be leaving behind, how he prodded me to reacquaint myself with my mother without considering the reasons why *I just fucking couldn't*—and it's easy to understand Josie's crest of resentment.

"But enough about my problems," Jo says, with a wave of her hand. "Which crisis is it that you say you've solved?"

"You have more than one?" I ask.

"Isn't that obvious?" She ekes out a smile.

"Well, I've resolved the Coke print crisis: I found your kid. Bart signed off on it, and we're good to go."

When I mention Bart, Josie's eyes pop almost intangibly, but just noticeably enough that I wonder if she'll pursue it. She doesn't.

"Thank God," she exhales, and slashes a Sharpie through an item on her list on her desk calendar. *I used to make those lists*, I think. Grocery lists. To-do lists. Katie lists. Best-damn-mother-of-the-year lists.

An hour prior, after filtering through the pile of plasticized-looking children, an e-mail popped into my inbox from Jack, confirming our date for the evening. And then I remembered that I already had the perfect child model: Allie. So I called Leigh, who seemed less than exuberant about whoring her daughter out for one of the nation's largest junk food and soda manufacturers, but who also made the mistake of having the conversation while she picked Allie up from school, and thus was cornered into doing it by a six-year-old.

"I wanna be in magazines!!!!!!" I heard her scream from the backseat of their Volvo wagon. Leigh sighed and asked if we could push the shoot until the afternoon, so Allie wouldn't miss school. I e-mailed Bart a snapshot of Allie from her birthday party, dressed in a prairie skirt and olive-green graphic tee, and then, just like that, it was done.

"God, you're a miracle worker," Josie says, when I explain the sequence of events.

I think of how far I've come, of how I've ended up back here half a decade after I'd done all of this before.

"You don't know the half of it," I say, standing to leave.

She grins a sad grin, and then, just as I'm turning out of her office, I look back, and watch any last-minute traces of joy drain from her face entirely.

☙

"OUR PLACE," as Jack referred to it in his note, was a cramped falafel dive on 114th Street and Broadway. The linoleum tables were covered with cheap paper place mats, and the aluminum chairs grated on the parquet floors when you slid them back to sit. Sitar music cooed out of the speakers that were perched near two corners of the ceiling. The air hung with the unmistakable scents of hummus and fried cooking oil, and every time that I stepped inside, pulling back the squeaky glass door, I thought of our first date.

If I'd been paying more attention on that evening, I realized later, far too much later when I was already sucked into heady love with him, I could have seen some of the signs. Signs that he wasn't going to be my savior or that he wouldn't be the flawless romantic writer whom I somehow imagined him to be on that initial date. The way that he talked about his meandering ambitions, of how he never really knew what he wanted out of life. *Such joie de vivre!* I thought, with euphoria. The way that his mother called him as he walked me home, and it didn't occur to either one of us that he shouldn't take the call. *Such a loving son!* I thought, my heart swelling at the very notion. And then I invited him inside, and we tore into each other in the way that you can do when you're first tugged toward someone and the curiosity is only outmatched by the boundless passion, and from then on, I stopped asking questions. At least until we were too far gone for answers, anyway.

Tonight, Jack is here before me, and I spot him at a cramped table tucked into the back corner. Still, even though it has been months since I came back, I am surprised, awed even, when I see him. He looks up from the pita chips he's been reaching into and finds his way to me, then smiles, his eyes crinkling like a paper fan, when he sees me.

"Oh my God, I'm so proud of you," he says, pulling me close, then holding me by the shoulders from afar, the way that a grandparent might his teenage grandchild who has gone through an unprecedented growth spurt. "I mean, seriously! Jill! It's amazing!"

I demur and pick up a menu, even though I order the same thing every time I'm here: the chicken gyro platter—and I do exactly that when the goateed waiter who looked like he might be perhaps getting his MFA in poetry while busing tables at night, ambles over and says, "So what's your pleasure?"

Halfway through dinner, Jack reaches around into his messenger bag and pulls out two envelopes.

"For you," he says, sliding one across the table.

With a furrowed brow, I engineer it around my plate, then flip it open.

"Oh, I didn't realize that you really intended to do this!" I say. I eye my plane ticket to Miami, which is tucked on top of Jack's handwritten list of suggested activities: Jet Skiing, South Beach, new restaurant openings.

"Of course," he answers and reaches over to weave his fingers into mine. "I've planned out every detail of the trip—all you have to do is pack and show up at the airport on time."

"You did this all this weekend?" I cock my head. "I thought

you were taking care of your mom." I pause, unsure of whether I should be amazed at what Jack can actually pull off when he aspires to it or upset that he wasn't aspiring to something greater. "And writing."

Indeed, I'd envisioned him either hovered above her sickbed or crouched over his laptop through all waking hours. Not sweet-talking airline representatives into upgrades to business class or booking nearly impossible reservations at celeb-packed Asian-fusion joints.

"The writing's going a little slower than I expected." He shrugs.

"What's the problem? Maybe I can help." I nudge some tabbouleh around a green pepper and swoop my fork in to grab it.

"There isn't a problem," he says. "It's just, you know, my mom is a distraction, and I wanted to be sure that I gave her my full attention."

With a mouthful, I nod my head in what I hope is support—even though I suspect that, mother or not, Jack might always find an excuse for the writing to go a little slower than expected.

"Anyway," he continues. "This isn't about my writing. This is about Miami!"

"Are you sure," I ask, "that you wouldn't rather spend that time at that writers' workshop we talked about? So that you hit the Thanksgiving goal you were aiming for?"

"Jillian! Seriously. You're killing me here."

"I'm just trying to be helpful," I say. But I don't add, because when we split seven years ago, you ruefully and regretfully told me that you'd orphaned your manuscript to spend more time with me, and that had you not devoted so much effort to what was now a torpedoed relationship, you might now have finally fulfilled your dream. And that I spat back that you never had any intention of fulfilling said dream because it was nothing more than a mirage, a mythical goal that you and your mother conjured up like an illusory end zone, that you had no intention of ever running toward. And that you crumbled in—I'm not sure what—rage, defeat, true pain—when I said such hateful things. Such that part of me always wondered if maybe you were right: that I hadn't been encouraging enough, nurturing enough, though I'd been plenty of both, and that when you slipped into the living room late at night to bang out a few pages, and I'd call you back, needy and hating to sleep alone, maybe I unconsciously didn't want you to get away from me, to take off on a new trajectory and potentially leave me behind. I'd been through that enough already.

"I know," Jack says kindly. "Don't worry about me. I'll write when I write." He raises his glass. "To Miami."

"To Miami," I echo, clinking my chardonnay against his.

I look down, and it's only then that I notice the date on the ticket. October 3. Three weeks away. The mere glance at it sends a jolt through my core, as if my chi were getting tangled all over again. This, after all, was the date that I was supposed to tearfully trudge into an East Village bar, order a cosmo to nurse my bruises after Jack and I were nearly ready to dissolve ourselves from each other, and then sidle up on a bar stool next to the man who would heal me. The man who would turn out to be my future. Henry.

I double-back at the date, then grab the ticket and stuff it into my purse. October 3. Now that dates and times have lost all meaning, so, too, I tell myself, can this one.

Chapter Sixteen

Allie, it turns out, was a supermodel in training.

"I practice every night in front of the mirror," she confides to me when we take a break for the photographer to reload his film, and she munches on Fritos. The grease on her fingertips shines under the glare of the studio lights.

Leigh's eyes widen in horror. "Allie! You do not."

"Yeah, I do, Mom, so? No biggie. I want to be in Victoria's Secret." She shimmies her shoulders like, I imagine, she's seen glistening, half-naked, nearly inhuman women do during prime time.

"That's it," Leigh sighs. "We're losing the TVs in the house."

Allie is called back to the set, and as she strikes her pose, a makeup artist darts in the frame to touch up her lip gloss and smooth off the crumbs from her chips.

"Easy with the makeup!" Leigh calls from the side. "Good Lord," she says to me. "If I wanted her to look like a pageant girl, I would have entered her in Little Miss New York."

I shrug. In fact, back in my old life, I'd considered sending in Katie's picture to the *Parents* child-model contest, so I wasn't entirely sure why Leigh is so disgruntled. Don't all parents want the world to coo over their offspring, as verification that their genes are the literal picture of DNA perfection, enough to make other couples froth with envy that their tots don't measure up?

Leigh's cell phone rings, and just as she excuses herself to the corner of the white-walled studio, Josie steps through the door. She glances around, then waves.

"Hey, what are you doing here?" I say, as she strides over in hip-hugging blue-rinsed jeans and a crisp pink oxford. "I've got everything under control."

"I know," she says, her eyes darting. "I just wanted to check in."

"He's not here, Jo," I say.

"What? What are you talking about?"

"Bart," I say firmly. "He's not here."

"What does that have to do with anything?" she says unconvincingly, as color spreads across her neck. "I'm here to make sure that the shoot goes okay."

Before I can answer, Leigh rushes back over.

"So there's a problem," she exhales. "My neighbor just called and, evidently, the basement pipes exploded and our house has flooded. *Shit.*" She stares down at the phone, as if she's intuiting it will ring. "I called Liam, but I can't reach him. How much longer do you need Allie for?"

"Oh God, at least another hour. Maybe two? They want to shoot her in different wardrobes so they can use her for the winter campaign, too."

"Shit," she repeats, then looks at me intently. "Well," she pauses. "What about if she stays with you?"

"Yeah, no, that's fine," I say. "Just sign the waiver that I'm her guardian, and you can pick her up after the shoot."

"No, that's not what I meant." She shakes her head. "It's already 4:30, and by the time I get home and deal with the plumbers and the cleanup, it will be hours . . . and well, Allie adores you, and I trust you, so could she just sleep at your place tonight?"

"Sleep there?"

"Well, yeah, turn it into a sleepover of sorts. I'll pick her up first thing in the morning and take her to school."

"Um, okay, I-I guess," I say with a stutter. "Jack's in Philadelphia for work, and I had dinner plans with a friend, but . . ." I mull it over: maximum bonding time with Jack's niece. This can't be a bad thing. "No, definitely. Let's do it."

"Thank God. Okay, look, you have my cell, call me if anything comes up, and I'll buzz you as soon as this mess is taken care of." She inhales and bats her bangs out of her eyes. "I'm so sorry about this."

"No, no, don't be silly." I wave her off.

Leigh calls out to Allie and explains her good-byes, and then she's off like a clap of thunder—one second here, the next she's gone.

"Good luck with that," Josie says, after we hear the heavy metal doors to the studio slam shut.

"How hard can it be?" I think of Katie and how I'd nearly mastered the art of domesticity.

"Harder than you think," she replies dryly. "You're not a mom."

I start to disagree but then grasp that she's not incorrect: for all intents and purposes, I'm nobody's mother. I'm saddened by the realization more than I expect to be.

"Well, I'm out of this blowhole," Josie sighs, and looks at her watch. It's impossible not to detect her bitterness.

"Jo," I start but am then unsure what else to say. Because I know that in the future, in the *real* future, she's happily content with Art, and that whatever life choices she made, whatever *hard* choices she made, she seems satisfied with them. And I also now know that if I hadn't come back, we never would have landed this print campaign, and she never would have been thrust so thoroughly back into her fantasy life with Bart. He never would have swirled around her head, like an escape hatch from her mundane doldrums, from the San Jose Opera, from a husband who now seemed to be a second-best choice.

Before I can speak, however, Bart walks in the studio, with the same nervous glance that Josie had cast about when she arrived earlier. The two lock eyes, and Josie erupts into a near-lunatic grin and then shuffles over to greet him with a peck on the cheek.

I watch her for a moment, then turn back to Allie, who has mesmerized both the crew and the photographer with her flawless charisma. She catches me staring and winks, then blows me an air kiss. I reach up to grab it, and she squeals in delight. Long after she's returned to posing, I can still feel the kiss on my palm, like a seared scar that, try as I might, just won't seem to fade.

☙

MEGAN MEETS US at Serendipity for dinner.

"Of course I don't mind," she says, when I explained our change of plans. "It gives me good practice."

"News to report?" I asked on the phone. I tried to remember when Meg announced that she was pregnant for the second time, but nothing jiggers in my brain.

"I can't test for a few more days," she responded, with either hope or nervousness: In both of our lives, the two are knotted so closely, they're nearly indistinguishable.

The restaurant is a throwback to a tea shop from my grand-mother's era. Vivid blue and red and yellow and purple Tiffany lamps hang from the ceiling like stained-glass windows, elegant wire-backed chairs cushioned with blooming pastel fabrics are tucked under marble-topped tables. The unmistakable scent of chocolate envelops the space, and around us, families clutter booths, toddlers sitting on top of their older siblings, moms leaning into fathers and laughing in their ears. This sort of laughter crops up when you're ensconced in something so quaint, so innocent, that it's easy to forget that outside the glass doors, another world exists entirely.

"Can I order a hot chocolate for dinner?" Allie asks. Serendipity is famous, after all, for their hulking sundaes and their frozen hot chocolate.

"Absolutely not," I tut. "Healthy dinner, then dessert after." I grab a napkin and dip it into my ice water, then rub down her hands.

"Come on," she whines. "Please?"

"Not even with a cherry on top." I glance at the kids' menu and twinges of the old me emerge; I'm more than a little horrified at the offerings: fried chicken fingers, (undoubtedly processed) hot dogs, pasta and butter. *I'd never allow this crap past Katie's lips. Never!*

Megan nudges me in the booth. "What's the big deal? Let her have the frozen hot chocolate for dinner."

"Yessssssssssssssssss!" Allie shrieks. "Lemme, lemme, lemme, lemme!"

"No," I say firmly. "Dinner first. Sorry, Al."

"Aw, come on, Jill. She's celebrating her first big shoot. She's a near star!" Megan grins at Allie who is now standing opposite us, perched on the sparkly red leather cushion, as if she's about to conquer the world. Or pounce on us like waiting prey. Whichever comes first.

"Uh-uh," I say. "Nutritionally, it's important that she get a mix of protein and fiber at dinner. It helps her sleep at night and ensures a deeper REM."

Megan rotates her head to cast a suspicious sidelong stare. "And you know this how?"

"*Parenting* magazine." I shrug.

"And you're reading this why?" Megan says slowly.

It's only then that I realize I have absolutely no excuse for amassing the knowledge that I've amassed, so, as a distraction, I cave.

"Fine, Allie, you can have the hot chocolate for dinner," I say, but Megan is still looking at me with peculiarity. "What?" I ask her finally.

"You're not pregnant are you?"

"Oh God, no!" I laugh.

"Then what's with the kid-knowledge and the parent magazines?" For reasons unclear to me, she appears bruised.

"It's nothing . . ." I race for an explanation. "I was in an office the other day, waiting for a meeting, and saw it on the table. So I flipped through it, you know, to kill time."

Meg doesn't respond but returns to reading her menu. After a minute, she says, "Why are you lying to me? I've known you since we were kids. You think I can't tell that you're lying to me?"

"Meg, Jesus Christ, it's nothing!" I wave my arm and try to hail down a waiter.

"Seriously, are you pregnant?" She stares at me, her eyes unavoidably welling.

"Oh my God, Meg. NO." I place my hand on top of hers. "Really. You're overreacting. It was just a silly article that I noticed in passing." I turn to Allie. "I tell you what, Al, not only can you have frozen hot chocolate but I'll let you order a banana split, too."

"EEEEEEEEEEEEEEEEEEEEEEE!!!" Allie screams, still standing on the seat of the booth, and throws her fifty-pound body through the air.

"At least bananas are healthy," I say with a guilty look to Megan.

"Hey, I'm not judging," she answers, holding her hands in the air, just as the waiter weaves his way over. "I say give the girl what she wants. That's my motto. God knows I'm going to be over-the-top with my kid."

She says this, and it strikes me violently, ruthlessly that this might never come true. That, unless something else has shifted in this new altered-reality, that sundaes and frozen hot chocolate and having the choice to say yes, or even no, won't be on Megan's future landscape. I watch her cajole Allie down from the booth and into a game of patty-cake and try to reassure myself. *So much is different this time around. So much and everything. So, too, might this be.*

Later, after we'd taken a horse and buggy ride through Central Park and after Allie had crashed from her sugar high, in which she demolished my apartment in under ten minutes, Meg and I gently strip off her pink plaid dress, tugging it gingerly over her head, and slip her white leather sandals off her tiny feet. I carry her to my bed, tuck her under the covers, and watch as her eyelids droop lower and heavier, as if weighted down with sand. I click off the night-stand light, but neither Meg nor I turn to leave. Instead, we are transfixed.

"I'm sorry about before," she says. "It's just this whole thing."

I don't answer; I just listen to Allie's lilting breath slide in and out.

"I'm just so focused on it, you know?" Meg continues. "Getting pregnant, staying pregnant . . ."

I reach over and clutch her hand.

"Sometimes it seems like too much." Her voice cracks. "Like it's the only thing in the world that I want."

I squeeze her hand harder, firmer, a tacit, wordless admission that I get it, and that she wasn't alone.

Eventually, we slip out of the room, not because we want to but because after a while, you feel strange to watch over a sleeping little girl who isn't your own. Even if she looks like an angel. And even if she reminds you so much, *too much*, of the angel you once had or the angel whom you so desperately hoped for.

After Megan leaves and I settle on the (scratchy goddamned) couch, I will myself to sleep, hoping to dream of nothing, but instead, dreaming over and over again of Katie. An angel no longer at my door.

Chapter Seventeen

The muggy October air in Miami shocks my system, such that nearly every pore declares mutiny with profuse and unstoppable sweating. By the second day, I've all but camped out in the resort pool in an effort to offer my body some relief. After my fingers have pruned, I slink out of the water onto my waiting lounge chair and reach for the SPF. Always with the SPF.

"You're not going to get *any* color down here?" Jack asks, setting down his book on the mini–patio table that sits between our loungers.

"Of course not!" I furrow my face and zealously rub the lotion into my forearm.

"But . . . you love a nice tan," he says, as I flip over and hand him the bottle to slather more block on my back. "That's part of the reason I chose Miami."

"The sun is terrible for you!" I exclaim, reaching for my linen hat, whose circumference outsizes a watermelon. And it's true: I'd learned all about the horrors of the sun via my diligent magazine reading in my old life. Wrinkles. Lines. *Melanoma.* I'd flip through the pages, then assiduously examine every mole on my body, holding up a mirror to peek at the ones on my back, and compare them all with the gruesome, gnarly pictures in the articles. And Katie never left the house without a full coating of SPF 50. Even in the rain. "You could never be too careful," a renowned Stanford professor was quoted as saying in the latest piece I'd perused in *Allure*.

"Um, okay," Jack answers with confusion, still rubbing. "But you spent all of last summer laying out in the park." *Don't remind me!* My skin nearly crawls at the thought of the damage I'd wrought in years past.

I turn my head away from him, pressing my face into the chair, and grunt a response. Slowly, I feel his fingers veer from my shoulders into the edges of my armpits and then slightly on the cusp of my breasts.

"Not now!" I try to sound serious, but mostly, I giggle.

"Now," he says, leaning into my ear.

"It's the middle of the afternoon!" His hands weave farther underneath my bikini.

"And that's a problem, why?"

He's right, I tell myself. *Just because you and Henry never had sex in the middle of the afternoon, or if you did, it was because it was your only window while Katie was napping, doesn't mean that you shouldn't run up to your suite and screw Jack's brains out.*

I push myself off my stomach, tie a towel around my waist, and grab his arm, then we race to our room, tugging, pulling, clawing at each other until twenty minutes later, I'm curled naked in bed, inhaling the sweetly cloying scent of suntan lotion and sex, and finally, it seems, blessed by a too-cold blast of air-conditioning, my body ceases to sweat. Just as I'm drifting into unconsciousness, that deep haze brought on by a great orgasm and strong sun, I hear Jack rustle in the sheets next to me.

"God," he says. "I could lie here with you forever."

Forever, I think. *What's that?*

But rather than answer him, I place my hand over his beating chest, and then soon, I am spent.

℮

THE RESTAURANT that Jack has chosen for dinner is impossibly hip, with smooth granite walls and towering bamboo shoots and models whose faces I double take because I wonder if I know them personally or have just seen them in one of my many magazines.

We're seated in the back, away from the pulsing bar and the even-more pulsing music, and though I've been back in my old life for nearly three months, I am struck with an overwhelming sense of surrealism. Sort of like déjà vu, only not really, since I know that I haven't been *here* here before. Because seven years ago tonight, not only was I not in Miami but also it was the fateful night that I, armed with the security of having met Henry, untied my anchors to Jack for good.

In the weeks leading up to the breakup, we'd spiraled from ailing to critical, and when he announced, yet again, that he was heading to visit his mother for the weekend, and failed to invite me along, I erupted. In retrospect, now with my neutered temperament, which clamped down on my niggly comments about his underachievements and overbearing gene pool, it seemed like I could have taken steps to prevent the blowout. *Maybe I overreacted,* I tell myself now, sipping a mojito and glancing at Jack, whose tan had brought out the blue in his eyes and whose hair had grown two shades lighter in just a few short days.

Back then, Jack asked me to rethink things. "This is ridiculous!" He shouted, loud enough that our neighbors could hear. "She's my mother! It's a weekend!"

"It's not about your mother!" I cried back. "It's about . . ." I shook my head and flitted my arms in a circle. "This! It's just all of this!" I didn't mention the kind-eyed man whom I'd met at the bar who seemed to interlock with me in the way that puzzle pieces might.

"Do you want me not to go see her?" He slammed a suitcase shut on our bed. "Is that it? Do you want me not to go, because then I won't fucking go!"

"That's not it," I said quietly. "It's so much more than that."

"Because we fight?" he asked. "Is this because of our stupid fights? Because everyone has goddamn fights. *Everyone!*"

"It's not about the fights, Jack," I said, then reconsidered. "Well, it is about the fights. Sort of. It just feels like we don't fit anymore." I thought again of Henry.

"This is bullshit," he said, though he stopped screaming and now seemed poised to explode into tears. "Fucking bullshit. Two years of my life, and then this. Out of nowhere."

"It's not exactly out of nowhere," I said, sitting on the bed.

"It's completely out of fucking nowhere," he answered, lifting his suitcase and heading for the front door. "Just like your goddamn mom. One day here, the next day gone."

The door slammed, and that's when I started to cry. Because while he might have been cruel, he might also have been right. Just the day before, we'd nursed cocktails with Meg and Tyler and toasted our fortune and circumstance, and now, this—yes, I could see how to Jack it did seem out of nowhere.

But no longer, I think, drowning a giant sip of the mojito. *Now I'm here, in this restaurant that my old suburban self wouldn't have thought worthy of going to, in a dress that my old suburban self couldn't have squeezed into, and with a man who my old suburban self never quite laid to rest.*

I shake myself out of the memory, just as our waiter arrives to take our order. *This is the here and now. This is the moment*, I think. *This is the time of my life.*

℮

Later, with my stomach happily dancing with mahimahi and crusty sourdough bread and rich molten chocolate cake and one mojito too many, Jack pays the check and takes my hand.

"I chose this place because they have the most incredible roof deck," he says. "Come on, let's go."

He pulls back my chair for me and guides me, arm around my waist, to the elevator. (Take that, *Marie Claire*! Chivalry is not dead!)

The doors ding open when we reach the top, and we step onto a mutedly lit terrace, with tiny white lights, like the fireflies of my childhood, dotting the stucco walls, and soaring potted palm trees looming from corners and crevasses. A jazz trio plays on an elevated stage to our right, and just ahead, I can see the ocean, its waves sweeping in, then out, then in again. Slim, crisp patrons mill about and the air smells of salt, just washed in from the sea.

We amble over to the ledge and stare out at the endless tide, its roar still detectable below the buzz of conversation, and then Jack turns to me.

"Jill, you know that I love you, right?"

"I do," I say, returning my gaze to the water. I'm mesmerized by its rhythm, how even when you think another wave won't come along, even when you think the beat won't hold steady, another crest rides up and there it is—the pulse of the ocean all over again.

"Look at me, baby. I'm saying something important here." His palm guides my cheek back to him. Jack inhales. "I know that as a writer, I'm supposed to have a way with words and all of that, but

I've thought about this over and over again, and I just don't have the right words for this moment."

It hits me, suddenly and viscerally, what is happening.

"And so," he continues and lowers himself onto one knee, "all I can say is, Jill, I love you more than anything, and I'd be honored if you'd marry me." He bats a curl of blond hair off his forehead, then reaches into his pants pocket and pulls out a box.

I can feel all my pores reopen, sweat marching forward, like an angry army, and my eyes are frozen wide, unable to blink. Blood rushes through me, and my mouth turns arid. I still haven't spoken when he slides the ring on my finger.

"So you will?" he says, rising to kiss me. I must nod my head or give some slight indication that, indeed, I will, though I can't remember giving such an acknowledgment, because the next thing I hear is raucous applause from the partygoers around us who have stopped sipping their martinis for just a moment to notice our passing flicker of a life moment. Jack swings me around in a bear hug and screams some sort of victory cry, reminding me of an ancient warrior who just slayed a beast, and the roar crescendos, then softens, just like the waves below.

Jack kisses my ear, biting just enough to tingle, then heads to the bar for celebratory drinks. *On the house,* cooed the cocktail waitress after making her way over to congratulate us.

I lean against the cool ledge and hold my left hand out for a view. The ring sings out—it is shining and round and big and hopeful—and by any standard, I should be bursting, *I am bursting,* to have it. I hug my arms in tight, wrapping my hands around my back, to ward off a cool breeze that strikes out of nowhere. The wind passes, and I release myself, staring down at my finger once again.

This was perfect, I think. *It wasn't intimate like Henry's proposal, and so what if his words weren't quite poetic, weren't quite*

what I'd imagined when someone asked me to swear myself to him
for life. It was pretty close to perfect. Perfect enough.

I run my thumb over the ring, trying to swivel it back and forth
the way that I'd grown accustomed to with Henry's, and it's only
then that I notice that the band is nearly choking my finger. That
it's wrapped around so tight that the better half of my ring finger
looks like an overstuffed sausage. I pull my hand closer and hold it
up to the light. It's hard to see at first, but then, I can feel the throb:
There, just to the right of my knuckle, is a tiny gash, no bigger than
a gnat-sized paper cut. Jack must have nicked it when he pushed
the ring on.

I raise my hand to my mouth and suck the pulsing joint, the
unmistakable taste of blood spreading across my tongue, and after
a minute, the pain subsides. I examine my knuckle again, turning
back and forth and back again under the dull glare of the tiny white
lights, and best I can tell, the cut is gone.

I catch Jack's eye from the bar and smile.

And yet, if I listened to my wiser self, my suburban self who
still clanged around in my brain when I let her, she would have told
me that though the wound was now invisible, it was never really
gone.

☾ K A T I E

By the time Katie was seven months old, many of my prebaby
fantasies had come to fruition: Baby powder did indeed fill
the air and her smile warmed me to my toes, but other things
lingered, too—my fear of damaging her, which manifested itself in overprotectiveness; Henry's new promotion at work,
which sucked away at the little time we had together outside
of Katie; the stale conversation between us, which circled
mostly (and only) about Katie herself.

"Katie pooped five times today!" I said, as we sat down to a dinner of grilled salmon I'd painstakingly marinated the night before *(Cooking Light!)*. "Can you believe it? Five times!"

"Should you call the doctor?" Henry asked, slightly disengaged.

"It seems like normal poop," I reply. "Nothing runny or anything."

"Well, I guess she likes to eat."

"Like her daddy," I said, smiling. "Poops and eats like her daddy."

Henry grinned and dug his fork into his fish, as I searched for something else with which to update him.

In real life, most marriages don't come undone with one big explosion. Unlike in the movies, most wives don't stumble upon lipstick on a collar or discover a hotel receipt in a blazer pocket. Most wives don't uncover hidden gambling problems or latent addictions or experience out-of-nowhere abuse that pops up one day and destroys everything. Some do, but most, no, not most. Most marriages unravel slowly, slipping drop by drop, like water ebbing through a curled palm, until one day, you look down and notice that it, your hand, is entirely empty. That's how most marriages dissolve and run dry. And, in retrospect, it's how mine came undone exactly.

"Oh!" I said with surprise that night at dinner. "And I can't believe I forgot to tell you! She's almost crawling! In fact, she's crawling backward . . . I saw her do it twice today. Ainsley says that Alex did the same thing one week before he did it the right way."

"She's practically ready for Harvard," Henry said, raising his glass for a mock toast.

"Speaking of which, we should talk about preschool," I answered.

And so it went. Two people who had spun concentric circles around the lives they'd created with each other, and now, the only thing that anchored us down, that anchored us together, was our daughter. So round and round we went. On the road to nowhere.

Chapter Eighteen

The time has come, I realize in late October, to annihilate my closet. Every morning, I'm lost in a sea of mismatched, crumpled clothes, unmoored shoes, and discarded coats and scarves and handbags. *Declutter your space, declutter your mind*, I tell myself on a soggy Saturday afternoon *(Woman's Day!)*.

Since our return from Miami two weeks earlier, we've been thrown into a tornado of wedding planning, courtesy, primarily, of Vivian.

2:00 P.M., Thursday, just as I'm heading into a crucial meeting on the winter Coke campaign: "Jillian dear, just when are you going to set a date? Tick tock! If we don't nail down the country club now, we'll never get it! How does April 9 sound?"

8:47 A.M., Monday, just as I'm stepping off the subway to head to the office: "Darling, it's me, Vivian. If we're going to do a spring wedding, I'm thinking that we should do coral roses and white lilies. It will be just lovely!"

9:29 P.M., Friday, just as I'm finally leaving work and meeting Megan and some college friends for a girls'-night-out much-needed drink: "Yoo-hoo, dear, it's imperative that we book a gown appointment ASAP! We're pushing this a bit too close already, and you absolutely need six months to get your dress before the big day!"

After Henry and I got engaged, we called my father and shared the news, then phoned Henry's parents to do the same. And then we both agreed that we wanted the event to be as intimate and non-frenzied as possible.

"Less of a circus, more of a celebration," he said at the time, and I nodded my head concurring. So I casually flipped through *Brides* and I conferred with him on simple flower choices, and I asked Ainsley and Megan along to try on gowns, but mostly, I let my father and Linda, his girlfriend, work out the fine print. It all seemed so unnecessary—stephanotis versus baby's breath, butter cream versus fondant, chicken versus steak. Did anyone ever look back at a wedding and say, "Thank God we opted for the cherry swirl in the middle of the cake because without it, it would have been a disastrous evening for all involved!" No. At least, that's what I told myself at the time, and with Henry's rational, always rational, opinion sounding in the background, it was easy enough to believe.

Now, maybe it did matter, I think, as I'm knee-deep in sweatpants that I hadn't seen since college graduation. Maybe the enthusiasm that you put out for the planning trickles over into your early days of marriage, and maybe if I'd seemed a little more game, a little more intoxicated with love for Henry, our relationship wouldn't have backfired so roundly. Besides, years of reading *Martha Stewart* and *InStyle Weddings* had led to near untoppable vats of knowledge: For an unhappily married woman trapped in suburbia with no hope of throwing a wedding anytime soon, I knew more than I'd earned the right to know about nuptial planning. So, after vetting Vivian's relentless calls, I agreed to meet her later this month to discuss details with the planner she's hired.

How did I live like this? I say to myself, spinning around the wreckage of my walk-in. *How did opening the closet door each morning not make you lose your mind?*

I stand on my tiptoes and reach for some partially folded sweaters, their arms hanging loose like a dead man's, which I hadn't worn since the year that Jack and I met. Tugging on the only one I can reach, I'm suddenly pelted with raining objects. The entire wire shelf comes careening down, and I jump back from the onslaught.

"You okay?" Jack calls from the living room where he's attempting to revive his manuscript.

"Alive," I say back.

"Almost done? I have a surprise for you."

"A few more minutes," I sigh. *Way more than a few more minutes.* Where was my *Real Simple*, complete with the perfect organizing tips, when I needed it?

I kick a pair of Levi's that I'd donned for my twenty-third birthday and crouch down among the debris. Piles of merino wool turtlenecks, musty from years of nonuse; my high-school yearbook with curled pages due to water damage from the apartment above; pashmina scarves that I'd bought in Chinatown when one in every color wasn't enough; mix tapes for boyfriends whose last names I could barely remember.

But then, peeking out of an old Yellow Pages *(I saved Yellow Pages??)*, a corner of a photo catches my eye. I cock my head to make sure that I'm seeing it correctly, but it's unmistakable. Adrenaline races through me, and my fingers shake almost on cue. I pluck it from the dusty urine-colored pages and sink to the floor, rapt and sickened all at once.

Though I had wiped clean every image, every reminder, of my mother, I'd been unable to release her entirely, and so, as I trekked from my childhood home to my dorms, from my dorms to my adult apartments, I'd always held on to one black-and-white picture, the way that a reformed binger might a piece of chocolate. Always there, just in case you need it. When Jack and I broke up the last time around, I'd moved out, and when packing up my things, I'd stumbled upon the photo. Still burning over my mother's note and unwelcome reentry into my life, I heaved the photo into the garbage bag, just as I had her letter. Gone and nearly forgotten.

But now, here it was all over again, like *Groundhog Day* for the emotionally impaired.

The shot was taken that same summer that my mother and I had lazed around the yard at dusk and chased fireflies until we were wasted. She and I are in her garden, her temple, as she liked to call it. Long after she'd showered and rubbed herself down in *Charlie* body lotion, she always smelled slightly of soil, and even today, I am reminded of her whenever the scent of dirt wafts through the air. We are perched between her tomato vines and her rows of basil and green beans, and she, with a bandanna in her hair and just a smudge of dirt on her left cheek, is wrapped around me from behind. I'm smiling straight into the camera, but rather than looking at the lens, she is casting down at me, a warm grin on her face, but one filled with sentimentality, not necessarily ebullience. She would leave us only five weeks later.

I stare at the photo with new eyes, eyes now of a mother, and it's as if I'm looking at it for the first time. In years past, hardened by fury, I'd always seen the photo as literal proof of her betrayal: that she could pretend to love me so vigorously but when the time came, she could disentangle her embrace and forget it entirely. But now I can see it as so much more: that perhaps, what she was doing that day in the garden wasn't so much as holding me with no love behind the embrace; rather, she was clutching me, as if I were a buoy and the only thing that might save her from drowning. Looking at it again, I can't believe that I'd never seen this clearly.

Jack pops his head into the closet, snapping me from my trance.

"You ready to head out?"

"A picture of my mother," I answer, holding it up for him.

He grasps it and pulls it closer, startled. "Jesus, you look just like her."

I shrug, then tuck the picture into my sock drawer and wade out from the mess, literal and not.

"Your surprise, m'lady," Jack says, ushering me to the front door.

I force a smile and follow, trying to erase the photo from my mind. Because what's most haunting isn't how closely I resemble my mother or even how clearly I can remember that day in the garden. No, what racks me most is how now, years later, I inherently recognize my mother's loving yet chagrined and weary expression because it's the same one that I wore like a mask since the very day that Katie was born.

℮

JACK'S SURPRISE, lo and behold, is a new couch. Which on paper, I understand, isn't particularly romantic or anything really to swoon over, but for him, it's a concession, and thus, for me, it is indeed something.

"My engagement gift to you," he says, as we're ensconced on the second floor of ABC Home. His arm sweeps around. "Have at it. Any one you choose."

My eyebrows dart down. "Where is my boyfriend and what did you do with him?"

"Fiancé," he corrects.

"Where is my fiancé and what did you do with him?" I peck him on the lips. I'm still not quite used to saying that.

"Well, you know, now that we're getting married, I do recognize that the couch of my bachelorhood should maybe take a hike."

I look at him with suspicion.

"Okay." He laughs. "And Leigh might have made a comment or two about how disgusting it was when she saw it last month."

Of course, I think, though say nothing.

I head over to a supple leather love seat and sink in. Jack opens his mouth to voice an opinion but I hold up a finger, and he snaps it shut with a smile.

"My choice this time!" I say, and he wordlessly plunks down next to me, like an obedient dog. If I'd gotten good at anything during my marriage to Henry, it was mastering the art of tasteful decorating.

A sand-hued, pebbled leather three seater on the other side of the floor looks exactly like what we need to spice up the living room, so I grab Jack's hand and weave through the sofas and couches and reclining chairs toward it. Just as we're about to park ourselves smack in the middle, a familiar stride wanders in front of me. The lanky torso, the sloping walk, I'd know it anywhere.

"Henry?" I say, then immediately regret it. My matted hair is tucked into a baseball cap, and my zip-up sweatshirt reeks of closet dust.

"Jill!" he says, his face ebbing into joyfulness when he sees me. He glances at Jack and extends his hand. "Jack, isn't it?"

"Uh, it is," Jack responds, reciprocating the shake but clearly having no recollection of their brief introduction at the Coke gala. Before I can explain the connection, a petite redhead slides over to Henry and slips her hand into his back pocket.

"Hey you," she says, as if we're not standing there, as if she's *not slipping her hand into my fucking husband's back pocket*!

"Er, hey. Celeste, this is Jill. A friend whom I know from around." Henry swipes his bangs and attempts to tuck them behind his ear. "And this is her boyfriend, Jack."

"Fiancé, actually," Jack interjects. "Just happened a few weeks ago!"

"Congratulations, you two!" Celeste squeals, like she's known us for decades. "How exciting! When is the big day?"

"Um, it's not set yet," I mutter. Henry freezes his face into a smile that he'd later reserve for horrid dinner parties that have lingered hours too long; at the first sign of it, I'd take it as our cue to start saying our good-byes. His "I'd rather be riding shotgun to the gates of hell than be here now" smile is exactly how we once classified it, after we'd rushed out of an evening at the Hollands', who were each screwing coworkers and who had made not-so-veiled references to their mutual antipathy the night through, and after we cried with laughter in the car as we drove home.

"Don't be silly," Jack says, rubbing my back. "It's set for April 9! Save the date! We're inviting everyone we know."

"Not everyone," I demur.

"The country club seats four hundred," Jack says to Henry and Celeste, as if this were a hard-won bragging right.

"Sounds like fun," Henry finally manages.

"I'm hoping it might be a bit more intimate," I say, too awkward to meet his stare. Mostly, I gaze at the floor.

"Oh, when I get married, I want it to be the biggest, most decadent thing anyone has ever seen!" Celeste says.

"See, that's what I'm talking about!" Jack laughs. "It's only once, so to hell with it!" He pauses. "So how long have you two been dating?"

Henry shakes his head almost imperceptibly, but Celeste answers for them both. "Oh, just a few weeks. We met on a blind date, and we couldn't believe it, right, Hen?" She pokes him. "I mean, *finally*! A date that I don't have to bail on halfway through."

"It's true," Henry says, seeming to regain his composure and slinging his arm over her shoulders. "Been on enough bad ones to finally deserve a good payoff. Paid our dues and all of that."

I smile roundly, pressing my cheeks into themselves and pushing my dimples in as far as they can go.

"That is just *wonderful!*" I say. "Wonderful!" I clap my hands for emphasis.

"It is, isn't it?" Celeste looks at me conspiratorially, as if I'm in on the secret. "I'm so over dating at this point."

"So you're already shopping for furniture together?" I can't help myself.

"No, nothing like that," Celeste flits her free hand about. Her other one seems firmly entrenched on Henry's ass. "I just need a new couch, and we were hanging out this weekend, so Hen came with me." If she weren't so casual about it, I decide, I'd have to hate her.

She's probably one of those free spirits who turns into a wild monkey in bed, I think, then nearly audibly heave at the thought. I glance around to make sure that, in fact, I *haven't* retched out loud, but none of the three seems to have noticed. Then Celeste removes her hand from his pocket *(about fucking time!)* and rises on her toes to kiss him.

"Come on," she says, tugging on his belt loop. "We have to find my dream couch before it gets too late. We have Darren's party, remember?"

Darren? Who the hell is Darren?

I smile wider and suspect that I might now resemble a mentally unstable chimpanzee. The creases of my underarms and elbows feel sticky and warm.

"Congrats," Henry says, leaning in to peck my cheek. My pulse throbs through my neck so fiercely that I'm certain we can both feel it. "And I'm sure that I'll see you soon." He shakes his head with a laugh. "No matter where I go, I just can't seem to dodge you, Jillian Westfield."

"I could say the same of you," I reply, unconsciously moving my fingers across my cheek.

He and Celeste round the corner, and I see him lean over to whisper something in her ear. She tosses her ginger hair around and giggles, the sounds of her mirth spreading their wings all the way back to where Jack and I now stand.

"Okay, so, back to business," Jack says, pointing at the golden leather couch in front of us. "Is that the one you want?"

Without pause, I sit down and tuck my clammy hands beneath me.

"Yes," I answer, unable to meet his eyes. "This is the one for me."

Chapter Nineteen

I have picked up the phone to call my mother at least eleven times before I can bring myself to punch in one of the numbers. The truth is, I don't know what to say and I don't know how to begin saying it. I'm not even sure when something shifted in me such that I decided to lower the bridge to forge our peace.

Most likely, it had something to do with Katie.

Katie, whom I now dreamed of nearly every night; Katie, whom I sometimes searched for in passing strollers; Katie, whom I so palpably missed, I felt wounded without her. I wondered if she'd forgive me for being gone, for being as selfish as I needed to be to safeguard my sanity, and for abandoning her to do so. And when I thought about that, and then thought about the firm grip of my mother's embrace that bright summer day in the garden, it was nearly impossible not to soften.

But now, with a dial tone in my ear and her letter pressed on my desk, I have nothing to say. How do I open? Do I call her "Mom"? Where has she been all this time? The questions felt heavy, insurmountable, and I wasn't sure I had the fortitude to hurdle them. A sturdy backbone, I could see now, was never my forte.

Just as I'm about to dial again, holding my breath as if I'm diving under frigid water, Josie ambles into my office. I quickly hang up, relieved for the excuse that isn't of my own making.

"I'm thinking about sleeping with Bart," she says, so fast that the sentence tumbles out like one consecutive word.

"What? You can't, Jo!"

"I absolutely can," she says, casually crossing her legs, like we're discussing something as mundane as ordering turkey versus tuna salad for lunch. "And I think I might."

I noticed that her hair is better highlighted than in weeks past and her skin flawless. The circles beneath her eyes have receded, and whether it's new makeup or just a new outlook, she looks fresher, happier even.

"Look, Jo, you can't. You're happy with Art."

"I'm not." She shrugs.

Yes, you are! You're fucking happy in seven years with Art!

"It m-might seem that way now," I stammer. "But with some perspective, this will pass." I try for something more convincing. "In fact, I read a study that said that when asked about their unhappy marriages five years later, nearly 82 percent of couples said they were now happy" *(Redbook!).*

Josie shifts. "It doesn't feel that way. It doesn't feel like this will ever turn around. Art wants to move to San Jose, and . . ." Her voice drifts, and she flops her hands helplessly.

"I understand."

"I appreciate that, Jill, I do. But until you've been married, I don't know . . . it's a tough row to hoe. And some things . . . well, sometimes people grow apart."

I understand! You don't get it! I really freaking understand!

"And you think that sleeping with Bart will make it all better?"

"Maybe." She shrugs again, but doesn't sound entirely convinced.

"Well, maybe it will," I agree. "But, you know, maybe it won't. Maybe your relationship with Bart will be as screwed up as your marriage."

"So you're acknowledging that my marriage is screwed up?" Jo laughs. "Tell me something I don't already know." She sighs. "I probably shouldn't be saying all of this to a newly engaged woman. I hope I'm not disillusioning you."

"I'm pretty sure I know what I'm in for." I lean back in my chair and massage the nape of my neck.

"That's the thing," Jo says. "You *think* you know what you're in for. I mean, you tell yourself that, of course, it's not going to be wine and roses and all of that bullshit for the rest of your life, but then, one day, you wake up, and your fucking husband has morphed into someone whom you barely recognize. And you sit there and you stare at him while he scratches his balls through his underwear at the kitchen table, and you think, 'This is *totally* not what I signed up for. I mean, who knows if I even love this ball-scratching, foul-breathed man?' And then you wonder if you love him more out of habit than out of anything else." She chews the inside of her lip and considers. "And I guess from there, all bets are off."

"And you don't think that one day you might wake up and think the same thing about Bart?" I ask. "That he might disappoint you in the same ways?"

"He couldn't disappoint me in the same ways," she says, her solemnity ringing clear.

"Well, then maybe in different ones," I say, pawing my engagement ring until I realize the symbolism and stop abruptly.

"Maybe," she says. "But I already know that Art's going to let me down, and with Bart, there's still the possibility that he won't." She heaves herself from the chair. "Anyway, it's just food for thought. Nothing I'm going to do anything about just yet."

I watch her go. "Be careful what you wish for," I call after her, and she pokes her head back into my office. "You just never know what you might end up with."

She nods and then darts away.

I reach for the phone once again to finally and firmly dial my mother. And as I do so, I try not to think of Jack. Or Henry. Or the disappointment my wishes might bring.

☙

MY MOTHER AND I have agreed, in a stilted two-minute conversation, in which my heart nearly exploded from my chest cavity, to meet at a tea emporium on Eighteenth Street at noon on Saturday. Which means I have to cancel a trip to Saks with Leigh, Meg, and Ainsley, in search of the quintessential bridesmaids' dresses, and leave Vivian none too pleased.

"Could you please just explain to her why I canceled?" I say to Jack the night before, after fielding her third message in two days. We're splitting Chinese food after begging off plans with Jack's coworker Austin and his wife because I am too emotionally exhausted to cope with small talk and martinis. Like so many other things about my old life, I'd forgotten that the nonstop social whirl was only so much fun, and that you can gorge yourself on too much of anything.

"Why don't you call her yourself?" he says. "I know that she wants to get closer to you." I realize that he's trying to offer a remedy, but coupled with the weight of my anxiety over my lunch the next day, mostly, I want to throttle him.

"Because," I spit out, and a sliver of broccoli flies out of my mouth, "I have bigger things to deal with than unleashing all of my various family issues and insecurities with your mother right now!"

"She might surprise you," Jack says, completely unaware of my mounting panic. "She's pretty good at stuff like this."

"Oh, for God's sake, Jack!" I slam down my chopsticks, and one skips right off the table, like a cartwheel in gymnastics class. "I know that your mother is your personal shrink, but I'm not looking for her to be mine. I just don't want to explain to her why I can't go goddamn bridesmaid dress shopping tomorrow."

His face clouds. "Suit yourself. Just trying to help," he says, with no malice behind it.

He probably was, I think today, as I push myself up the subway stairs and head eastward toward the tea shop. *He probably seriously thought that his mother could fix this, just like she fixes all of his shit.* I snort out loud, unsure of whom to feel sorry for: me, Jack, or Vivian.

Soon, too soon, I'm in front of the quaint bakery that I chose on the phone—*neutral ground,* I remember thinking, as if the tea emporium were Switzerland and my mother and I were lords of war.

The scent of baked butter floats through the air, and classical music that I can't quite place but that I should know because I played every goddamn famous composer for Katie when she was a baby, lilts in the background. The brunch crowd has descended, so while I'd envisioned recognizing my mother in an instant, I find myself scanning the tables, my stomach nearly rising up through my throat, partially hoping that she didn't show, partially hoping that she wouldn't let me down yet again.

My eyes are darting from table to table, booth to booth, when I see a hand wave toward the back. I turn toward it, and there she is. I'd know her anywhere, even though it's been two decades and even though I'd convinced myself that I'd bleached her from my memory. Her black hair spills over her shoulders, her skin is unlined and lightly tanned, and her face, though tight from the unavoidable tension of the situation, seems calmer than I remember, as if she's softened over the years.

My first instinct upon seeing her is to flee. My foot rotates and I can feel my legs spinning around, propelling my body in any direction other than toward my mother, but I clamp down. *No. We've done that before. We know how that version ends. Besides, remember Katie.*

So I push out my breath, swallow deeply, and forge my way through.

"Jillian," my mother says, her voice welling, as she rises to greet me.

We flank each other, each unsure what to do. I extend my right hand, but she pulls me in for a nearly claustrophobic hug. I inhale and search for soil, for the scent that for so long reminded me of her, but there are no notes that smell familiar.

"I took the liberty of ordering some tea and sandwiches," my mom says once we sit. She pauses, as awkward as I am. "You look beautiful. And thank you for calling."

I nod and avert her eyes.

"I have a lot to explain."

I nod again but say nothing. Mostly, I am trying not to cry.

She shakes her head. "I don't know where to begin, really. It's a lot of years . . . there's so much . . . I just . . ." She stops and composes herself. "I should start by apologizing. What I did then . . . well, I see now, for reasons I'll explain, what that must have done to you and your brother."

"Thank you," I offer quietly, just as a tear spills down from my left eye. I want to be bitter, angry, furious, but I'm also tired of carrying around the weight of that rage, and now, seeing her, in this moment, nervous as a cowering mouse, and terrified and repentant, it feels easier to let it go, like air slowly ebbing from a balloon, until there's nothing left to buoy it. To buoy my rage.

"It's all very hard to explain," she tries again, then corrects herself. "No, it's not. That is my excuse, but it's not hard to explain. I've been telling myself that it's complicated so I don't have to face up to the guilt of the situation, but it's not complicated. I made a horrible decision. Period." She manages a laugh. "My therapist would be so proud of me. Accepting responsibility."

The waiter arrives with our pots of tea and minisandwiches. I reach for one and peel at the crust.

"What happened?" I say finally, forcing myself to ask but repressing it, too, so fearful of her answer. *It's because you didn't pick up your goddamned room!*

"I just . . . you know, this is going to sound awful, and it's okay, you can hate me and judge me for it; I expect that." She drops her eyes down to her hands. "But I just wasn't ready for all of it—for motherhood and the obligations that it brought, and for my marriage and the complications that we had . . ."

I wipe two tears off my cheek. They are sprinkling down at random, so I look not so much as if I'm crying, rather that I have something lodged in my eye.

"None of this meant that I didn't love you. Or Andy," my mother says firmly. "I was just young . . . and I didn't . . . I didn't know how to cope. Your dad and I married at twenty, and when . . ."—she clears her throat—"when I left, I wasn't even thirty, and I had it in my head that there was *so much more life out there,* just so much more to do than sit at home and be a mother . . ." Her voice drifts off, then she rights herself. "This is all coming out wrong. I'd prepared it all, but now, it's not coming out the way I want."

"I'm not sure what to say."

"I know," she responds. "I know. But, take this however you need to, but my love for you and your brother . . . it never wavered. I missed you every day of my life. I just didn't know how to juggle both of those things: my love for you and my need to get out of what felt like chains." She shrugs, though there's nothing casual in the movement. "I was young. It's not an excuse. But I didn't know what else to do."

The first time that I held Katie, after an anguished, brutal labor that was nothing like they described in the copious magazines that I'd read, after I pushed what I believed was an impossible push and I felt her head and then shoulder and then legs roll out of me, I was so beaten down that my body had nearly gone numb. Then they placed this alien, swollen, bloodied being on my chest and said, "Here you go, Mommy," and rather than drown in a flood of love, I felt nothing. I didn't say this to Henry, who was seeping tears of joy from behind his video camera; I didn't, in fact, breathe mention of this to anyone. Not to Ainsley, who was wallowing in the dredges of postpartum depression and who might have understood, not to my new mommy friends whose lives seemed as shiny as their tricked-out thousand-dollar strollers.

But I held Katie underneath the harsh hospital lights and smiled and cooed, and she squirmed and wailed, and I looked down at her and waited for that rush of emotion to come. And yet it didn't. I was relieved when the nurses came to gather her for her first bath.

We swaddled her up and took her home, and still, I waited. I pressed my nipple in her tiny, greedy mouth, and I rocked her to sleep and I sang to her when she woke. And still, I waited for the tidal wave that everyone describes as unconditional maternal love. From the first moment, Henry, the most logical, stoic being I'd ever encountered, was smitten, and yet, here I was, the picture of motherly perfection, with a void where my adoration should be.

Finally, when she was six weeks old, I heard her stir in her crib, so I dragged myself in to begin the routine: diaper, nurse, burp, sing, nap all over again. Katie was staring at her pink floral bumper guard and must have heard me enter. She startled and started to wail, and my insides curdled at the sound of it. But then, I poked my face over her crib, and she shifted her head and our eyes locked. *She can see me!* I thought. She hushed immediately, and a tiny smile crept across her pink rosebud lips. And I felt it: that rush akin to a drug-fueled high that mothers explain as indescribable, that tug of love that knows no boundaries. Once I stumbled upon it, it would rest like a bass note inside of me: always there, but occasionally blending into the rest of the medley of my life, such that at times, I'd have to press my ear up and listen closely to ensure that it was still there, still keeping rhythm.

Today, looking at my mother, I couldn't help but remember those early days with Katie, when I wondered if I'd made a mistake that now couldn't be undone. And it was hard not to see how closely our cloths were cut.

We chew on our sandwiches thoughtfully, silently.

Finally, I say, "So why now? It's been eighteen years. Why now?"

"Well, that's where there's more to tell." She swallows.

I nod and wait, as she reaches down into her purse and slides out a photo, then pushes it across the table.

I shake my head. "What's this?" The shot is of my mother on the nose of a sailboat, a younger girl sitting below her, and a man, whom I presume is my mother's husband, with his arm thrown over her shoulder.

My mom clears her throat and speaks carefully. "This is your sister." She waits for a response but I have none: I feel as if I've been pierced in the gut, like an ice pick is jutting over my skin, then through it, so she continues. "She's nine now, the same age you were when I left you." She pauses, and I see her searching for a way to make this right, though rage is creeping into my gut, and I want to tell her to quit, to stop now because there's no possible way, in fact, to make this right. "I see her now, and how precious she is, and Jill . . ." Here she reaches across the table to my sweaty hand, which I immediately pull back from her grasp. "I look at her, and I can't believe that someone as young as her, with all of her innocence, might have to endure a life without her mom."

I stare at my mother for a beat too long and realize with the force of a flying fist that this was a mistake, that all of the healing that I thought this might bring, all of the wisdom that I assumed I missed out on the first time around by spurning her, well, *fuck that*, I think, surprising even myself with my vitriol.

"So you're sticking around for her, but couldn't bring yourself to do it for me? Protecting her fragile nature while leaving me and Andy to fend for ourselves abandoned on the roadside?" I finally spit out. I reach for my bag. "You know, we're done here, Ilene. I don't know what you were hoping to gain from this, but whatever it was, I don't want to be part of it." I stand to go, holding back furious tears.

"Jillian, please, let me explain. Please don't leave like this." Her voice is pleading. "I'm trying to make it up to you."

"There is *nothing* you can make up to me now," I seethe. "Nothing."

She flops her hands helplessly, and I race to the door before she can see me crumble. That's the thing about the people I love and me: One of us is always leaving the other, even when our intentions promise otherwise.

Chapter Twenty

That is it, that's the one," Ainsley says from the cream chenille chair at Vera Wang. She picks up her cup of decaf. "That is definitely the one."

"You think?" I swivel in front of the three-way mirror and arch my neck to see the back. Dozens of hand-sewn buttons trickle down the spine of the gown, and the flesh of my back is naked and exposed. "Meg? You like it?"

"Uh-huh," she answers, though she seems noncommittal.

I turn and face front again. "I do like it," I say, running my hands over the beaded bodice and the rich, heavy silk organza. "But shouldn't I, like, *know* know, when it's the right dress?"

Ainsley shakes her head. "I think you just find one that you love, and that's that. You don't have to break down in tears and have an epiphany or anything like that." She cocks her head. "I'd tried on about five dozen dresses when my mom and I just said, 'Enough, this one is beautiful, so let's go for it.' " She shrugs. "Worked well enough for me."

"Thanks again for coming, you guys," I say for the tenth time that afternoon. Vivian had tried to insert herself into the plans, but I wouldn't have it. Somehow it was as if now that I'd committed to marrying Jack, she was willing to embrace me as her own, and in doing so, I was expected to forgive all of her previous affronts and sins. And though I tried to do so in many ways—answering her daily phone calls, humoring her grotesque wedding plans—mostly, I did this for Jack or, more honestly, mostly I did this so that Jack and I could move forward rather than explode in the way that we did the last time around. But regardless, while I greatly understood the irony that now I had two women who longed to be my mother, neither of them was welcome to accompany me in search of the perfect gown. In fact, I'd shuttered any last thought of my own mom out of my mind; thinking of her on a day such as today gave her more weight than she deserved.

"Let's try on a veil," suggests Deidre, the polished brunette salesgirl. "That will help complete the look."

Ainsley and I nod, as she darts to the back, and as Meg flips listlessly through a look book.

"Meg, you okay, sweetie?" I hike up the gown and step down from the pedestal.

"Fine," she nods, then arranges her face into what I suppose is a smile, though she shows no teeth, nor any happiness. "You look beautiful, J, just beautiful."

I sit on the ivory love seat next to her. My gown poufs on both sides of me.

"You sure?" *Is she pregnant? Is this when it happens again?* I try to shake a memory free, but nothing comes. The truth is that seven years ago, I was so lost in the haze of mending my wounds from my breakup with Jack and falling into the heady swirl of love with Henry that I lost track of Meg. We would meet for the occasional drink and swap e-mails peppered with relevant details of our lives, but time got away from me, and in fairness, I suppose from her, too. And so, I have no recollection of the exact date she lost her second baby. I knew back then, but it isn't permanently embedded in me the way that, as her closest friend, it certainly should have been.

"I'm fine," Meg says, then flaps her hands in front of her face, as if that can stop an onslaught of tears. "I just got my period this morning, that's all."

"Oh, Meg." I pull her into me, and the dress crinkles.

She shakes her head and moves back. "No, no, come on, this is a big day for you. I don't want to ruin it. I've waited twenty-seven years to go wedding dress shopping with you!" She grins compassionately, selflessly, and I can see the truth within it.

I squeeze her hand, just as Deidre returns, holding forth a fluttering floor-length veil. I step back on to the pedestal, and she expertly combs it into the crest of my neck.

"Oooh," Ainsley claps. "It's perfect."

"It is," Meg says. "You look exactly how I'd pictured you would when you walk down the aisle."

"Really?" I ask.

"Really," they both say simultaneously, as Deidre nods her elegant head behind them with vigor.

For my wedding to Henry, I'd dress shopped alone. Not intentionally but because I stumbled upon what would become my wedding gown in a vintage store in Sag Harbor where Henry and I were weekending. He had gone to the farmers' market two streets over—this was back when he still had the time to grill—and I ambled through the quaint streets, in and out of kitschy shops that sold tackle and kites and handmade blankets. Eventually, I wandered into Rock of Ages, and as I filtered through the racks, I uncovered a simple, timeless sheath. I ducked behind the Asian divider that served as a dressing area, slid it over my head, and emerged to size myself up in the mirror.

It was, as Ainsley and Meg said today, perfect. The spaghetti straps curved against my collarbone, and the silk clung to my breasts and glided over my stomach. I looked at myself and *knew*, just knew, as they say. It was, in retrospect, one of the last things I had a firm grip on in the coming years of my marriage.

And now, standing in front of the mirror at Vera Wang, everyone else, it seemed, knew, too. Only they knew that *this one*, beaded and buttoned and strapless and regal and so distinctly different from the gown I'd worn when I'd betrothed myself to my other love, was the one for me.

So I turned to Deidre and told her that I'd take it. My instincts had proven wrong the first time, and now, it was a relief for someone else to decide.

@

MY MOTHER HAS called me three times at work, but I haven't called her back. I tried to seek advice from Jack but he offered little clarity.

"Do you think I'm making a mistake?" I asked him two nights ago. Jack was hovered over his laptop, attempting, I guessed, to eke out his manuscript, but mostly relieved that I'd wandered into the bedroom and interrupted.

"Jesus, I don't know," he said, and spun his chair in a circle. I flopped on the bed and pulled a pillow over my head.

"I just want someone to tell me what to do!" I said, my voice muffled. *Tell me what to do, Jack!* I'm surprised by the thought, given my resentment at Henry when he tried to do just that.

"Well, you know, it's a tough situation," he answered. "That whole sister thing . . ."

"Right," I said, sitting up. "I mean, she's had a daughter all this time—I have a *sister*—and she expects me to just roll with it?"

"Well, to be fair, what else was she supposed to do?"

"Um, I don't know—*tell me?*"

"But she did try to tell you," he echoes. "And now you won't talk to her. Maybe it's not black and white."

"Duly noted," I said. "So you'd return her call?"

Jack plopped on the bed and kissed the underside of my elbow as an answer, and then he worked his way up to my neck. And from there, that was as far as we got on my mother.

Later, while Jack slept, I replayed his passing comment. *Black and white.* I remembered how I left Jack seven years earlier, after one fight too many, and turned it off completely, as if someone flicked a switch in me, and then I thought of how I ended up back here to begin with: tired and lonely and fed up with my stale, crusting life, such that I might have literally willed myself out of it. Black and white. Maybe there was something to it.

And now, today in my office, my mother's number is once again displayed on my caller ID, her fourth call since I left her with her minisandwiches and cooling tea and the photo of my button-cute half-sister who, if I'd peered at any closer, might look a little too much like my own daughter for me to stomach.

I consider Jack's words, and make a small movement to pick up the phone, but just as I do so, the ringing stops. She's flipped into voice mail where, surely, she won't leave a message. I know this because I'm learning that my mother and I aren't so different, and while she might be brave enough to punch in my digits, she's not so sure of herself as to leave a lasting reminder that she was there.

I sigh with both relief and a small amount of regret, and then notice the time. *Shit.* I am way behind approving graphics and copy for the Christmas print ads. My hands scramble over my desk, rooting through old memos and half-eaten granola bars, to find the images and layouts. I squeeze the bridge of my nose and exhale, urging myself to find the mental space for this but still feeling mostly depleted. I don't remember resenting work in my old life as

I'm slowly growing to in my new one. I am in the office nearly round the clock, helming the team and reporting to Josie. Every moment that doesn't circle around my wedding seems to circle around ad copy and new ideas and storyboards and Photoshopped images and "finding the quintessential Coke models," as an exec put it to me recently, as if certain people literally bubbled this stuff from their noses.

Half a decade ago, I remember thriving on the camaraderie and the joy of launching a new idea and the thrill of the occasional late night when the team pulled together like Olympic relay racers, working to cross the finish line before the buzzer ran out. But like so many things, I'm starting to wonder if I've remembered wrong, if I've recast my past in a better light because it's so much easier than considering that while the present isn't a cheery Rockwell painting, neither was my history. That, in fact, it was just life, nothing glorious, nothing shabby, and while I like work well enough, it was still work, and that, perhaps, when I got pregnant and Henry suggested I quit, that I welcomed the chance, rather than resented it.

Or perhaps not. The edges are so blurred these days between reality and fiction, between this life and the other, that nothing seems linear anymore. Nothing seems concrete, and I often find myself trying to decipher what is real, as if I might have dreamed or imagined all the rest.

I am arched over my desk, my shoulder blades cramped and deep into comparing a gray-hued font with a grayish-silver-hued font, when Gene buzzes from his desk.

"Cute boy here to see you," he says, masking his enthusiasm to let me know that he's still annoyed that I kept him here until 11:30 the night before.

"Jack," I answer. "Send him in." I reach my hand over my shoulder to massage a throbbing knot.

"Not Jack," Gene answers. "Definitely not Jack. And I already sent him back."

Before I can reply, knuckles rap on my doorjamb, and Henry pokes his head inside. I jolt like a rat away from a trap. Even when we dated the first time around, Henry didn't make office calls, so seeing him here, out of his element in so many ways, is both disconcerting and welcome. Not that in my prior life, Henry needed to stop by: Back then, I was home by 7:00, and he was never later than 8:00. The balance, at least for the first few years, was still there.

"Hey." He smiles and his entire face illuminates. It's a smile that I barely remember. *When did you lose that?* I think. *Did I stop noticing or did I seep the happiness right out of you?* "I was in the building at a meeting and remembered that you worked here. Thought I'd stop by." He saunters in and sits, that loopy grin still splashed across him.

"Hey," I say back. "Sure, of course, I could use a distraction." I gesture to the mountains of work stacked atop my desk. "Er, it's nice to see you." *Too nice*, I realize, as my blood pressure noticeably skyrockets.

"You, too. How's your couch?" *Is that a euphemism for my boyfriend?* I wonder. My forehead wrinkles.

"Good," I say. "Comfortable. Yours?"

"Oh, well, I wasn't looking for one that day. Celeste was. But she didn't end up getting anything." *Is that a euphemism for they broke up?*

"Too bad." I shrug. "They had nice couches."

"Yes, they did," he answers and grins. *Is that a euphemism for you want me?* My eyebrows dart down. This coding system was beginning to confuse me.

"So how did things go with your mother?" Henry asks.

I can't believe that he remembers! The Henry I married wasn't nearly this thoughtful.

"Oh, I can't believe that you remembered," I say aloud.

"Of course." He folds his hands underneath his chin, as if his remembering were the most natural thing in the world.

Then why couldn't you remember to bring home fucking milk when I asked you to? Why couldn't you remember when I had a goddamn girls' night out, which I so desperately needed to reconnect with my old self, and you'd schedule a work dinner anyway?

"I met her for lunch, and . . ." I pause. "It was complicated."

"How so?" he asks.

"In a lot of ways, but, you know, I'll manage," I say, as I feel myself slipping into my old married patterns with Henry. Talking about a lot of things, revealing very little.

"Hit me with 'em." He shifts his legs in the chair. "Come on, spill." *Who are you and what have you done with the man I married?*

I sigh. "My mother has a daughter, which I guess means that I have a sister. And this girl is the same age now as when my mother left . . ." My voice drifts. "She told me about her, and, I don't know, it all seemed like too much. Like she was maybe trying to repay her debt to me because of this girl whom she looked at every day and felt guilty about, not because it was the right thing to do by me."

"Man, I'm sorry," Henry says. "That must have been hard."

"What are you gonna do?" I shrug. "That's life."

"I guess, but it's still hard. So what now?"

"Now, I deal with Coke's shiny new Christmas campaign!" I throw my hands in the air in mock celebration, but Henry doesn't laugh.

"I'm serious, Jill. What now?"

This is not what you do! You are not a prober! You don't ask the hard questions; you don't crack the facade that our life is any-thing less than perfect. Stop it this very second! We forged an entire marriage without asking each other for deeper explanations to an entire bevy of problems! You never stopped to ask me what I wanted with my mother! It was only "do this, do that," or "this is what I think is best," as if you were the one who had to deal with the carnage of your decisions.

"Oh, Jesus, I don't know." I clear my throat. "I just wish some-one would tell me what to do. . . . I'm not, it seems, very good with figuring out what I want, what's best for me."

"Sometimes it's hard to assess." Henry nods. "Instant gratification versus long-term reward." *There's my old Henry! Rational to the bone.*

"What would you do?" I ask, surprised at how easily it slips out when I'd rebelled against his advice on the subject for so long, more surprised at this quiet confidence that we have found in each other. Between Katie's demands and Henry's work and my need to create a crisp, perfect household, I can't remember the last time one of us leaned on the other in this manner.

"Oh, shit, I don't know. I'd probably take a hard look at what matters more: getting to know my mother or risking that she might hurt me again." He pauses. "I'm analytical, though—I try to find the most logical solution possible, you know? Both my parents are scientists, so that's probably why." He shrugs.

I know! I want to scream. *Enough with your backstory! I know that they're both professors at George Washington, and that, bar-ring our wedding and a few other choice moments, much of your energy is spent compartmentalizing your emotions, buffing them down to "the most rational point," as you used to say whenever we would devolve into a screaming match, and you'd inevitably tell me to stop being irrational and "get a grip." So I did stop being*

irrational and I did get a goddamn grip, which is why we stopped
fighting and eventually stopped communicating and why I ended
up seven fucking years in the past, all to get away from the haunt-
ing and suffocating silence that comes with being perfect.

I don't say any of this.

Instead, I offer, "See, that's the thing: I obviously don't *want*
her to hurt me again, and I'm not sure how I can move forward in
any sort of relationship with her, knowing that."

"Well, yeah, that's definitely the risk. But, I mean . . ." He
pauses and considers exactly what he's trying to say. "Isn't that
sometimes the point? No risk, no gain?" He clears his throat. "My
dad is a math professor [*I know!*], and he's always calculating the
odds of things, what the odds are—real odds, not due to luck or
fluke or anything like that—of say, a bus crashing into the car in
front of it, or us getting to school on time when we left the house
five minutes late if he drives forty-five miles per hour; you know,
quantifiable stuff like that."

I nod my head. I've heard all of this before, mostly from Phil,
Henry's dad, who could spin nearly anything you say into a math
problem, which led to many dreary and insufferable dinners and
conversations. It also surely didn't help nurture Henry's softer, more
compassionate gene. But I realize now, as I stare at my former husband and old love, that maybe his prodding and his niggling nagging about my mother was his way of watching over me. In the
future, I took it as judgment, as his way to look down on, not out
for, me. But I sense none of that today, only compassion.

"So anyway," he continues, "I mean, this one is harder because there's emotion and all of that involved, and my dad would
say it's thus a flawed formula . . . but you have to weigh the odds
and assess how likely it is that you're risking more than you're
gaining."

I'm about to answer when Gene buzzes me again.

"You're late for the copy meeting," he says flatly, then clicks off.

"Oh crap, I have to run." I stand and grab random documents strewn across my desk and in a pile on the floor.

"No problem," Henry says. "Hey, whatever happens, let me know, will you?" He pulls a card from his wallet and is about to place it on my desk but thinks otherwise, smartly recognizing that it might never be seen again. So he hands it to me directly. "Oh, and have a good Thanksgiving," he says on his way to the door.

"You, too." I smile, then realize that technically, this should be our first Thanksgiving together and that I should be headed to his childhood home to meet Phil and Susan, his physics-professor mom.

"Going home?" he asks.

"To Jack's," I say with a shrug. "You?"

"To Celeste's," he says, mirroring my posture, then forcing a grin. "You gotta do what you gotta do." *So I guess that wasn't a euphemism for they broke up, after all.* I'm punctured.

"Have a good one," he says again, lingering, in no hurry to move on. "And don't forget the formula: risk or gain. Which one is more likely?"

"I won't forget," I say, looking at him one last time just before I turn down the hall toward the conference room. "In fact, I'm thinking it over as we speak."

ℰ HENRY

Henry first nudged me about my mother when Katie was seven and a half months. I remember it clearly because it was

just after she started crawling, which changed the literal trajectory of my day. No more plopping her down while I ran
into the kitchen for an iced tea. The first (and last) time I did
that, I returned to the living room and she'd vanished. Panic
spread through my veins, and I raced around shouting her
name with hysteria for the longest minute of my lifetime, as if
she could say, "Yes, Mama, I'm right here," until I found her
tucked under the piano bench, cooing softly and pawing the
gold pedals.

I don't know why Henry started in with it—probably because he suspected that I might find motherhood more fulfilling if I came to peace with my own disrupted youth. He'd
bring it up in small ways: Maybe he saw an older woman on
the street whom he thought looked so much like me, maybe
he'd mention an article he'd read in the *New York Times*
about child rearing and how we pass along our own sins to
our offspring, try as we might not to. Maybe he'd just casually mention her when I'd be smack in the middle of prepar-
ing dinner, asking, ever so nonchalantly, if my mom was a
good cook or if I knew if she had an aversion to basil, if it
made her gag reflux kick in, as it did mine.

At first, I didn't mind so much. At first, it just seemed
like he was trying to peel off a layer and dig a little deeper
into discovering more about his wife, and just about all of my
magazines told me that this was a *good thing* for a marriage.
Oh, to have a relationship in which your husband still finds
you mysterious, they would sing! So he'd make his passing
comment, and I'd try not to let the edges of my mouth curl
under, and I'd instead smile pleasantly enough and shrug off
his inquiries.

But soon, it became clear that Henry's comments were
part of a larger plan, a bigger objective, the goal of which was

to forge some sort of reconciliation between me and the woman who left me behind.

"You never pushed me to do this before," I said one night, my voice frigid with unexpressed anger because I just *wanted him to shut his piehole about this fucking subject,* a feeling I hoped was made clear by my refusal to turn around and face him while I was washing the dishes.

"I just think it's important," he replied. "I think it's important for Katie to know her grandmother, but I mostly think it's important for you to get answers to all of your questions."

"I don't have any questions," I said flatly, scrubbing, scrubbing, *scrubbing* this goddamn spot of grease that *refused* to relinquish its grip on my pot.

"You have plenty of questions," he said, not unkindly, though I didn't see it this way at the time. "And they're valid questions that deserve answers. I think," he paused to consider his words, "that getting some answers might make you a happier person. Might, you know, help you figure things out."

"I don't need to figure things out!" I seethed. "And I resent the insinuation that I'm confused or unsettled, that I'm not entirely fucking happy right now, with you and with Katie, and without *that woman*," I spat out the words, "in my life."

I slammed down the pot, shook off my rubber gloves, and retreated to the nursery to check on Katie. I sat in her rocking chair, gliding back and forth and back again, with only the nightlight for illumination, until I heard Henry plod into our bedroom and retire.

Who asked you? I thought. *What gave you the fucking right? As if you think you have all the answers!* I steamed.

I rocked and I rocked, eventually sliding down onto my-self and resting my feet on the ottoman and falling into a fit-ful slumber. Never once, not even for a moment, did it occur to me that my husband, he who truly loved me, even when he felt so far, so very, very far away, might be right.

Chapter Twenty-one

Jack and I are on the train, tucked in the last passenger car, on our way to his parents' house for Thanksgiving when my phone rings. The car is clogged with holiday travelers, all rushing to see loved (or not-so-loved) ones for the obligatory turkey feast, and our breaths collectively stifle the air, such that the windows drip with condensation and I nearly suffocate from my maroon wool scarf. My cell keeps buzzing, and I unwrap the scarf from my neck, tossing aside the work memos I was scouring, and scavenge through my overnight bag for my phone. Jack doesn't glance up; he's fully enmeshed in rereading the first five chapters of his novel. It's as far as he's gotten in the four months that I've been back here, but it's progress, I suppose. He's showing it to Vivian tonight, and even he admits that he's more than a little queasy at the thought of doing so.

"So don't let her read it," I suggest as we're packing.

"Of course I'm letting her read it," he says, throwing five pairs of boxers in his suitcase and leaving me to wonder just how long he plans on staying or why he needs to change his underwear so often.

"But it's making you crazy. You're so worried about her opinion that you're barely concentrating on whether or not *you're* happy with it." I turn to retrieve a sweater from the closet, and I'm startled by how much I see my own self in my words—how I was so busy trying to please Henry that I never stopped to consider my own happiness, or, just as important, whether or not he wanted to be pleased in such a way in the first place. I glance at myself in the closet mirror and see the surprise of the realization wash across me.

Jack sighs. "Jill, look, this is just how it is. Please don't get up in my face about it."

"Okay," I say and drop my navy cable-knit into the bag. "Consider it dropped." *What's the point in changing him?* I tell myself, though a wiser part of me whispers that *change* is the point entirely.

As my cell rings and rings and as a couple behind us debates the ethics of hanging chads, Jack chews on the cap of his pen, then makes a note in the manuscript, muttering to himself.

"Yello," I say over the din of the train's engine, loudly enough to break Jack from his trance. He shoots me an annoyed glare, and I shrug.

"I'm pregnant!" Meg screams on the other end of the line. "I'm pregnant, I'm pregnant, I'm pregnant!!"

I press my finger into my free ear and turn into the window to afford a little privacy.

"Sweetie, that's amazing!" I hear myself say, though I feel as if I'm saying so from inside a tunnel, so far removed from the actual words. I'm frantically spinning backward, confirming that *no*—I shake my head slightly—*she wasn't pregnant at Thanksgiving last time around. I would have remembered that. Surely, I would have paid attention to that.* My mind flips back and forth, like a children's picture book, as I search for any sign that this is *new* news, not new old news.

No, I think firmly. Last time around, Henry and I drove to D.C., stopping at a TCBY on the side of the road for snacks, even though it was sleeting outside, and singing along to country music as we went. Henry, I learned on the trip, was tone-deaf, but this didn't stop him from singing to virtually every twang-filled, crooning, heartsick tune that floated from the car radio.

"I'm just a misplaced country boy," he said to me sheepishly at one point.

"An off-tune one, be that as it may," I said, smiling.

"Well, you found my first flaw." He winked, and then turned back toward the road.

Eventually, as our ardor eroded, I grew weary of his country music, and he listened to it only when alone. Truth told, I have no idea if he still sang along, and if not, if he stopped because of me.

But certainly, as we careened down the highway toward his parents' house on that Wednesday before Thanksgiving, Meg never called to announce pregnancy number two.

So now, on the train to Vivian and Bentley's, this was certainly good news to behold. Since I'd come back from seven years forward I've too often suspected that I'd set off a destructive chain of events that would never have occurred, *shouldn't* have occurred, were it not for my return. It's easy to feel this way: I do, after all, have a map of the previous course of events, so any deviation from someone else's designated path is, no dodging it, directly my fault. I wanted to come back to change *my life, my history,* but I never contemplated how that might tweak the outcome for so many others. Like Josie and Bart. Like Henry and Celeste.

But now, there was Megan and Tyler, and as she confides that she's only five weeks along, so let's not get our hopes up, but she's feeling positive and no morning sickness yet, but she's certain she'll be barfing any day now, I can't help but feel like things are exactly as they should be.

Outside, the world rushes by me. I stare out of the train window, and pine trees blur into other pine trees, and deadened fields, crusty from the winter, flow into other browned and deserted grasses. I watch it all whiz by and think that my coming back has changed things, sure, but sometimes, *change is exactly what you need.* As Henry might have once sung, *some change is going to do you good.*

❧

THIS IS MY FIRST Thanksgiving with the Turnhill clan. The year before, I'd joined my father, Linda, and Andy in Florida, and the year prior to that, Jack and I hadn't been serious enough to merit a discussion on where to spend the holidays. So, while I've burrowed myself into his family tree, thanks to that sparkler on my finger, and Vivian has certainly extended her (formerly clamped-shut, never-to-be-pried-open) arms, still, I feel off balance.

I have tried, however, to come prepared. While my preference would be to slum it in jeans and a T-shirt, I am demurely dressed like a Connecticut prep-school graduate, complete with a honey-colored cashmere crew, a tweed pencil skirt and peep-toe lizard-skin shoes. *Peep-toe shoes!* I think as I slide them on. *Who wears heels to dinner in their own home?*

Vivian did, is the answer, and thus, so did I—though I'm alarmed to remember how often I wore heels to dinner in my old life: how Henry would burst through the door, and an apron-clad, exquisite wife, complete with a piping hot dinner, would be waiting.

I descend from the stairs into the living room, and Leigh catches a glimpse of me.

"Oh my God." She laughs. "You look like one of them!" She gestures her elbow toward the library, where her two sisters and mother huddle in front of the fireplace. Leigh, I notice, is in pressed black pants, a matching turtleneck, and flats with a shiny silver emblem on the toe. The balls of my feet practically cry out in envy.

"Just trying to do my part." I shrug.

"More like 'just trying to play your part,' " Leigh says, and though the words could be piercing, they actually burst with sympathy. She smiles at me kindly. "Come on, let's get a drink. This can be a long evening."

Two bourbons later, I am helping Vivian reheat the (catered, preordered) stuffing (that she doesn't cook), when she blindsides me from behind.

Pressing close, too close to me, she says, "Jill, now that you're going to be part of my family, I'd like you to consider calling me 'Mom.' "

I spin around. We're now close enough that, were this a movie (and were she not my future mother-in-law), the audience would shift with anticipation in their seats, hoping that one of us might leap toward the other and burst the sexual bubble. As it was, I take a step back and nail my head into the oven door.

"Oh, Vivian, I'm, uh, I'm really . . ."

She smiles at me like a possessed Cheshire cat, and I'm suddenly reminded of *Alice in Wonderland* and how I bought Katie an original copy for her first birthday, knowing, of course, that she couldn't yet read, but dripping with excitement to pass along the story of the girl who slides down the rabbit hole, all the same.

"I'm sorry," I say in a panic, squeezing out from between Vivian's breath and the heat of the oven, and racing for the bathroom.

I plunk on the toilet and try to gather the air that seems clotted in my lungs, try to stop my heart from nearly detonating in my chest. I run my clammy hands over my forehead and tug at the pearls around my neck. Everything feels like it's closing in on me, and I exhale to try to will it away, but still, the claustrophobia persists.

A small voice sounds through the door.

"Aunt Jilly? You okay?"

Allie, I think. "Fine, honey. I'll be out in a minute." My voice is an octave too high.

"Hurry, I have something I want to show you." Her footsteps fade as she runs with abandon down the hall.

I stand, ignoring the sudden dizziness, and splash water across my cheeks, then peer closer into the mirror.

Thanksgiving had long been my least favorite holiday, and for many years, it was all my family could do to suffer through it in stoic silence, pretending that nothing had changed, despite the absent place setting where my mother once sat. Our first Thanksgiving without her—just seven short weeks after she left—my father valiantly but ultimately fruitlessly toiled the day through in the kitchen, intent on crafting a homespun celebratory feast, as my mother had done with seeming ease for all the years I could remember. I'd stand in the kitchen door opening, my five-year-old self or seven-year-old self, and watch her move from oven to stovetop back to oven, checking on the turkey or the gravy or the stuffing, and she never once stopped moving. As if nothing were more natural, as if she couldn't have been more content.

And then she was gone.

And try as he did, my father's turkey was too dry, and the gravy too salty, and the yams so lumpy I just pushed them around on my plate even though they used to be my favorite. But we smiled and smiled the dinner through, even though the tears that sat just behind the cusps of our eyes said more about our misery than our grins ever did.

I stare into the mirror, now, in Vivian's powder room, and muffle a cry. For my feet that are pressed achingly into my peep-toed heels when they'd so much rather be free. For my father who tried to shoehorn a rosy sense of familial happiness into our holidays when, surely, all he, too, wanted to do was scream. For my old self, who seemingly woke up one day as a country-club-ready, chipper-in-all-moments, shiny supermom, as if she crept in overnight like a zombie and seized my mind while leaving my body untouched. And for the me now, who, try as she might, felt hauntingly similar to that old self, the very one she was trying to outrun.

I slide down the putty-colored wall onto the cold tiled floor and focus on my mother, on how she hummed under her breath while she toiled in the kitchen, so lost in herself that sometimes she didn't even notice me watching. And then I remember how I used to do much the same: singing to myself while folding laundry, literally whistling while I worked around the house. But none of these musical musings filled me with any joy. If anything, they masked the more honest sounds, the guttural ones that I was too fearful to let escape.

I lean against the wall and the radiator clicks on, emitting a sudden whoosh of heat. I sit there until time blends into itself, and as my back muscles spasm and Allie once again begs for my presence outside of the closed door, I'm struck with a sudden and immediate realization: that I might be able to hide from my mother, but it's clear that I can't outrun her, not when what I'm mostly sprinting from is not her memory alone, but the way that her memory has planted its roots inside of me and grows bigger with each passing year, until my sense of my mother is so intertwined with my own sense of self that I can't tell which is which any longer.

Chapter Twenty-two

I've begged off a staff meeting to find a sliver of free time, and my mom has agreed to meet me at the south gate of Central Park at lunch. It's an unseasonably mild day for early December, though it snowed earlier in the week, so the lawns are bathed in slush, and puddles threaten on every sidewalk corner. As at the tea emporium, she is there early, and I see her from my corner perch long before she sees me.

She is chewing the inside of her lip, and while I imagine this should endear her to me, it instead angers me all over again, shooting shards of her betrayal, of her plea for sympathy, of the news of my sister through me like hot lightning.

Henry, my old Henry, would be proud of me, I think. He'd pushed me relentlessly, until his hints were no longer subtle or even all together padded with softness, to forge a reconciliation, and so, if he could see me here, toeing the literal line between my childhood self and my adult one, surely, he'd be proud.

But as I watch my mother glance through the passing crowds, searching strange faces for mine, a familiar one, it occurs to me that pleasing Henry, *making him proud*, has nothing to do with any-thing. Before, in my old life, I felt much the same, only it wasn't really the same feeling at all. Before, back then, I was cocooned in hostility, the way that it's so easy to be when the person closest to you isn't telling you what you want to hear or isn't taking the time to listen clearly to what it is that you *need* them to hear.

Instead of shutting down with Henry, I consider, I should have listened more. Listened to why this reconciliation with my mother mattered to him. Told him why it felt like too much to bear for me. Maybe then, instead of digging emotional graves for ourselves, we could have forged an understanding that would have pleased us both equally. Because the Henry I've come to know in this second chance would have preferred that, and I realize, as I see my mother check her watch once again, I would have much preferred that, too.

I start to move toward my mom, but still, something holds me back, like I'm trapped in a giant impermeable bubble that won't allow me through. I freeze and exhale, trying for the first time in so, so long to listen to what it is that I need to do for myself, not what I think needs to be done for the future and not what I'm doing to escape my past. Just here and now. Me, myself, and I.

I'm not ready, I say. *I'm not ready to let this all go. I wish that I were but it can't be so easy. Stop pretending that it's all so fucking easy. As if you should be able to forgive her just because she beckoned.*

The words resonate within me, echoing and ringing clearly, and I know that they are true. So rather than cross the street and gloss over the scars that still lie within me, I pull my hood tight over my head, turn down the avenue, and, like a ghost, am gone.

ℰ

"OH MY GOD, what is that smell?" Later that night, I hear Josie's voice from the hall before I see her in my office.

"Chinese," I say, gesturing to the spread in front of me. "You want? We ordered way too much."

"Don't be so sure," Meg says, her chopsticks diving into her paper plate. "I'm eating for two."

"Hey, congrats!" Josie kisses Megan on the cheek and grabs a dumpling with her fingers. "What are you doing here on a Friday night?"

Meg tries to answer but her mouth is too full, so mostly, she grunts and gestures toward me.

"Forgive her," I say. "She's nine weeks pregnant and this is the first time she's eaten in about a month."

"Morning sickness up the wazoo," Meg chimes in after finally swallowing.

"Ugh, I had it with both of mine the entire pregnancy," Josie says, committing to dinner by reaching for a plate. "Everyone swore that it would pass after the first trimester, but nope, kept vomiting right until I delivered them."

"Yeah, but really, wasn't the heartburn the worst?" I say. They both cock their heads in confusion, and I realize my mistake. "Um, I mean, that's what I've read. That the heartburn can be the worst."

"Oh, the whole fucking thing was the worst." Josie waves her chopsticks in the air, and I notice she's still wearing her wedding ring. She hasn't breathed a word of her potential dalliance with Bart in nearly two months. "I don't care what all those books out there say, pregnancy is *not* the best time of a woman's life."

Meg freezes for half a beat and stares at her, as if Josie has just told her that the world is flat. Then she dismisses it.

"Well," she says carefully, "I think it's pretty wonderful. I mean, it's such a powerful feeling knowing that I'm growing a *human* inside of me."

I smile and try to soften Josie's cynicism. Because Meg, after all that she's gone through, or perhaps, after all that I've seen her go through in my previous life, does not deserve even a flea nip of cynicism. Though, I note to myself, she does echo the sound bites from the dozens of books on mommyhood that I'd piled next to my nightstand in anticipation of Katie's arrival.

"Sweetie, it is pretty wonderful," I say. "And you're going to produce the cutest human being ever." *Second to Katie,* I catch myself thinking, and I can't seem to shake her chubby cheeks from my mind.

"No, but seriously, Meg, what are you doing here on a Friday night?" Josie asks again.

"That would be my fault," I offer, pouring the container of mu shu onto my plate, still seeing Katie behind my eyes. "Every year, Meg and I plan an afternoon of last-minute gift shopping, and this year . . ." I gesture to the debris and to-dos in my office, "I couldn't leave. So she came to me. We're doing it all online."

"Not quite the quality time I envisioned, but eh, free Chinese food, so I'll take it." Megan laughs.

"Those Coke fuckers, right?" Josie sighs. "And I haven't even started my shopping." The Coke execs scrapped our planned copy for the new print ads at the last minute, which meant brainstorming anew.

"Speaking of pregnancy," Meg says, then pauses, reaching down into her bag.

"Which we weren't exactly," Josie notes.

"Close enough," she counters, then produces an envelope from her purse. "Here, I wanted to show you." She navigates the envelope around the food cartons and slides it over my desk. I run my fingers under the flap and pull out grainy black-and-white snapshots. To an untrained eye, they might look like alien shots taken from a spycam in space, but to a mother, they are proof, palpable proof, of both the being and the love that are growing inside of her.

"Oh my God, Meg." I move my hand to my mouth and feel my nose tingle. I look up and see that her eyes, too, are full.

"That's our little one," she says, and for the first time tonight, her pallid, pregnant skin flushes with blood, as if the thought of her baby literally brings her to life. "It was taken last week when we saw the heartbeat." She shakes her head. "The most incredible thing I've ever seen."

I stare at the little bean and remember my own appointment, just on the cusp of my second trimester. My stomach was just beginning to pooch, and the technician slopped cold gel onto my abdomen, such that I recoiled at the sensation. Henry held my hand as I lay on the exam table, and we both gazed up at the monitor, gazing in wait, as the tech moved her wand over and about until I felt her apply pressure and *bam*, there she was. Katie. Up on the screen. With tiny arms and legs and a bloated stomach and a perfect circle of a head. She somersaulted around inside of me, though I couldn't yet feel her, throwing her own private party in my uterus.

"You've got a handful there," the technician said to us, as we watched silently, too overcome with awe to answer. I wiped a stray tear off my cheek and caught Henry doing the same.

When we left, the tech printed out some snapshots of our baby, of our potential, and for hours after, I sat in our half-boxed-up apartment and stared at the images. So full of surprise and hope and disbelief. I just stared and stared, certain that I would love this baby more than anything I'd loved before, but less certain about everything else that came with it: the move to Westchester that was now barreling ahead, the job that I'd soon resign from, the mother I could be when my own mother's shadow threatened at too many turns. But love this baby, that, I could do.

Tonight, Josie moves closer to my desk to gaze at the ultrasound, and then Meg inches in, too. The three of us huddle around the image of Meg's future: Josie, the battle-weary one who feels shortchanged by it all; me, the desperate one who doesn't know what to cling on to and what to let go; and Meg, the hopeful one who still has so much left to uncover. But as the lights of the city glow in the window behind us, we all look much the same: mothers who sit in wonder and wait for the children who will inevitably change their lives.

Chapter Twenty-three

The snow has fallen heavy and wet overnight, and when I wake up in my childhood bed on Christmas morning, I am, for a second, discombobulated, lost between my present and past, between my youth and the adult I've grown into.

The sugary scent of griddled pancakes lures me from my room, and I pad my way into the kitchen, where my father, in a forest green robe that still has a tag hanging from the sleeve, hovers over the stove.

"Merry Christmas, J-bird," he says, stepping away from the oven and kissing my cheek. "From Linda. She ran into town for coffee." He twirls around, and a droplet of batter flies off the spatula and lands on the refrigerator. "You like?"

"Uh-huh," I answer, then cock my head at the sound of running water above us.

"Andy," my dad says. "He got in from Singapore late last night." He flips two pancakes off the griddle and onto the plate, then slides them onto the table. "Sit," he commands. "And eat. You don't look so great."

I dump a liberal amount of syrup on top *(Sugar! Why It Will Suck Five Years from Your Life!)* and wrestle off a piece of the pancake with my fingers. I stare out the window of our dining nook, and it's as if the world has frozen over. Icicles hang like chandeliers; tree branches sink under their own weight. My mother's garden, which had long been overrun with unwieldy weeds and deadened plants, is covered in a blanket of snow, masking the joy and betrayal that once symbolized everything about how I defined myself.

My dad pulls out the chair next to me and plunks down. His plate rattles as he does so. He, too, focuses outside, and I wonder if he's thinking about her, about her garden, about all of it, just as I am.

"I saw her," I say finally. "I met Mom. Awhile back."

His chewing slows as he ingests more than just his breakfast, and in the silence, I can hear him swallow.

"I'm glad for you," he says finally. "If that's what you want." He clears his throat.

"It's complicated." I shrug. "I have a sister."

My dad doesn't flinch as I expect him to. Instead, he just nods his head. Eventually, he says, "I know."

"What do you mean, 'you know'?" A lone robin lands in the yard as I turn to face my father.

"I've . . ." He pauses, and his eyes shift downward. "I've occasionally been in touch with your mother."

"What?" My surprise flares like a firework. "Why would you do that? Why wouldn't you tell me?"

"Oh, Jilly." My dad sighs. "You've just been so . . ." He searches for the right words. "Stoic or bitter, I don't know . . . at her and the whole situation that I didn't want you to be angry with me for forgiving her. It just seemed . . . easier to let you come to terms with it if and when you wanted to."

I rub my temples and notice that the robin has moved on, gone as quickly as it came. I stuff a piece of pancake in my mouth, trying to hear, really *hear*, what my father is saying. About my anger at her, about how I tried to block it out, and about how instead, maybe I've let it consume me.

"Why did it happen?" I ask when I've finally swallowed. "I mean, why did you decide to let it go?"

"I don't know if there's any specific reason," he says. "It's just, well, you know that marriage is complicated." He bites the outside of his lip. "After a while, I realized that she was the one who left, but maybe I didn't do enough to make her stay."

"That's ridiculous!" I say. A piece of spittle flies all the way to the window and lands with a silent splat. "You were a wonderful husband to her."

"I was," he concedes. "At times. Other times, I don't know," he says, his shoulders offering a limp gesture.

"That's just ridiculous," I repeat. "*She's* the one who left. *She's* the one who made the choices that ruined us."

My dad's face quivers like I slapped him. "She didn't ruin us," he says softly. "And I'm sorry that you feel that way. I tried to preserve as much of your happiness as I could."

I pause and reconsider my words, whether or not I still believed the mantra that I'd fed on for so many years, now that I'd abandoned my own child and now that I understood the loneliness that can eat up your whole life.

"I'm sorry; that came out wrong," I say. "You're right, she didn't ruin us. I don't even know why I said that."

"You said that," my dad says, "because you spent so many years believing it. Unwilling to see that even though she left us, she didn't leave us in total wreckage. Some wreckage, but not total." He manages a laugh. "Besides, I think I did a pretty okay job."

"You did." I smile. "You really did." I lean over to kiss his unshaven cheek. "So let me ask you something: If you've forgiven Mom, why haven't you ever asked Linda to marry you?"

"Ha! Are you kidding me?" My dad grins. "I've asked her at

least half a dozen times. She's just never said yes. Says I'm too old and too much of a slob."

"Oh, I . . ." I'm breathless with the way that my understanding of everything has been turned on its head. "I guess I thought you never wanted to remarry. That's always what I assumed." I push out the clump of air in my chest and try to get a grip on my pulse.

"Nope," he said, standing and running his hands over my hair. "I'd marry Linda in a heartbeat." He pauses. "Jilly, don't get so tangled up that you think that everyone will walk out on you like your mom did. And even though she did what she did, I suppose she had her reasons." He kisses me on the top of my head. "It's never easy, you know, marriage and all of that. You'll find out soon enough."

It's true, I think, running my finger through the syrup on my plate and mulling over my upcoming nuptials to Jack. *Everyone says it's hard, but it's hard in ways you don't grasp until you're in it. How hard can it be? you say. I mean, so he'll leave his socks on the floor and he might be a little cheap about money and occasionally, he'll fart at the dinner table, which will really, really annoy me, but come on, how hard can it be?*

I hear the noise from the shower above recede, then my brother's heavy footsteps reverberate on the ceiling. Linda bursts through the door with shouts of "Merry Christmas" and hot eggnog lattes for us all.

I watch my dad and Linda disappear into the den, him sliding his hand on the small of her back. I turn back again to the desolate, sleeping landscape out my childhood kitchen window and wonder how I could have gotten so much wrong for so long. And what's more surprising than any of these revelations is who I now want to share them with most: Henry, the very man who set me off running, just like my mother did two decades earlier.

ॐ

AFTER YEARS OF living without my mother, my father has finally mastered the art of cooking. I've tried to help all afternoon, but he just shushes me out of the kitchen, shooing me off with a "what do you know about fine cuisine?"

You don't know the half of it, I want to say, remembering the *Gourmet*s, *Bon Appétit*s, and *Cooking Light*s that I organized by season in my sprawling suburban chef's kitchen.

My brother has trudged straight back into bed after guzzling his latte, and Linda has retreated to the bedroom. I flip through some football on TV, then glance over the newspaper headlines, and finally, with the house silent other than the clanging of pots and my father's mutterings to himself in the kitchen, I slip out the front door and into the frozen world outside, which feels like another planet entirely. The snow crunches underneath my weighted steps as I wind down the street.

I replay my conversation with my father and blend it into my old life with Henry. How maybe we both failed each other in our own ways.

When Henry got promoted to partner, he called me from the office to break the news. I was seven months pregnant, bored and swollen in our new home, and was elevating my feet on the couch, with *Days of Our Lives* in the background, and a tower of parenting magazines on the floor.

"This will mean a lot more work," he warned. "And before I accept it, I want to be sure that you're okay with it."

"Of course!" I practically squealed. "It's incredible, and I'm so proud of you." And I was.

"You sure?" He hedged again. "Because really, I mean it when I say that I'll be traveling a lot. A lot."

"I'm sure," I reiterated, not hearing, not really listening to the veracity of his words.

"Good," he said, and I could hear him break into a smile. "Because I already accepted it!"

Later, months later, when his nonstop schedule had torn him away from the family and when my resentment had festered and was rising into a slow boil, and when I clamped down even further on that resentment, as if putting a lid on a tea kettle can keep it from warming, I considered our exchange. And how, in those few short words, we'd equally betrayed each other: me, by pretending that I had everything that I needed, and him, by assuming to know what I needed in the first place, with no real understanding of that need at all.

Why didn't I just say something, I think today, panting as I ascend my neighbor's hill, the same one Andy and I used to fly down, feet off our bike pedals, with gleeful abandon. *Why didn't I just say, "Be here. Be present. Give me what I need." Why was I so incapable of saying something so simple?* Despite the frigid temperatures, I feel sweat pool on the waistband of my jeans, as I consider how big a difference this tiny shift might have made in the scope of everything. *Maybe he would have heard me; maybe I could have started hearing him, too.*

Finally, when my thighs are pleading for a reprieve, I loop back to the house, which smells like pumpkin pie and nutmeg, and gallop up the stairs to my room. Then I reach into my purse, extract my wallet, and tug out Henry's business card.

He has scrawled his cell phone on the back, and so, before my nerves get the better of me, I poke his numbers into my pink phone that matches the wallpaper and bedding in my girlhood room.

I'm flipped into voice mail, and his message is familiar as always. It is, I surmise, from my perch on my strawberry-hued bed, the same message that he still has today. Or in the future. It's all muddling together now.

"Er, Henry, it's . . . Jill. Jillian Westfield." *How weird is this?* I flip onto my stomach. "Um, for some reason I was just thinking of you. So, er, I just wanted to wish you a Merry Christmas." *No, you didn't! You wanted to say so much more.* " 'Kay. Bye."

I throw my arm around my ragged stuffed bunny that I'd slept with since I was four and lie still. Then, in one frantic movement, I reach for the phone again, redial, and press the receiver so closely to my ear, I can hear the crackling across the line as I'm connected.

"Henry! Hey, it's me! Um, Jillian. Um, actually, you're going to think I'm crazy, but um, I was thinking about it and wondered if you wanted to meet for coffee." I pause and inhale. "Erm, not today, obviously, because it's Christmas." I emit a semipsychotic laugh, which, if he knew me better as he once did, would signal that I was nearly vomiting with anxiety. "But, uh, maybe tomorrow. I'm back in the city. Er, if you're around. Not sure if you are. Oh, maybe you're at Celeste's." I feel my face redden. It didn't even occur to me that he's at Celeste's. *Shit.* "Um, in which case, disregard this. Ha! Yes, just ignore me completely! Ha ha! Okay, good. You have my number. Oh, maybe you don't. Well, it probably came up on caller ID. Great. Er. Um. Thanks, bye."

I throw the receiver back into the base and feel my pulse spin like a loose grenade through my neck. I feel like I should want to regret it, like I should want to rewind the past few minutes and take the messages back. But surprisingly, I don't. Surprisingly, though my heart might burst with frenzy, for the first time in a long time, something feels right about going after what I think I might need.

I roll over on my bed and let out a hyena giggle that falls into itself and turns into heaping, overflowing euphoria that doesn't let up until my pillow is nearly soaked with mirthful tears. I sink into my childhood bed, into the literal home where I lost so much, and I realize that here, too, is where something—my voice, my needs, my groove?—just might be found.

※

HENRY HASN'T CALLED back by dinner. I try to remember where he spent his holiday that first year that we dated, but I'm stuck between Vail with his college friends and at home with his parents. I know that he did each during one of the years that we dated or before we dated or around when we dated, but they've all blended into one another. Now and then. Past and present and future.

I distract myself by calling Meg, then Ainsley, but no one is picking up. I consider diving into the pile of work that I've slugged home, but I can't stomach the depression that accompanies trudging through copyedits on a snowy Christmas evening.

The front door slams as Andy heads out to meet some high-school friends. He will, no doubt, return just before dawn and sleep the day away. The better not to have to face his return home.

"We're putting in *It's a Wonderful Life*," my dad calls up to me. "Linda's popped the 'corn. Come on down."

I'd forgotten all about it, about my father's requisite tradition. He started it the year my mother left. I suppose it was, in his way, his attempt to show us how changed our lives might have been without our mother—even though we were seething with rage and I, at least, refused to even begrudgingly admit that what time I did have with my mother was precious indeed. So every Christmas, my father would gather Andy and me on the couch and pull an Icelandic blanket over our knees, and we'd recline and consider the story of George Bailey, who wanted to give up on his life until he saw how much his life actually mattered. Eventually, I stopped equating the movie with my mother, and Andy and I would race to fill in the dialogue before the actors said the words themselves.

And now, it's come full circle: the man who has given up on his life and wishes to be absolved of it, my mother and her abandonment, and me and my own.

I heave myself from my twin bed and scurry down the stairs, my polka-dotted pajama bottoms dragging as I go. As I toss popcorn into my mouth and watch the lights of the TV bounce off the living room walls, I consider my decisions, my setbacks, and how I got here, literally *here*, seven years in the past, running from my choices, so ready to turn away from the path I'd opted for with my own free will.

It's so easy to give up on it all, I think, as Clarence, George's guardian angel, descends to earth to save George from himself. *It's so fucking easy to toss it in and call it a day.*

But then I think of Katie, of our first Christmas together when she was nearly one and toddling through the house, her mind so determined to take those first few steps but her body not quite ready. I watched her and thought she was so brave—falling over and over again, but always getting up with a laugh and trying anew.

And now, I watch poor George and realize that Katie might have had it right the whole time: She wasn't being brave, she was only moving forward. Stumbling and getting back up. Falling and refusing to be cowed. Why, as her mother, didn't I see this? Why did I tuck my tail under and run? Why didn't I consider, I think now, with my dad half-asleep by my side and a deserted popcorn bowl on the coffee table, that maybe Katie was my guardian angel all along?

Chapter Twenty-four

H enry hasn't returned my call. I'm trying not to consider the implications of this fact two days after Christmas, as I hover over my desk, feigning busywork but mostly bored and listless. And by trying not to consider the implications, all I have done is further obsess about the silent, lifeless, *why won't you fucking ring?* phone.

It's a dead zone, this time between Christmas and New Year's. Jack is in Antigua with his family, a vacation I gracefully declined months back, before our engagement, and my apartment is so quiet that it leaves me nothing to do but think, so I've returned to the office as a default.

I have clicked through all of the online holiday sales, looked up the weather in both Vail and Antigua, and added some stemware to my registry, when out of nowhere, a silly banner ad with an unusually well-endowed bride and her barely aging mother sends my mind flashing to my own mother and how maybe it's time to start saying something real in the conversation toward healing. How I'm the only one who is going to be able to set aside my baggage and how I'm responsible for owning that. *Really,* I think, *maybe this is what Henry was trying to push me toward, with all of his nagging about reconciliation. I just wasn't able to see it that way, so his words always seemed to come out wrong. Maybe his intentions were always pure, and that has to count for something.*

I close my office door, hearing the latch snap shut, and uncover a pen and pad in my top drawer. I might not be ready to wash it all clean, but I am ready, I know, to begin to try.

Dear Mom,

I'm sorry that I wasn't able to meet you last week. I shouldn't have promised something that I couldn't deliver. It wasn't my intention to disappoint you. I understand why you want to get to know me now after so many years. And I want you to know that part of me is grateful for that desire. But another part of me feels like, felt like, I should say, it's all too much, too soon.

I want to forgive you, I do. I'd even like to say that I'm ready to forgive you, but this isn't a blackboard that can just be erased with one fell swoop. Every day, I'm reminded of what you did to me. For years, I pretended that I wasn't, but now, it's clear that nearly everything about who I've become has been defined by learning to live with the belief, and the isolation of that belief, that my mother didn't love me.

I am a chameleon, Mother. I sell myself out to the person who bids high enough with his love. If he gives me enough, I can become whomever he needs me to be. As long as he promises devotion, I'm his, blocking out my instincts to become who I want, to say what I want to say. Because, I've long feared, if I expose my true self, if I speak up and say no, he might leave, just as you once did nearly two decades ago.

And even now, with your request to start anew, I feel myself doing it all over again: giving myself over to you because you show up, ready and heady with your love. A chameleon never stops trying to blend in, it seems.

It's time, however, for me to start sinking into my own skin, not

just that of what others want to see. To start facing who I am, who I
need to be. I can't blame you forever, and I don't want to. I'd like to
become an adult who is responsible for her own path and for her own
happiness. And I do hope that one day, we can be fully enmeshed in
each other's lives.

But on my terms and at my own pace. And for now, it's enough
for me to know that you're out there, ready and waiting. I hope this
is enough for you, too.

All best,
Jillian

I lick the inside flap of a DMP envelope and taste the stale gum on my tongue. Then I press the seal closed, carefully pen her address on the front, and drop it into my outbox where it can be ushered out into the world. It isn't everything, I know, but it is something. I know that, too. And for me, a small step is victory enough.

☙

An hour later, I'm still high on the euphoria of saying what I finally needed to say, when Josie buzzes over the intercom and convinces me to tag along while she battles the post-Christmas crowds and returns some of her gifts. I grab my army green puffy down jacket, my fisherman's hat and matching mittens, and meet her in the lobby.

"Wow, you look well rested," I say. I haven't seen her in a week; she and Art had bused the kids down to Naples for the holiday.

"It's the sun," she says dismissively, waving a leather-gloved hand, then picking up her shopping bags and moving toward the revolving glass door, which normally spun around nonstop with employees, but today, sat still.

"So how was vacation?" I ask as we hit the street, the biting winter air nipping at my neck like termites. I tug my jacket zipper as high as it allows, but still, air sneaks its way in.

"Good," she says without much conviction. "No, it was good," she reiterates, more forcefully this time.

"And Art?" I ask. A deliveryman nearly mows me down on the sidewalk, and I dart aside just in time to avoid collision.

"Still hell-bent on San Jose." Her face contorts into a wistful smile.

"And you? How are you?"

"Still faithful." She lets out a grotesque laugh that sounds more like a howl of a dying seal. "Still faithful," she says again more softly.

"Well, that's good." I push open the glass door to Saks, but neither of us can get through: too many tourists rushing out in a wave. Finally, we edge our way in, and the pumped-in heat rises over my cheeks, warming them in an instant. We tug our hats off together, in sync.

"I suppose it's good," she answers, as we weave our way through the cloying, perfumed air of the cosmetics department. "Bart is back in San Francisco."

"Oh," I say with surprise and maybe relief. *You are happy in seven years, goddammit!* "For good?"

The escalator whisks us up and Josie shrugs but doesn't respond. It occurs to me for the first time that this wasn't just a dalliance in her mind, that, perhaps, just like when I came back for Jack, there was something real behind Josie's desire, *the thought of a rescue from her current life,* even if it wasn't a perfect fit, even if there weren't any reassurances that she'd be any better off this time around. It was the illusion that she *might* be that fed her, the knowledge that she didn't think she could be any worse off, at least, than where she found herself now.

Don't be so sure, I think. Instead, I say, "I'm sorry, Jo. I am."

"It would have been nice to have the option," she answers, as we step off into the women's department.

"You don't have to tell me that," I say.

She cocks me a sidelong look. "What are you talking about? You have this amazing guy who is gainfully and well employed, who placed a fat rock on your finger, whose family seems to adore you . . ." She trails off, as if she needs to provide no further explanation.

"You're right," I say. "Though I bet that at some point, Art had a checklist of strong points, too." *Funny how everyone's life always appears shiny on the outside.*

Her face goes blank, and I'm unsure if she's lost in a moment of trying to remember what those attributes were or if she's realizing that a checklist is meaningless, like a flimsy piece of paper left too long in the elements that erodes over time.

Before she can answer, my cell rings, and I root in my bag to grab it. Josie heads toward the counter, and I snap the phone to my ear. *Henry? Oh please let it be Henry!*

The static crackles on the other side of the line, and I repeat "Hello, hello" two times until I finally hear Jack. His voice sounds as if it's underwater.

"Hey! I finally got a signal!" he shouts so I can make him out. Only there's a delay and gap between Antigua and Saks, so mostly, I hear, "Ey . . . Inally ot ignal." It's like Pig Latin for rich tourists in the Caribbean.

"Hey," I say, my voice raised three decibels, my finger wedged into my free ear.

"Only have a second," he says. *Ly ave econd.* "I was talking to Mom and she wants to throw an engagement party in a few weeks. Sound okay?" *Ound kay?*

I hesitate and wander over to the shoe section, plunking down on a leather couch and staring at myself in the mirror. Does that really sound okay? The pomp and circumstance of Vivian's friends, tornadoing around us with their air kisses and their Hermès scarves and their catered pâté-covered crackers, reminding me of the carbon-copied image of my old Westchestered self. Do we really need to turn our nuptials into more of a public spectacle? As if the four-hundred-person ceremony isn't enough, isn't exactly what I didn't want to do in the first place?

"No," I say quietly, with an air of authority that feels unfamiliar yet not unwelcome. A tiny beadlet of sweat trickles down my neck. "No, it doesn't sound okay."

"Can't hear you!" Jack shouts, and a burst of static clogs the line. "So it's okay?"

"No," I say louder, and three shoppers turn to look at me. "I don't want to do it." My confidence accelerates like a gassed-up engine. "Please tell your mother that I don't want to do it!"

But we've been cut off, my fiancé and I. I am speaking into a black hole, a void, empty air, and I stare at my phone, willing him to call back so I can set him straight. But the phone doesn't ring, not from Henry, not from Jack, so eventually, Josie waves at me from the counter, and we shuffle to the office, shoulders sagging, morale low, and all we can do is wait for the cold breeze to usher in the winds of change.

❧ H E N R Y

What I remember most about my husband was the ease with which he moved through life. I'd watch him sometimes, just shaving in his boxers or lying on the living room rug with Katie, and wish that I could absorb even a sliver of his confidence. It was as if he decided, maybe because the world to him worked in almost mathematical ways, that this was *how* his life would hum along and therefore, all would be well. No need for unnecessary worrying or second-guessing.

I don't know if Henry knew how unraveled we'd become. Or maybe we hadn't become that unraveled. Maybe I just didn't know any better, and, like my mother, maybe all I knew was how to flee rather than to dive into the foxhole with my husband and wait out the missiles.

Two weeks before I found myself back in my old life, Henry snuck up on me in the kitchen. Katie was asleep and rather than join Henry in the den, I was wiping down the cabinets. I can't remember why I felt so compelled to clean just then, only that I did. That it seemed like an easier alternative than making small talk with my husband. I was standing on the step stool, trying to rub out the greasy smudges around the handle of my upper cupboard, when, out of nowhere, he was behind me.

"Come on," he said. "Come to the couch and watch something with me. You choose. I'll throw in a foot rub." I could hear him smiling.

"I can't right now," I replied without turning around. My right arm never stopped scrubbing.

"Jilly," he said softly, placing his hand through my belt loop. "Come down. These don't need to be cleaned right now. I'm finally back home for a few nights, and I want to spend time together."

But I just shook my head and pressed back out-of-nowhere tears. So he padded out of the kitchen and, I presumed, retreated to the couch where he listlessly flipped through TV channels alone.

What I should have told Henry, I realize now, is that he

felt like a stranger. That his efforts, which I suppose I should have appreciated, felt like efforts from someone who inhabited my house but not my home. That his touch felt like the touch of a man whom I barely knew.

But now, looking back, I can see that Henry was still trying to guide our ship. Guide me down from my figurative step stool and back to the bunker where we would weather the storm. That, yes, we'd gotten off track, and though the night was black and the storms would be dire, I could still cling on tight and face down the spiral. Eventually, the skies might have cleared, and Henry and I might have emerged scathed but not broken, changed yet still complete.

But like so many other things, these are the lessons that often only come in hindsight. Now I have mine. And I can only do with them what my time now allows.

☺

Chapter Twenty-five

Jack and I have RSVPed to *Esquire*'s annual black tie New Year's Eve party. With my closet in such disarray, I'd even braved the Christmas rush two weeks back on my lunch break and bought a decidedly non-me dress for the occasion: tight and black and clingy and so unlike anything I'd ever choose to wear in my suburban life that I hardly recognized the sultry skin and firm body that flashed in front of the mirror when I spun around in the dressing room at Bloomingdale's.

When I wake New Year's Eve morning, our bedroom is darkened and gray, like it's hugged with fog, though I know that I've risen late enough for the sun to be up. I'd been dreaming about Henry again, as I had been nearly nonstop since Christmas and since he's failed to return my phone call. It's all I can do to pry open my eyes and escape the dream that feels so much like a memory, even though I know that this isn't so.

I yank the shades open with one willful tug, and discover the cause: Outside, it is pouring snow. Portly, tumbling flakes have piled on the windowsill, stacking up to well over a foot and barricading the light that normally spills into the room. I vaguely recollect the storm from years past. Where was I? It comes back to me in pieces. With Henry. I do remember that.

I crawl back into bed and tug the comforter over me, then reach for the remote and flip on the TV. Red bars glare across the bottom of the screen: *winter storm warnings, winter storm advisories, do not leave your home, all flights canceled.*

All flights canceled! I perch up on my elbows. *Jack is homeward bound in*—I check the clock—*one hour.* He'll be stranded! I pull myself all the way up. *Shit! What about tonight?*

It wasn't, I considered, a grave catastrophe not to spend New Year's Eve with Jack, but it certainly seemed depressing to have to spend it alone. Besides, I'd read enough *Glamour*s to semibelieve the old adage that whom you kissed on New Year's Eve was whom you were destined to kiss the year through. I was too weary to mentally calculate if this had proven true in my romantic history, but it seemed like a wise enough mantra. If I were to kiss no one, what did that mean? That this whole thing, this whole coming back here was for naught? That not only would I not end up with Jack but I'd also end up alone? No, *no, this just wouldn't do.*

I rolled over and called his cell but got sent right to voice mail.

Five minutes later, I'm nearly hypnotized by the angry red bars that continue to flash on the screen, when my cell vibrates on the covers. It shimmies across the bed, as if it's running from my grasp.

"Jack," I say breathlessly, "where are you?"

"Henry," a different voice answers. "And I'm in New York."

"Oh shit! Henry!" I actually say this out loud.

"Nice to speak with you too." He laughs. "Sorry to disappoint."

"No, no." I shake my head and try to refocus. "Er, you know, just thought it was someone else."

"Obviously," he says dryly but not without good humor.

We both pause.

"Hey, sorry it took me a while to get back to you. I was in Vail."

And they don't have cell service in Vail? I think, then reprimand myself for sounding like a jealous girlfriend.

"No worries," I say. "I just wanted to wish you a Merry Christmas."

"No, seriously, I forgot my cell at home, so that's why I couldn't call back. I just got home last night."

"Ahead of the storm," I say, reiterating the obvious.

"Whoo yeah. Anyone coming in today is screwed." I hear him open his refrigerator door and take a swill of what I imagine to be orange juice. Most likely directly from the carton. I know this because no matter how many times I asked him to use a glass, he never did, at least not when he thought that I wasn't watching. But I was—always watching. Always there to swoop in with a towel to wipe up the residue that the carton would leave or snap at him when he'd actually use the glass but distractedly leave it on the counter for me to put away. As if using the glass was the favor to begin with and putting it in the *(fucking)* dishwasher was more effort than he could muster. When we first moved, I made off-hand, occasional comments, "Could you please put the glass away, Hen?" or "It really grosses me out when you swig from the carton; I use it, too, you know," but changing him was like trying to alter Morse code: It was too ingrained and thus impossible. So I stopped asking and thumped the glasses into the sink and then the dishwasher, all the while wanting to aim them more firmly at his head.

"So, anyway, now that I have you on the phone, what are you up to tonight?" Henry says, swallowing his drink. *Definitely straight from the carton,* I think, though now, it all seems sort of funny, sort of hilarious, like a perverted cartoon of a mouse who keeps going back to get the cheese and gets his tail caught every time. But he just doesn't give a shit because he wants that cheese so badly. *Henry, my poor demented mouse.* I shake my head as a smile spreads across my face at the thought.

"Er, well, we have plans. Jack and I do. But, um, he's supposed to fly home today—"

"No way that's happening," Henry interrupts.

I glance back over at the TV. The red warning bars are still pulsing at the bottom.

"Yeah, I guess not," I say. I can nearly hear my blood quickening, and immediately, I'm nervous.

"Well, here's an idea. You suggested coffee in your message, so, want to come over to my place for dessert and coffee? We can watch the ball go down and be all corny like that."

I snort to myself, despite my nerves. Henry *loved* the stupid Times Square ball. Nonchalant as he pretended to be, he was *obsessed* with that thing. In fact, we'd spent every New Year's Eve of our married life ushering in the New Year by watching that glittery ball descend among a crowd of crazed, drunken revelers. I realize, suddenly, that Henry is trying to impress me today, feigning his coolness, his quasi disinterest in the ball when he is fervently hoping that I'd agree. *We're not so different, you and me,* I think. *We've both mastered the art of concealing ourselves so well that it's no wonder that we finally imploded.*

"What about Celeste?" I ask. "Won't she mind?"

"Oh, she's in Florida," he says, as if that's some sort of explanation.

I pause and listen again to a news reporter who has had the misfortune of being assigned to braving the elements. "Grab your skis or snowshoes because that's the only way anyone is getting in or out today," she says, snot dripping from her nose; her eyes and lips are the only other exposed parts of her body.

Jack, it seems clear, will not be here by the stroke of midnight to greet 2001 by my side.

"Sure," I hear myself saying to Henry. "Sure, let's do dessert and coffee. I'll be there around nine."

We hang up, and I pull the covers over my head and burrow underneath, wondering if and when I'm going to wake up and discover this, *all of this*, was just a mad dream or a nightmare or even a little bit of fantasy. But after I lull back into sleep and after I'm awakened by my cell phone ringing yet again and after Jack confirms his extended vacation, I look around, fully cognizant and in no way dreaming, and realize that this life, *this time*, might just be for good.

❧

How mail carriers do it, I do not know, but per its motto, the U.S. Postal Service does manage to hurdle through what the news is now calling "the worst storm in two decades" and deliver the day's mail.

My superintendent throws it against my front door, and it lands with a thud. Gingerly, because I have spent the past twenty minutes coating my nails in pillow-soft pink, I slip my palm over the knob and shuffle the letters in with my bare foot.

I flap my hands in the air, much like a chicken does wings, until my nails seem bulletproof, and lean down to retrieve the pile and filter through it. Mostly, it's catalogs, companies I've never heard of crying out for me to purchase their on-sale dog beds, their on-sale Christmas ornaments, their on-sale long johns.

I pick up the only other noncatalog letter for the day, running my fingers underneath the lip of the envelope, which whispers out a crackle in exchange. An unfamiliar Christmas card awaits inside. Hand-cut snowflakes and silver sparkles dot the front, and some of the glitter sticks to the tips of my fingers as I flip the card open.

"To Jillian," it says in the ballooning scrawl of a child who

hasn't quite mastered her cursive. *"Happy New Year!! I hope this is the year of your dreams!!! Love, your sister, Izzy."*

Below it, my mother has written, *"Thank you for your note. It is enough to know that you're out there. And I hope you don't mind the card. She wanted to."*

I stare at the card for so long that eventually the writing and the sparkles and the snowflakes blend into themselves, creating a master composite of light and color that is only broken when I wipe away my tears and catch my breath. Then, I walk into the bedroom and slip that card into my sock drawer because I don't know where else it might belong.

❧

THOUGH MY NEW black dress, short and flirty, is crying to be worn, the weather mocks me and doesn't surrender, and trodding through foot-high snow simply doesn't seem survivable in such a getup. Besides, I tell myself, as I wade through my closet, *you are not going for alluring tonight. You are going for "we're friends," tonight, and friends don't let friends wear skimpy black dresses.*

I settle on a black V-neck sweater and jeans. Innocuous enough. Deflecting enough. I stare at myself as I dot my eyes with liner and float mascara over my lashes and peck my cheeks with blush and convince myself that *I am not nervous.* My sweaty palms and moist underarms, however, plead to the contrary, and I swipe on an extra layer of deodorant, like that can somehow calm my sticky dry mouth and my tumbling stomach.

The snow has finally ceased when I make my way out of my building. Though it's stopped, the damage it has left is remarkable: Cars are buried so deeply that they simply look like lumpy igloos on the side of the street; store owners and doormen are bundled like Eskimos, shoveling their sidewalks, virtually in vain, in an attempt to make them passable; pedestrians, the few of us who are braving it, are slipping and stomping and nearly hiking their way down the block. The city is at a quiet standstill: There are no cars or buses or taxis on the roads, no airplanes overhead, nothing but a hush of recently fallen snow and the smacks of the shovels digging into the mess and futilely pushing it elsewhere.

Henry lives only eight blocks away, but tonight, the route takes nearly half an hour, and I arrive late, panting and sweaty, my thighs aching from wading through the depths of the storm. I buzz his apartment, tucked in the back of an unassuming brownstone, and the door beeps and clicks open. As I step into the front entry, I'm dizzy with déjà vu. The scent—a touch of mildew mixed with Pine-Sol—is too familiar, and for a moment, I lose my balance, slapping my gloved hand up against the tiled wall for balance.

Finally, the vertigo passes, though the sense of discombobulation does not, and I haul my way up the creaky steps to his third-floor apartment. He opens the door before I can knock.

"Hey, come in," he says, sweeping his arm out like a maître d'.

"Sorry I'm late," I manage, though my intestines have now somersaulted, and I suspect that a better countdown than the one to midnight might be the one to how soon I need to rush to the toilet.

"As long as you're here before the ball drops." He lets out a nervous laugh and swipes his bangs, but they fall, as they always do, right back into place. "You look cold. What's your pleasure? I have beer, wine, water, eggnog . . ."

I catch a glimpse of myself in his front mirror: my nose cherry-engine red, my hair matted and splayed at the ends from my wool hat. Color rises to my ears as I wipe away the film of mucus that has settled in above my lip. *You're friends*, I tell myself. *Besides, Henry likes you when you're immaculate, when you're tailored and crisp and Lilly Pulitzered. Crumpled and damp is better for our purposes tonight anyway.*

I peel off my coat, hang it on the front doorknob, and exhale. *Relax! Just freaking relax!*

"Wow, eggnog!" I say, moving into his living room to survey the place. "You really went all out."

"Full confession," he says, hands up like a newly disarmed bank robber. "I ran down to the deli downstairs and picked up whatever they had." He laughs. "We will be decidedly *ungourmet* tonight." He pauses to survey me now that I've peeled off the protective elements. "You look *great*."

"Well, I'll take an eggnog," I answer, deflecting the compliment. *You are not supposed to like me dressed like a rodent! That is not your thing!* "Deli style or not."

I watch him for a moment in his tiny galley kitchen, barefoot in his faded jeans and rumpled navy cable sweater, then turn back toward the expanse of the apartment. It is spare, more so than I remember it, with a black leather couch and an oversized TV screen that is on but muted, and a beige rug with a tiny ribbon pattern that's only noticeable if you're sitting on the floor. Honey-colored built-in bookshelves line the back wall, and they're gorged with stacks and piles of hardcovers, most of which, I already know, are autobiographies of famous explorers or historians or politicians or examinations of science and medicine and the world at large. A wooden desk peers out over his living room window, and other than a computer, it is virtually bare: no picture frames, no cluttered mail.

Is this how I became so linear? I think. *Is this why I flitted around the house to ensure that nothing was out of place, so nothing ever shifted for him?* I twist my engagement ring around my finger, and remember how, when we moved to the suburbs, I was determined to pull together a magazine-worthy home, how desperately I needed to leave behind my scars from my mother and the mess of my old closet and my desk and, really, of my former life. *No,* I say to myself now. *Henry isn't why you became what you be-*

came. It's not so simple as that. Though maybe his need for order is what drew you to him in the first place.

Henry nudges me from behind. "Your drink, ma'am."

I turn, taking the eggnog, foamy in a glass beer mug, from him, and smile.

"A toast," he says, raising his bottle of Amstel.

"To what?" I ask, though I raise my glass just the same.

"To . . ." He hesitates and thinks. "To life. To time. To 2001. To the way that we got here and the places we're going."

A rush of tears floods my eyes, but I blink them back before he can take notice. "I'll drink to that," I say, then sip my actually pretty-good eggnog, though not as good as the homemade version that I'd eventually make for our various neighborhood Christmas events.

"So what happened with your mom?" Henry asks, depositing himself on the couch.

"Well, what's more interesting is what happened with my dad, actually," I reply and join him. "Turns out, he forgave her a long time ago." I shrug. "I guess he feels like he holds some responsibility in all of it."

"He probably did," Henry says simply. "Where there's an effect, there's usually a cause."

"So says your professor of a father," I say with a grin.

"So says he." He smiles back. "But, I mean, for the most part, it's true. That's always what I've found most difficult about relationships, how . . ."—he swigs from his beer and searches for the phrasing—"how tough it can be to change in conformance to the other person. It just seems like one person is always changing too much and the other not enough. And then the cause and effect just makes it worse. You feel like you've given too much, but then keep giving because the other person doesn't . . ." He drifts off. "It's just never easy. Not for me, at least."

"Not for me, either," I say, wondering why Henry and I have never spoken frankly like this before, or, if we did, back in the whirlwind days of our dating life, why I'd forgotten such conversations when life pushed us in other directions.

"But you're marrying Jack," he offers. "It must be different with him."

"It is," I offer, though the words are neither forceful nor direct. I consider how much I've bent on the wedding planning, on his aimless ambition, on molding myself into a perfectly crafted version of who I thought he needed me to be. It wasn't altogether different, I realized just as I had in Vivian's bathroom when the image of my future self startled me into tears, from what I'd done in my marriage to Henry. And, the thought pummels me, if the problem didn't lie with them, then it lies with me, rendering this whole trip, this whole *fucking experience* inconsequential because my history wasn't what I needed to change. I was.

"Oh, I almost forgot! Dessert!" Henry says, puncturing our pregnant silence and bounding off the couch, flushing away the morbid realization that was creeping into my consciousness.

I hear wrappers crinkling and a minute later, he returns with a platter of powdered doughnuts, Twinkies, fluorescent pink Snowballs, a Twix bar, and a mound of Skittles.

"Nice," I giggle. "Very upscale."

"Only the finest is served here at Casa Henry," he says, grabbing a butter knife and delicately slicing off the end of the Twix, then popping it in his mouth.

He rests the plate on the coffee table, sits next to me, and reaches for the remote. I tear into a Snowball, unnaturally colored as it might be, and press the sacchariney coconut into the roof of my mouth until it dissolves, sending trickles of artificial flavoring and sugar down the back of my throat. Henry turns up the volume on Times Square.

"I know it's strange, but man, I love this." He gestures toward the TV, reaching for a Twinkie. "The whole thing. The crazy tourists, the confetti, Dick Clark." He sighs and takes a bite. "I think I've seen it every year since I was a kid."

I watch him watching the revelry. His straight nose and his creamy skin and his pillow lips, so much like our daughter's, the little girl who isn't even yet a blip, a seed in his mind. *How could she be, after all?* I think. *He can't know what the future brings.* But then I consider that now, lost in the maze between what has happened in the past and what has already transpired in the future, neither can I know what the future brings. I glance at him, inconspicuously now, trying not to appear too obvious, and ache—literally physically ache—for my daughter's straight nose and her creamy skin and her pillow lips, and I stop myself from reaching over and sliding my fingers down the bridge of his nose and onto his lips, as if that might somehow connect me to Katie. As if that might bring her back or ignite a series of events that would still allow her to be, to thrive, to live.

Henry notices me staring, despite my efforts, and cocks his head.

"You okay?" he asks.

"I'm fine." I wave my hand and swoop down for some Skittles, but my dampened eyes betray me.

"No," he says firmly. "You're not."

I look at him for a beat too long. I can remember it clearly now, that Henry and I weren't always broken, that there was a time when we were our true selves for each other, when our nuances weren't lost, when we weren't putting forth so much effort to be what we thought the other wanted that we taxed ourselves empty. It wasn't that we didn't have what we needed to begin with, it was that we, the both of us, let it seep away.

But tonight, I can't explain any of this to Henry. I know that he wants to hear it, to listen to why I'm so weighed down, but the explanation is just so outlandish, so *ridiculous*, that even I, with my new understanding of my future husband, can't bear to unload it.

Knowing that he wants to know is enough.

So instead of answering, I excuse myself to the bathroom, and when I return, it is nearly midnight.

The glittery silver ball is descending and the crowd is furiously chanting down the numbers and the biting winter air, clear now of snow but still frigid and uninviting, swirls the confetti through the air. Henry looks over at me and smiles, giddy with boyhood excitement, and I, too, am caught up in the moment, my eyes wide and my grin bigger.

With five seconds to go, he looks over at me, and because I know him so well, I already know what he's thinking. He brushes aside his bangs, and I see him consider it, consider moving closer, but then we are at *three*, and then at *two*, and then finally *one*, and in that literal second, there is a bubble between us, each staring at the other, each willing the other to move. But then I see the moment pass inside of him, wash right over his eyes, so he leans over, kisses me on the cheek, and whispers, "Happy New Year, Jilly," just like he would whisper for the next six years to come.

Later, he insists on walking me home. We trudge through the piles of snow and beyond revelers who, in spite of the storm, seem to crowd the streets in drunken packs, and my face nearly freezes from the chill. But after he's deposited me safely, and I rush inside toward the warmth of my lobby, I realize that while my cheeks have gone numb, there, that spot where he kissed, seems to burn hot enough to warm me from the inside out.

WHEN I WAKE the next morning, there is a message from Jack. He'll be home in two days, and Happy New Year, where are you?

I wrap myself under my covers until it seems too gluttonous to stay in bed any longer. I peer out my window, and the sun has risen, strong and bright, and already, the snow is dissolving into streaky drops on the glass, into flooding puddles on the street.

I walk to my closet and pull open my sock drawer and tug out Izzy's New Year's card. I rattle around in the kitchen drawer until I find some tape, and then I paste it up on the refrigerator, a daily reminder of a nine-year-old who hadn't yet found a way to conceal her true colors.

I sink onto the kitchen floor and gaze up at her card, with its lopsided snowflakes and piles of glitter. *That is how life should be,* I think. *Shiny and imperfect but, despite the flaws, still full of promise for the year to come. How did I miss that in the first place?*

Chapter Twenty-six

 B ut why can't you just go along with it?" Jack is saying, as he steps out of the shower and wraps a towel around his tanned, lean waist. "I mean, she wants to throw us a party, and she's already started making the calls and doing the planning, so come on, Jill . . ." He trails off and moves closer, kissing me on the neck, as if that will convince me.

"I just . . . don't," I say, pushing him away. His face clouds into a bruise. "Besides, the wedding is in three months; do we really need an engagement party *now?*"

I'd read enough bridal magazines to know that, in fact, engagement parties were thrown for an *engagement,* not because the mother of the groom was once again looking to insert herself into a relationship and had grown bored at the lull in the planning.

"How's the writing going?" I ask, hoping to divert his attention, hoping to hear that perhaps Jack's New Year's resolution was to finally, *finally* find something, anything, writing or otherwise, that ignites his fire. Life with Jack has started to feel like we're playing on a loop: circling everything, going nowhere, and it's hard not to acknowledge that his lack of direction, his total complacency with his lot, is part of the problem.

But he ignores me.

"It will be small, tasteful," he insists, wandering into the living room to retrieve his dry cleaning from the front hall closet.

"It's not an issue of size," I say, following him in. I spy the time on the cable box. "*Shit.* I have to run."

"So we'll talk about this later?" he says.

"Why? You heard me," I answer, stabbing my arms through the sleeves of my coat and throwing open the door. I knew it was a small thing, even a petty thing, to refuse this engagement party, but it seemed like a good place to start—to start saying no, to start crafting a better version of myself, rather than an echo of the old one.

"Come on, Jill," he weaves his arms around my waist and kisses me fully on the mouth. "Just think about it."

"Really, Jack, there's nothing to think about," I say flatly. "I just have too much on my plate, with your mom's nonstop wedding plans and craziness at work, and this is just the last thing I want!"

"Think about it," he repeats, as I'm running down the corridor toward the elevator. I don't reply and instead fling myself into the open door of the car going down.

Josie has left me a message that she needs to see me in her office at 9:00 A.M., and though I'm uncertain as to why, I suspect that the Coke team has been less than pleased with one aspect or another of our ideas for the spring campaign. You would think that this would be easier—creating ads that I'd already seen before—but I've spent countless hours, too many hours, I suppose, attempting to remember the commercials and print layouts and copy from six years ago, and . . . I just can't. They are details, like so many other life details, that at one point occupied a temporary space in my brain and now have jumped ship and drowned themselves. So I'm working solely with my own imagination, skills, and creativity, and I fear today, as I hustle into the lobby of my office building, that this simply isn't adequate anymore. That I've cashed in all my talent chips and that maybe the pot I assumed lay within me, a pot that I grieved through my years of full-time mommyhood, wasn't such a bounty to begin with.

Josie's staring out her window, her back toward me, when I rap on her door.

She swivels her chair around and wanly smiles. She is still tanned, but now, underneath her browned skin, she looks ashen and drawn.

"Oh God, I screwed something up, didn't I?" I say before she can speak. "Coke hates the new ideas. Jo, *I'm sorry.* I feel like I'm spinning my wheels with these ideas and not getting *anywhere.*" I toss my bag on the floor and sink into the chair opposite her desk.

"I haven't heard anything from them," she says with surprise. "I've actually thought what you've been coming up with is good. Quite good. You don't?"

"Oh, well, er . . . I think maybe I've just lost perspective. You know, we've been working so much that it's like a vacuum, and I can't get a grip on the quality that I'm producing." And this was true. Maybe my shortcomings were simply imagined, and I was a broken barometer whose gauge fluttered about freely.

She nods, then chews on her words. "Well, I'm pleased, and as far as I know, they're pleased."

"So . . . what's up?" I furrow my forehead.

"I have some news."

"Oh my God, you're not pregnant, are you?" I clap my hand over my mouth.

"No, no, definitely not pregnant." She manages an ironic laugh, and I can tell that she's thinking, *I'd have to have had sex to be pregnant.* And I know she's thinking this because I'd think it so often in the last days of my marriage to Henry.

"I'm, well, I've let the other partners know that I'm leaving." She casts her eyes downward and picks a stray cuticle.

"Leaving what?" I say with genuine confusion.

"This. Here. I'm leaving the firm."

"For where? Why?" *This isn't what happens in your life story! You stick around to create award-winning, world-recognized campaigns!*

"Well," she says after she clears her throat, "I'm moving to San Jose. Art wins." She shrugs. "We're going."

"But Jo, you love this job!" I sit up straighter in my chair.

"Sometimes," she says simply. "Sometimes not really."

I look at her for a moment: I'd never really considered it, that Josie wasn't here because she loved it. Of course I knew that the job took her away from her children and her home life and other parts of herself that she might want to nurture, but never for a moment did I realize that what she was getting in return wasn't adequate bounty for her, that she might have fallen into this path and been unable to correct her course until now. That life swept her up and before she realized it, her children were half-grown and her husband barely knew her, and while she could craft a hell of an ad campaign, that didn't feel worthy of much.

"I . . . I don't know what to say," I answer finally. "But I'm happy for you, Jo, if this is what you want."

"Who knows what I want." She shrugs, then sips her coffee. Her red lipstick leaves a ring around the lip of the mug. "But, more important, I called you in here because I spoke with the partners, and we all agree that while you won't be named an official partner, we'd like to see you take over most of my responsibilities."

I don't answer, though I feel words spinning around my brain, lodged there, unable to come out. This is all happening much too quickly, the changes, the shifts; *none of this is supposed to happen. I don't want to be a partner at DMP! I don't want to log in longer hours over tedious copy and bargain with clients who don't know what they want in the first place!* I physically twitch in my chair. Because, best I can remember, work is what I loved most from my former life, and now, that, too, is just a figment of memory, no more or less real than anything else about whom I thought I used to be.

"I'll think about it," I say to her, exactly what Jack had hoped to hear an hour back.

"You'd be great," she says, smiling genuinely for the first time in our conversation.

Probably, I think. *But it's like Henry once said: risk or gain. What did I stand to lose more of, now that I was getting every-thing—the ring, the man, the job—that I ever wanted?*

℮

Meg is meeting me after work at Tiffany. Vivian has alerted me that her friends are simply not satisfied with my pitiful registry, and thus, has implored me to ask for more.

"Dear, they're going to buy you something anyway. So please let them know what you'd like! It makes everyone feel better about the process," she said in a voice message on my work line earlier in the day. *Which is funny,* I think, *because that's exactly how it worked out the last time, when Henry and I married.* I didn't miss the formal place settings or the sterling candlesticks until we moved to Westchester, when I swirled myself into a desperate housewife whose china patterns were as important as her manicures.

Jack has begged off the task tonight, citing an issue deadline, and truly, I don't blame him so much. When we first registered, he gallivanted around Crate and Barrel, clutching the scanner like an armed robber, but after thirty minutes, he listlessly flopped in an oversized love seat, and I more or less did the same. Somehow ac-quiring these physical representations of our union seemed less

appealing than either of us expected. Five minutes later, we left and
instead went out for a drink.

Though just six o'clock, the sky is blackened with clouds, and
the avenues are illuminated solely by the streetlights. The sidewalks
have refrozen, thanks to arctic air that's pushed in from the north,
and I'm slowly shuffling toward the store, moving along cautiously,
my arms slightly askew for balance.

Meg is on the corner of Fifty-seventh and Fifth, bundled with a
furry hat and a full-length down coat that disguises what I assume
is a blossoming bump underneath.

She waves when she spots me halfway down the block. Just as
I'm about to reciprocate, I hear the sharp screech of car brakes,
then the clamor of taxi horns and the sick crunching of metal, and
finally, the shrill shriek of people all around me. Everything slows
down in a way that I might have wished it to in my old life, and
frames of frantic masses and a battered streetlamp flash before me.
My legs are lead, my boots weighting me down like anchors, and as
I push forward, I feel as if I'm swimming through the ticking seconds of time. I look for Meg, but she's no longer there, and instead,
a taxi is crushed into a mailbox on the corner, and a crowd has huddled around it.

Someone yells, "I've called 911," and suddenly, my cells grant
me freedom, and I rush forward, pushing my way through the huddle, forgetting about the slippery, treacherous pavement underneath.

Meg and two others are flat on the ground, each of them bleeding, none of them conscious. I emit a strangled, frantic cry, then
kneel down to comfort her, but someone pulls me back.

"Don't touch her," the stranger says. "You could make the in-
jury worse."

The minutes spin, and finally, soon, too long—I have no idea—
I hear the blare of sirens screaming down the avenue. Paramedics

jump out and the circle of the crowd grows wider to accommodate them. The EMTs busy themselves with work, taking pulses and gently shifting limbs and, in the case of an elderly man who lies perpendicular to Meg, compressing his chest, then breathing into his mouth until he chokes out gasping air.

"She's pregnant," I cry to the pair of paramedics who are lifting Meg onto a stretcher. "She's pregnant!"

I see alarm rise over their faces. "You know her?" one asks.

Yes, I nod, unable to say more, as an earthquake of sobs makes its way through me.

"Come with us then." A strong arm tugs on my elbow, and I'm whisked into a blaring, too loud ambulance. Meg, her eyes still closed and with a line of blood snaking down her forehead, follows on the stretcher. One of the EMTs places an oxygen mask over her mouth, and the other slams the door closed with a heavy thud that shakes the entire vehicle.

The siren continues to swirl, cutting through the icy night air, and the tires spin beneath us. We rush down the avenue and over the streets and hurry forward toward the hospital, hoping, furiously, that time will creep ahead slowly enough for us to catch up and undo the damage that we are certain will come.

☙

I AM BARGAINING with God in the waiting room. Tyler is pacing the halls outside of the ER, and Jack has gone to hunt down semi-digestible coffee, and I am left alone with my guilt and blame.

Please God, let Meg keep the baby. I will marry Jack and never complain about anything ever again. Thank you very much. Love, Jill.

Dear God, I know that I've been asking for a lot lately, and that you've been very flexible in terms of accommodating me. But if you just do me this favor—keep that baby in there—I'm open to pretty much anything you need. Jill.

God, are you there? You name the price, you can have it from me. Just keep Meg out of it. This is between you and me, not her. If you've sent me back here to make your point, you've made it. Please let that baby live. All best, Jill.

The doors to the waiting room fly open and a balding resident tugs a surgical mask over his head, then weaves his way through waiting patients toward me.

"You came in with Megan Callahan, correct?"

I nod and lick my lips, waiting for the penance that I'm destined to pay. Because I know, in my gut, that if I hadn't come back, *if I hadn't asked for so fucking much,* that none of this would have happened. That Meg wouldn't have been waiting for me outside of fucking Tiffany and that she wouldn't have been mowed down by a taxi that lost control on black ice and that her baby would still be thriving inside of her as it was supposed to be.

I remember, for a fleeting moment, that, in fact, it wasn't supposed to be—that last time around, this baby was nothing more than a gasp of hope for Meg and Tyler—but that doesn't seem to matter now because *this is the reality,* not then. And *this,* clearly, is my doing.

I look around for Tyler, but he's nowhere to be seen, and the resident presses on.

"She's stabilized," he says. "She took a very bad bump to the head, but she's conscious and talking."

"And the baby?" I ask, barely managing to breathe out the words.

He nods. "We have a heartbeat," he says, and I feel my face crumble, purging tears flooding my eyes. "But we're not out of the woods yet," he continues delicately. "She'll be here for monitoring for a few days." He starts to walk away, then says over his shoulder, "If you'd like to see her, you may."

Meg's room is silent, except for the sound of two beeping heart monitors that echo each other, and when I enter, I think she is sleeping, so I slowly start to creep back out. But then she opens her eyes and turns to me and smiles.

"Come in," she says. "I'm up."

"Oh, sweetie." I try to say more but choke on the swell of emotion. I move to the bed and clutch her hand.

"I'm fine," she says, squeezing mine harder. "Just a few bruises and bumps."

"The baby . . ." I say.

"Look at that." She nods her head toward a monitor just beside us. "Look at my baby's heart. Thriving. This baby will be fine." Meg's eyes are bright with promise.

"I hope so." It sounds flimsy, disbelieving.

"I know so." She doesn't let go of my hand.

"How can you?" I ask, though I suspect that I shouldn't. After all, I know how her pregnancies end. All four of them the last time around.

Meg sighs and shakes her head. "I have to. *I have to.*" Her voice catches. "When I miscarried . . . I just . . . I don't know what I would do if I can't be a mother. *Truly. I don't know what I would do.*" Tears streak down both cheeks.

Her words bounce inside of me and something resonates, sticking hard, something that I missed the last time around when I wasn't present enough to notice the finer details. Meg's fog after her miscarriage, her fevered obsession with her fertility, her pure belief in the power of motherhood, the way she cocooned further into herself and away from the rest of us. Looking at her now, I know that she didn't fall asleep late at night on a Los Angeles highway. That

Meg was far too conscientious for such an error, and that the accident had never fully made sense to anyone who knew her well. But now it did. Because I hear it in the desperation of her voice. That *truly, she didn't know what she would do* if she couldn't become a mother, and so, when frustration turned to despair and despair melted into burrowing depression, Meg, devoid of hope, opted out of life rather than trying to find a new outlook on it. And now, this time, she had her chance to change all of that. And yet, my coming back created different wreckage, new wreckage that might lead to the same result after all.

Meg and I are quiet except for the beeping of the monitors, ensuring us that yes, there is life inside of her, fighting to keep going, fighting to be heard. I clutch her hand and think of Katie, and hope that this time around, I leave more than destruction in my wake, that I leave a bit of altered destiny in it, too.

Chapter Twenty-seven

The hours ebb into days and the days ebb into weeks, and soon, I'm starting to forget all of the nuances about Katie that I once couldn't live without: the ring of chubby skin around her neck, the way her arms locked around me for a hug, her warm feet that I would lean over to kiss when she'd just awakened. And as I lose a grip on these details, I begin to wonder if I haven't made up this journey entirely. Like Katie and my life with Henry and the discontentedness that came along with it weren't all just some strange flash-forward, a glimpse of what might be if I don't leap down the aisle with Jack and avow myself to him.

Late one January night, after Jack has fallen into a heavy slumber, I am racked with fitful sleep, and so I rise, pull on my sweatshirt and boots, and make my way downstairs into the frigid night air. The streets are nearly empty, an aberration for New York, but the subarctic temperatures have pushed everyone inside, and so other than the occasional dog owner, anxiously waiting for his beast to relieve himself, I am alone, the shadows of the streetlamps my only company.

My hands lose sensation—I've forgotten my gloves—and I duck into a twenty-four-hour drugstore. Fluorescent lights glare overhead, and Muzak attempts to mute their harshness, and I wind my way toward the back, shaking my fingers to encourage blood flow. I don't realize where I am until I'm there—in the baby section—and with still-numbed hands, I reach for the lotion, Katie's lotion, and pop open the lid. I inhale and the scent of lavender overtakes me, and my head spins so quickly that I reach for the shelf to ensure that I don't topple over.

In a rush, like a montage, I remember slathering on the lotion every night after Katie's bath, toweling down her hair and giggling together when she'd shake it like a wet dog. I remember tugging on her jammies, then reading her books, then pulling her in so close that the lavender, *this lavender*, would linger on my neck the evening through, gone only when I rose the next morning.

No, she isn't imagined, I think when I finally regain my breath and the sting of my tears has slowly abated. *She is as real as I am. She is as real as I need her to be.*

Only now, trapped in my time warp and with my future so altered, I don't know how to make that so, how to get Katie back and how to get what I need.

❦

JOSIE IS IN my office, running through a list of her contact names who will become my contact names when she leaves in three weeks, when Leigh unexpectedly drops in with Allie. My future niece bounds over the piles of paper and cardboard boxes that litter my floor and wraps me in a smothering hug.

"Can I steal you after work?" Leigh says.

Josie shrugs a compliant shrug and gives me an off smile, so I say "sure," and agree that I'll meet Leigh at the tearoom in the Plaza.

Hours later, before I shut down for the night, I call Meg, as I do daily now, to see what I can bring her and how she is coping with bed rest, which she has been placed on through her twentieth week. While so much is tumbling out of control in this new old life, I am determined to ensure that at least one thing—Meg and this baby—do not. *Not on my watch*, I think nearly every day. Armed with my hindsight, *not on my watch*.

Tonight on the phone, Meg is as she always is: listless but satisfied. She has all she needs, with her burgeoning tummy and her hope for her future, and sometimes, when I drop by with groceries or DVDs or just to chat, I'm envious of my friend who is so close to losing so much. Because despite that risk, she is content. I see this when she rubs her belly, and her eyes shine bright, and she talks about baby names, even though I wish that she wouldn't because I somehow think it's a curse.

I log off for the day and navigate my way through the crowds to the Plaza. The lobby smells of expensive, floral perfume and carpet cleaner, and guests come and go, the elevator button ringing in beat with their pace. I amble into the tearoom, but Leigh and Allie are nowhere to be found, so I wave over the hostess, a lanky, blond six-footer who is undoubtedly an aspiring model.

"Excuse me, I'm looking for a mother and her daughter. They might have put their names down. Leigh and Allie?"

"Oh, right this way," she says with a wink. "They're in the private room."

That's odd. I wrinkle my forehead and follow her through the parlor. She pushes open a door, then moves aside and allows me through.

"SURPRISE!" The volume of the welcome overwhelms me, and I stagger back two steps in dazed confusion.

Jack rushes forward from the crowd and kisses me.

"I knew you would protest, so we did it in secret," he says, smiling like he is the smartest man in the world.

"Wh-what are you talking about?" I stammer, trying to pin this down. Is it my birthday? Have I so lost track of time that I forgot my birthday?

"Our engagement party!" he says, then kisses me again. "I didn't want you to worry about it, so Mom and I thought this would be the perfect solution!"

I pull away from him, and unwrap his arms, like a twist tie on a bread bag, from my waist.

"This is an engagement party?" I say with disbelief, trying to contain my irritation, knowing that guests are watching. "I specifically *asked you not to do this*!"

"No, I asked you to think about it . . . you didn't answer," he offers. "Oh come on, it's fun," he says, either not detecting or purposefully ignoring my rancor entirely. He turns around to look at the hundred-plus guests. "Everyone is here."

I scan the crowd and mostly see Vivian's well-tailored country club set. I notice Josie in the back, alone and nursing a drink, and my father awkwardly making small talk near the buffet, but no one else with whom I need to share the supposed joy of my nuptials is here. Meg isn't here. Henry isn't here. Nothing is different here and now than it used to be: The people whom I need most are gone, and the ones who remain do nothing to help me get to where I need to go. Different names, different faces, but the end result is still the same.

Suddenly, it feels like too much, this party, this life with Jack—all of these people who are so similar to the me that I'm set to become in seven years, the me I've grown to loathe and have tried to outrun in vain. *It doesn't have to be this way*, I finally hear myself say. *There's more than one choice in whatever road you choose. Flats instead of heels. Nurturing Katie instead of constant mothering. Gray instead of black and white.* I feel Jack's hand pressed into the small of my back and an angry bruise grows inside of me. *I told him what I wanted and still, he didn't listen. I finally found my voice, finally stopped pretending to be what I thought he needed me to be, and still, it wasn't enough.*

I spin around and fly out the door of the room and through the cushy tea salon and down the steps in the front of the hotel. I hear Jack calling me back, tailing me through the lobby, but he stops when I reach the sidewalk, unwilling to chase me to whatever destination I flee to. Then I hear another voice, and turn to see my dad, nearly at my heels.

"Don't do this," he says, between gasps. "Don't run because you feel like you're out of options. You're better than that. I should have told you that years ago, but talking was never my thing. *You're better than that.*"

I shake my head at him. "I'm not like her. I'm not leaving because I'm out of options. I'm leaving because I have them."

He pauses, and I see something shift inside of him, then a wry smile turns his worrying face into a kind one. He looks back at Jack, then pulls me into an embrace.

"Then go," he says, pushing me away from him. "Go to wherever those options take you."

I nod, then sail down the streets, down the avenues, breathless and cold and sweaty all at once. I run and I run and I run, as I always seem to do, only this time, for once, there is a tiny seed in me that knows that I'm running toward something, not just running from it.

Chapter Twenty-eight

I pace the streets endlessly, unsure of where to go, what to do. I can't go home—I can't face Jack and his passivity. He'll hold his hands up and say, "Whoa, babe, it's not a big deal, can't you calm down," and then he'll try to wash it all away by kissing me or distracting me or pretending that he's not complicit in creating the ruins of our relationship. As if by leaning in and watching my mouth move, he was actually listening to who I was and who I needed to be. *Maybe that's why he never pushed me toward my mother: Maybe he simply didn't love me enough to understand what was best for me, even if I didn't know what was best for me in the first place. And maybe that's why I never pushed him harder in his aimlessness; maybe I didn't love him enough, either. Maybe it was all a lot simpler than it seemed, like one of Henry's mathematical life solutions.* The thought stirs something, and for the first time in seven years, it's as if our undoing might finally make sense, that this wasn't a relationship worth saving. It was a relationship that was a stepping-stone to something better.

I wander until I find myself outside of Henry's, to maybe where I should have been all along. Because now, with freezing air on my ears and the debris of my relationship on my shoulders, I can't ignore that this whole thing, that being back here, trying to undo the past might have been a horrid, wretched, and irreversible mistake. Not because things might turn out differently, though yes, there's that, too. But because what I needed to change seven years in the future had nothing to do with Jack or Katie or my mother or even Henry. Now that the patterns of my future life have replayed themselves in my past one, the thing that seems apparent is the only person I need to change is, in fact, me.

I reach for a garbage can outside of his building and vomit. Two pedestrians whisper to themselves as they pass me by. But for once, for the first time really, I ignore those whispers and those judgments and everything that comes with them, and I try instead to stop the waves of regret that now manifest themselves in nausea as they rip through me.

How could I not have considered how this all might end? I hurl again, spewing out slimy bile now that my stomach is entirely purged. *How could I have been so focused on reinventing both myself and my life that I never mulled over how much I had to lose? Risk and gain. Katie. Katie. Katie.* I can't shake her name from my mind, where it spins on repeat like a bad pop song.

I ring Henry's buzzer three times, but he doesn't answer. Either asleep or with Celeste, I realize as my insides drop all over again. I sink onto his front stoop and try to remember my old life, what made it so abhorrent that I might have permanently leapt from it with no hope of getting it back.

I get caught in a memory of when I was newly pregnant with Katie.

I had been ill with morning sickness and called into work to take the day off. Henry, before he rushed into the office, ran to the corner deli to buy me Saltines and ginger ale.

When he returned, he pressed a cool washcloth to my forehead and rubbed my back and then he said, "Why don't you take the rest of the week off? You're running yourself down."

"Why don't I take the rest of my life off," I answered. "It's not like we need the money."

"You'd want to quit?" I could hear his surprise.

I flipped over to face him. "Would you care?"

"Er, no, I guess not," he said. "As long as you feel fulfilled."

"Why wouldn't I feel fulfilled?" I asked, without a trace of foreshadowing. "I think I'd like it—being a full-time mom." Even as I said it, I knew that part of me didn't believe it and wasn't sure why I suggested it in the first place. But Henry couldn't have known that. Truly. I threw it out with such hope and conviction, that even the best of partners couldn't have seen through something so opaque.

"So do it," Henry said, leaning down to kiss my forehead. "Quit. Whatever makes you happy."

From the cold stoop in front of my future husband's deserted apartment, I'm flattened at the memory: both at how Henry hadn't coerced me into my decision and how wrong I'd gotten it for so many years. Time can play that trick on you, I realize. Obscure some of the good things and skew some of the bad, such that they blend together and you can't get your bearings on which is which and on what to hold on to as you wade through the muck.

I wipe the mucus from my face and the mascara from my numbed cheeks, and I pull myself upright. It is still dark, though I know that dawn will come soon, and I have to hurry, I have to be on my way. I'm not sure how and I'm uncertain where, but try I must—I have to make my way back home.

Chapter Twenty-nine

T he train to Westchester is nearly empty. It's too early for the reverse-commute crowd, and no one else needs to head to the suburbs before 7:00 A.M. I listen to the clanking of the wheels and the hum of the engine, and try to catch some sleep, but none will come.

At the station, I hail a cab, and we wind through the hushed streets, with their looming arbor trees and their shingled houses and their garages stuffed with SUVs and minivans. I remember touring our own home for the first time. Our real estate agent was lukewarm on the place, but as soon as I saw the pink nursery and the granite kitchen, I swooned. My high heels clicked on the hardwood floors as Henry tagged after me, and I turned back to him and said, "This is it, this is the one." He was less certain but he wanted to do right by me, so we put in an offer and moved just a month later. *It had been both of our doing*, I realize now, staring out the window at the houses whizzing by. *No one person was guilty, no one person can be blamed. Henry just wanted to please me, and I him. And we rotted ourselves in trying.*

The taxi deposits me at Ainsley's front door, which she answers with confusion, still in her pajamas and sipping a steaming mug of coffee. She shivers from the air that blows in.

"It's 8:15 in the morning, Jill! What are you doing here?" She surveys me, disheveled and unshowered from the day before.

"I need your help." I push my way past her and into the kitchen, where in six years, Katie would say her first word, "Mama."

She pauses before following me in. Then I hear her slippers shuffling behind me.

"Coffee?" She raises the carafe.

"Sit down, I'll help myself," I say, moving toward the cabinets, grabbing a mug, then opening another drawer for the sugar, and finally, yet another for a spoon. I do all of this without effort, without thought, gliding around the kitchen as if it's my own.

"How do you . . . ?" Ainsley starts, then shuts her mouth abruptly. I can see that I've given something away—I've only visited Ainsley's twice before, at least in this new life—but now, it's irrelevant. The guise doesn't matter.

"Look, I need some information," I say, sitting down opposite her. "Don't ask me why. It's too hard to explain."

"Is Jack cheating on you?" Her eyes grow wide. "I don't know anything about it!"

"What? No! Wait, *what?*" I scowl. "What are you talking about?"

"Oh, nothing. I just . . . you look like you do . . . so I assumed you had a fight . . . and now you're here." She waves her hands in the air. "I figured you were trying to track down some dirt on him or something."

"No," I mutter. "No, nothing like that." Though part of me is disturbed at the idea of Jack's unfaithfulness. Even though I'm desperately running back to Henry, part of me still hangs like clinging lint to Jack. I try to shake it loose but it loiters. *Maybe that's just how it will be*, I consider. *Maybe part of me will always be tied to him, no matter and irrespective of how much I love Henry.*

"No, look, I need to know how to find your masseuse—Garland," I say. I'd already called information from the train, but the spa at which he works in the future has not yet opened.

Ainsley's eyebrows skew downward in confusion. "What? I don't know what you're talking about. I don't even have a masseuse."

"Of course you do!" I cry and my voice nearly cracks. "Garland. Black hair, huge arms. All of you guys love him!"

"Jilly, I think maybe you should lie down." Ainsley places her hand over my arm. "You don't look well."

"I'm fine! I'm fine! I just need to find him." My pitch snakes into hysterics, and I can feel a tear squeeze its way out of my left eye. *Garland is my chance to set this right.* It hadn't occurred to me that he might not be around to do that.

"Okay, okay, let's look in the phone book," Ainsley says soothingly in a tone she'd later reserve for her son's renowned meltdowns. She rises and pulls out the Yellow Pages from underneath a cabinet, and the pots and pans next to it clang in response. "If you just need a massage, how about someone else? I've heard great things about the one down at the club."

"No." I shake my head and begin to purge real, unstoppable tears. "It has to be him."

She thumps the phone book onto the table, then flips it open toward the middle.

"Machine . . . mass waste . . . massage. Here we go." She runs her finger down the entries. "I don't see anyone named 'Garland,' though there is a 'G. Stone.' Could that be him?" She looks up at me hopefully.

"Maybe, I don't know. I'll try." I tear out the entire page, then grab Ainsley's car keys and kiss her forehead, her mouth still hanging agape. "I'll be back before you even know that I've gone."

And then I hurry out the door, like a flash of lightning—one minute there, the next leaving only electricity in its wake.

⟡

THE ADDRESS FOR G. Stone is off the main street in town, past the kitschy coffee shop where I'd grab my nonfat lattes between Katie's playdates and just north of Mrs. Kwon's dry cleaner. I kill the engine and stare at the slightly dilapidated, black-shingled home with fading gray paint curling on the corners of the wood-beamed facade. I'd never noticed it in the two years I'd lived here in my former life. The shades are pulled shut, and the house appears totally motionless, resting, not yet ready to be woken. But still, I am here, so I push open the door to Ainsley's SUV—and this time, I do hear the dings as it waits for me to slam it closed—and when I finally do, yes, then, just as before, six months back and seven years in the future, I hear the quiet.

The bricks that line the walkway are cracking—snow is nestled into the crevices, and frozen leaves crunch below my heels as I make my way toward the door. I ring the bell, and it echoes throughout the house, much like I imagine it would in a horror movie, right before the heroine meets the reaper. I hear footsteps, and when the door swings open, it is him, Garland, a reaper of a different sort, and my voice lurches forward to speak but my mouth is too dry to do so.

"Can I help you?" he says finally. I suspect that I've woken him. His normally lush, wavy hair is matted on one side of his head, and a well-worn burgundy bathrobe has been cavalierly tied around his waist.

"Yes," I exhale finally. "I, I . . . don't know how to explain this . . . but . . . I think you did something to me . . ." I pause to see if he has any recollection. *Don't you know me? Don't you know what you did to me?* I search his face like a lost mountaineer a map, but he is a blank canvas. Because, of course, he doesn't know. Of course, I admonish myself, *it was seven years in the fucking future! How could he?*

"I, well, I need your help," I continue. "That's the easiest way to put it."

He tilts his head and reminds me of a cocker spaniel awaiting a treat, but he also seems to take pity on me, so waves me in. A teapot whistle sounds in the background.

"Tea?" he asks.

"No." I shake my head. He motions to sit in his living room, then wanders off and returns cupping a warm mug that smells like farmed grass.

"So what seems to be the problem, Jillian?"

"You know my name! How do you know my name?" I press myself forward to the edge of the chair. A hot-wire surge flies through me.

"I have no idea," he answers, and his face contorts into confusion. "I, er, really, I have no idea." He seems to be searching for a memory that is just on the edge of his brain, yet still unattainable. "Have we met before?"

"Sort of," I exhale. "Though I don't really know how to explain it."

But because I have no other hope, I try. I tell him about my "what-ifs," and about Jack and Henry and my mother and Katie, and how turned around I got, wishing for things that I didn't have, lamenting the things I had, not realizing how much of it fell within my hands, within my scope, and how nearly all of it circled back to me and my doing and my strong, capable self, even when I didn't believe it to be so.

Garland nods his head while I lay out the story, and when I'm done, he says, "But I'm still not sure what you're doing here. What part I play in all of this." His brow furrows. "And why I seem to know you and your name, when I'm certain that we've never met."

"Well, that's the thing," I say slowly. "You were the one who sent me back."

Garland looks at me for three beats, like I've just told him that the world is flatter than paper and the tooth fairy dances among us and that Santa Claus flies freely come Christmas Eve. And then he lets out a deep, disbelieving chuckle.

"Come on," he says. "There's no way that I was the one who did that. I mean . . . how on earth . . ." He shakes his head, then laughs again.

"I don't know," I say, trying to contain both the panic and my rising anger. "But you did. You unblocked my chi and you set something off and the next thing I know, I'm seven years in my past in my old apartment with my old boyfriend in my old life."

He stops laughing and stares at me pointedly, seriously. "I unblocked your chi?"

"Yes." I nod. "That's what you told me."

He stands and starts to pace, mumbling to himself under his breath. Then he halts abruptly and turns toward me.

"I've been doing some reading, but . . ." He pauses, then continues. "Well, I've been doing some reading on the mind-body-spirit connection, and chis and auras, and all of that . . ." He waves his arms in a circle, as if that's an explanation for *all of that*, but I look at him perplexedly, so he keeps talking. "I've always long believed that the mind influenced our bodies and souls in powerful ways, ways that humans never quiet grasped, so, I started researching it . . ."

"And? How does this help me?" I stand to bring him back to focus.

"I've started tinkering around with clients' pressure points, you know, to help free their toxins and their minds, and well, I guess their chis . . ."

I run my hands over my face. "I'm sorry, Garland, I still don't see what this has to do with me. I just . . . I just want to get back to normal, back to my old life. I need you to get me there."

He sits on the couch opposite me. "Oh, Jillian. It doesn't work like that. You can't just go back to *there* unchanged. All of this is connected. All of this is a full circle." He waves his arms again.

"Just send me back there!" I shriek hysterically, as tears tug themselves down my cheeks. "Just help me get back!"

Garland's head jerks back abruptly, as if the force of my cries made a literal impact. He exhales. "I can't promise anything," he says, rising to pull out the massage table that is tucked to the side, against a glass china cabinet that is instead stocked with purple- and moss- and gold-colored candles. Two of its shelves are entirely empty. "It's up to you. It's all ultimately up to you, what you're thinking about, what matters most, where you want to end up when everything is loosened and freed."

I nod and wipe my damp cheeks, then I climb on top of the table and mash my face into the donut cushion, just as I had so far ahead and so long ago. Garland brushes aside my hair from the nape of my neck, and I hear him push his breath out, so I try to do the same. His fingers flit over my scalp and twist themselves through my mane, and though every cell in me wants to relax, they only seem to rebel and puff up with more tension and anxiety, like a cheese soufflé that might at any minute explode.

I think of Katie and my body heaves, but I won't let go of her face in my mind, of her butterfly kisses and her sweet breath as she falls into slumber when night tumbles in. I think of Henry and how we both got it wrong, how we twisted ourselves into versions of each other's expectations without ever giving voice to what we were asking and how much we could each bend. I think of my mother who must have believed she had bent too far, and of my father who later agreed that he maybe could have placed an arm under her back when he saw it arching, and then I feel Garland's hands dig into me, kneading out my pain, kneading out the past.

He leans in closer, his breath on my neck, and whispers, just as he did a lifetime ago, "Your chi is blocked. I'm going to work to unblock it, but you'll feel some pressure."

He pushes into my shoulder blades, and an explosion of fireworks moves through me. Red circles flash beneath my eyelids, and my breath grows measured and heavy. I move beyond the pain, and I bite down on my lip and think of Katie and Henry. What if I hadn't married Henry? What if Katie had never been born? Looking back on it now, with Garland's fingers pressing me free, I can see it from an entirely different view: not one of lost opportunity with Jack and my whole other life, but one of lost opportunity with this one. *This life. The one I should have chosen all along.*

What if I hadn't married Henry? I ask myself again, the answer now as clear as cut glass. *What if I hadn't married Henry?* And then, the world goes black.

Chapter Thirty

The sheets beneath me feel unfamiliar, like crisp, new linens that need to be washed before they soften, and my pillow is damp with sweat. Crusty saliva crowds the corners of my mouth, and my throat is sandy and dry. My temples throb, and my pulse thumps so strongly that the beats ring in my ears.

I roll to my side and sit up gingerly, swatting my knotted hair from my eyes. The room looks strange, different, yet also welcoming and a small reminder of home. Gone are the poufy silk window treatments, replaced by simpler, dark wood blinds, and gone too are the elaborate modern-print rugs that I opted for because I'd once read about them in *Metropolitan Home*, swapped for simple, cushy wall-to-wall cream carpeting. A pile of laundry is mashed in the corner, tucked away just enough that it's not an eyesore, but still there, calling out to be washed, dried, and folded.

Katie!

I throw my sleep shade onto the rumpled covers and tear out of the room, down the hall into the nursery. But it's a nursery no longer: Instead, I find a mess of an office, with a desk topped in floating papers and memos, and a treadmill that appears to serve more as a clothing receptacle than an exercise contraption. My hands filter through the clutter—letterhead with my name and Josie's maiden name on top, business cards with the same, letters of introduction to clients whose companies I've never heard of, a photo of Meg and a child I've never before seen—and I shake my head furiously because *none of this makes sense. Where is Katie? WHERE IS SHE?* I race toward the kitchen and shriek with fright when I fly through the doorway.

"Jesus Christ!" I scream. "You almost gave me a heart attack!" I clap my hand to my chest.

Henry is sipping from the orange juice container and makes a quick motion to return it to the fridge when he sees me, like a boy whose mom has caught him flipping through porn. He slams the re-frigerator door closed.

"And a good morning to you, too." He surveys me. "Um, maybe you should put some clothes on? Not that I mind, but you know, the neighbors." He gestures out the window, and I look down and notice, just as I did six months and seven years ago, that I'm naked.

I ignore him. "Katie! Where is Katie?" Panic is filtering through me, and I can do little to stop its flood. I can literally feel it racing through my bloodstream and pour into, over, and on top of my heart.

"She's with your mother. Jesus, Jill, what's wrong with you?"

"What do you mean, she's with my mother? Why the hell would she be with my mother?" I spin around and look for clues to Katie's whereabouts, like that will somehow intersect all of the missing pieces. I rush into the living room—a newer, less showy living room, I notice, without the gilded lamps or the custom-made couches, but a comfortable living room all the same—and grab a stray pink sock that Katie must have tugged off at one point and that no one noticed until now.

"She's with your mother because it's Monday," Henry says slowly. "Like she's with her every Monday."

I hear him, and yet it doesn't register. "This? What is this?" I wiggle the sock at Henry in a frenzy, my voice reaching a new, unexplored key.

"Er, it's Katie's sock," he says, bewildered.

"Yes! It's her sock!" I shriek, then begin to sob.

Henry's eyes grow to the size of globes, and he moves closer, wrapping himself around me, and I inhale his minty shampoo and his menthol shaving cream, a scent that was once so familiar, I stopped noticing it entirely.

"Jilly, sit down. You're obviously not well." He eases me back toward the sofa, where we sit, me, naked, him, in a pressed suit, ready for work.

I gasp for air, and Henry rubs my back until my lungs seem to reopen.

"So she's fine? Katie? She's fine?" I wipe my nose with the back of my hand and look up at him. It's only then that I notice my solid gold wedding band back on my finger. I roll my thumb over it, back and forth and back again, as confirmation of its existence.

"Of course she's fine. Why wouldn't she be? You were just sleeping late and didn't feel well last night, so I didn't wake you when your mom got here early to pick her up."

I nod, though none of this adds up. Going back in time was fluid: I already anticipated the events to come, at least initially. Returning is more jarring because I've missed so much; there are too many holes empty and unfilled.

"Okay," Henry says. "I'm going to call Josie and tell her that you can't get her at the airport today. We'll send a car."

"Wait, *what*? Why would I be picking Josie up from the airport today?"

Henry stares at me, starts to speak, then stops and stares again.

"For your presentation. You've been working on it for months." He exhales. "Jilly, I think we should call the doctor." He rises to grab the phone.

"No, stop." I pull him back down. "I just . . . I'm just a little foggy. Give me a minute." I chew the inside of my mouth and feign an attempt to look calmer. Then I force a smile. "See, I'm feeling better already."

Henry gazes at me, unconvinced, then we both jump when the doorbell rings.

"Shit," he says. "My ride."

"Your ride? To where?" It comes out shriller than I hoped, given that I'm aiming for an illusion of serenity. Though I'm certain that I'm ready to bare more of myself to Henry, I'm equally certain that starting off with "I just came back from seven years ago" is not the best place to begin.

"My ride . . . to work. Um, like every morning when Tyler picks me up and we take the train." Henry's face has shifted from confusion to alarm. "But I'm not going in. Hold on, let me tell him."

"No, no, go." I wave my hand in a flurry. "I'm fine. Just . . . groggy. I'm fine."

He cocks his head. "You're not."

I inhale and try to absorb it all. Katie, Tyler, Henry. I'm back and yet something isn't quite the same, something clearly has shifted. Something that feels welcoming, safe, and a lot like the place I call home.

"No, really," I say, standing to meet Henry's gaze. "I just need some time alone to clear my head."

The doorbell rings again, more urgently this time, and I see him hesitate.

"Go," I say firmly. "Go without a second thought." And be-cause he can hear the honesty in my voice, he does, kissing me before he leaves and promising to call to check in when he catches a break in his day.

"I'll try to be home to tuck her in," he says before he's out the door, though I already know that he might not be, and I also know that it won't be a slight against me if he isn't.

I run my tongue over my lips, tasting Henry's acrid coffee residue, and I watch him as he ambles down the sidewalk toward Tyler's car, a minivan, the type you buy only when required due to multiplying offspring, and I see Henry turn back toward the window just before he ducks inside. I flash my shaking hand up in a form of a wave, and he smiles and does the same. Then I tug the blinds shut, and I wander back into the depths of the house, *my* house, and I begin to redraw the lines of my broken life.

I find Katie's room tucked into what was once a den, back behind the kitchen, and it smells of banana bread. I sink into the rocking chair, the one in which I would sit to nurse and lull her to sleep. Slowly, now, my eyelids droop, too, as security washes over me like the warmth of a blanket fresh from the dryer.

I close my eyes and I rock and I rock, tumbling into a peaceful slumber, one with kind memories of the days gone by, but mostly with hopeful anticipation of those yet to come. Because I trust that Henry will go into the city and he will work as he always has, but this time, when he returns to me, I, the whole version of me, will be here waiting. Here and now. Then and before. Always.

℮ JILLIAN

I should have known, I suppose, from all the early signs. But I've never been good at reading the signals, picking up the cues from the figurative tea leaves. Henry had taken Katie out to breakfast so I could go for a run when I finally realized that something was off.

The house was quiet but not nearly as neat as I'd have liked. I remember thinking this as I wound my way through the first floor to the master bathroom. Henry's socks peeked out from underneath the couch, the morning paper was strewn every which way across the rug, and a lollipop wrapper from Katie's dessert last night littered the coffee table. *(Sugar! Why It Will Rot Her Teeth from the Inside Out!)* But I fought the maniacal urge to clean, clean, clean, like I'd done in the past, and instead focused on the task at hand. That's how I lived my life now. I would never come to full peace with my urges toward domestic fastidiousness, with my need to create a sparkly veneer of life, but I could accept these faults and move forward. Just knowing that they were within my control was enough to tame them. Most of the time, anyway. Like an addict, sometimes I still slipped up, but never was it so severe that I couldn't talk myself down, that I couldn't think of how prosperous my life was, how lucky I was to inhabit it, and how easy it would be for me to lose my footing all over again, Garland and my blocked chi or not.

I reached the bathroom just as another wave of nausea consumed me, and I grabbed a white plastic stick from underneath the cabinet. I removed Katie's potty seat from the lid of the toilet and squatted and peed over the stick as instructed. I'd done this a few times over the past several months but nothing so far.

This time around, unlike with Katie, it had been *my* idea to try for another child, and it felt unfamiliarly powerful to be in command. I tried to do that more often these days—to listen to my internal cues and honor them. So when Katie turned two, and I realized that we'd both be okay, that we'd both emerge from this whole mother-daughter thing without permanent damage, I also realized that I'd like to try it again, only this time without the self-doubt and the self-loathing and the self-induced need for perfection.

I finished peeing, and plopped the stick down on the sink, then tried to busy myself by tweezing my eyebrows while I waited. And soon enough, there. There it was. The literal sign of my future. Though I'd been expecting it, still, I was shocked, breathless even. And more surprising than the plus sign was my initial inclination to panic, to flee like hell straight out of there.

But no. I caught my breath and I exhaled and I remembered how far I'd come, how I'd tripped down a rocky path and so nearly lost my grip on everything that mattered, and then I thought of Katie and my unbreakable love for her, and how I could already feel that same love growing inside of me.

I looked in the mirror and saw blood running flush through my cheeks. Soon, the beat slowed inside of my neck, and my hand fluttered down to cup my abdomen, and I gazed at myself—so changed and yet so not—and all I could do was smile.

Yes, truly, now, I was home.

Acknowledgments

If there is such a thing as publishing heaven, Shaye Areheart Books is it, and I can't believe my good fortune to have landed here. Most writers are lucky to have one fabulous editor. I was lucky enough to have two, both of whom are worthier than I deserved. I will always be grateful to Sally Kim, who with kindness, genius, and dedication, nurtured this book long after her responsibilities had expired, and to Shaye Areheart, who gave me more attention, support, and wisdom than surely her schedule allowed. My team at Shaye Areheart Books—Kira Walton, Annsley Rosner, Rowena Yow, Karin Schulze, Sarah Knight, and Anne Berry, among others—was more than I could have ever hoped for: the perfect trifecta of intelligence, talent, and wit.

Most writers are also lucky to have an agent who advocates on their behalf, but I'm lucky to have one who goes way beyond just being my advocate: Elisabeth Weed, as if I haven't told you this a thousand times before, you rock, and I'm thankful each and every day that you responded to my introductory email. Soon we shall conquer the world! (Yes, readers, she knows that I'm joking. Sort of. We're always both sort of joking.)

To Michelle Winn and Andrea Mazur: Thank you for your

friendship and for talking endlessly with me about our own "what ifs." You made this a better book, and you make my life a better place to live.

To Amy Stanton, Melissa Brecher, and Paula Pontes: Thank you for our girls' nights, which keep me sane, and for reminding me that where you come from is as important as where you're going.

To Laura Dave: Thank you for the perfect epigraph.

To my friends at FLX: Thank you for providing companionship during my solitary days in my office, and thank you for sharing in my triumphs every step of the way.

To Randy and Tamara Winn, Barbara and Barry Scotch, Matthew Scotch, Molly Scotch, Linda Childers, Debra Netschert, Larramie, Rachel Weingarten, Jennifer Lancaster, Sarah Self, Meryl Poster, and Kate Schumaecker: Thank you for the various unsolicited ways that you offered help, support, critiques, cheerleading, shoulders, and friendship these past few years. I'm constantly indebted.

To my parents: Thank you for your pride in my success and for the knowledge that you'd be proud of me whether I was published or not. Thank you also for those last-minute babysitting fill-ins that I usually forget to thank you for.

To my husband, Adam: Thank you for your good humor and your wry smile when I told you about the subject matter of the book; thank you for not caring if people will confuse this fiction with our real life; thank you for occasionally putting your dishes in the dishwasher and every once in a while picking up your socks from the floor.

Finally, to Campbell and Amelia: Thank you for providing more unfiltered joy and untouchable love than I have ever known. I might have written a book about "what ifs," but with you, I have my answers.

About the Author

Allison Winn Scotch is a frequent contributor to numerous national magazines and is the author of *The Department of Lost and Found.* She lives in New York City with her husband and their son, daughter, and dog.

About the Type

This book was set in Bauer Bodoni, originally designed by Heinrich Jost and released by the Bauer Type Foundry in 1926. The typeface is based on the "modern style" Bodoni typefaces created by Giambattista Bodoni in the late eighteenth century.